CAPTIVES OF THOTH!

''Open the lock! All occupants out!''

Starbuck keyed the intercom to reply. ''Your request is contrary to the interstellar rules of space commerce.''

''You have one minute to open the lock and debark all passengers and crew! If you do not comply, we will order the space port defense batteries to open fire on you. A state of armed conflict exists here. Interstellar rules have been suspended. You are on territory controlled by the Black Path of Thoth. You now have forty seconds to debark . . . or die!''

A MATTER OF METALAW

LEE CORREY

DAW BOOKS, INC.
DONALD A. WOLLHEIM, PUBLISHER

1633 Broadway, New York, NY 10019

DISCLAIMER

All intelligent beings and worlds portrayed herein are believed to be non-existent, and any resemblance to any being or planet is statistically improbable but also undoubtedly possible—the number, variety, size, and workings of all possible universes being what they are.

First Printing, October 1986

1 2 3 4 5 6 7 8 9

PRINTED IN U.S.A.

TO:
Lisa and Bill

Preface

METALAW—DEFINITIONS AND RULES (CANONS)

Law: A system of rules of conduct and action governing the relationships between intelligent beings. These precepts are classified, reduced to order, put in the shape of rules, and mutually agreed-upon.

Metalaw: A system of law dealing with all frames of existence and with intelligent beings of all kinds.

Intelligent being: An organized system having all of the following characteristics:

a. Self-awareness.

b. Time-binding sense — able to consider the future, conceive optional future actions, and act upon the results thereof.

c. Creative — able to make bi-sociative syntheses of random matrices to produce new concepts.

d. Behaviorly adaptive — capable of overriding the pre-programmed behavior of instinct with behavior adapted to perceived present or imagined future circumstances.

e. Empathetic — capable of imaginative identification with another intelligent being.

f. Communicative — able to transmit information to another intelligent being in a meaningful manner.

Zone of Sensitivity: A spherical region about an intelligent being that extends out to the threshold of sensory detection, physio-bio-psycho-socio effects, or some arbitrary boundary within those limits that is announced by the being.

THE CANONS OF METALAW:

First Canon (Haley's Rule): Do unto others as they would have you do unto them.

Second Canon: The First Canon of Metalaw must not be applied if it might result in the destruction of an intelligent being.

Third Canon: Any intelligent being may suspend adherence to the first two Canons of Metalaw in his own self-defense to prevent others from restricting his freedom of choice or destroying him.

Fourth Canon: An intelligent being must not affect the freedom of choice or the survival of another intelligent being and must not, by inaction, permit the destruction of another intelligent being.

Fifth Canon: Any intelligent being has the right of freedom of choice in life style, living location, and socio-economic-cultural system consistent with the preceding Canons of Metalaw.

Sixth Canon: Sustained communication among intelligent beings must always be established and maintained with bilateral consent.

Seventh Canon: Any intelligent being may move about at will in a fashion unrestricted by other intelligent beings provided that the Zone of Sensitivity of another intelligent being is not thereby violated without permission.

Eighth Canon: In the event of canonical conflict in any relationship among intelligent beings, the involved beings shall settle said conflict by non-violent concordance.

Chapter One

It was like a silent scream in his head.

Peter Starbuck had to stop what he was doing because of it. He waved his hand in the air over the bed and turned on the light.

"What's the matter?" Triga Rimmon wanted to know. Things had been going fine . . .

Starbuck lay back on the pillow and stared at the ceiling. He had trouble getting his emotions under control. That was something highly unusual for him. He finally replied in flat tones, "An AI Team has just been lost."

"What?" Triga couldn't believe it. She rolled over and brushed her hair out of her face. "How do you know?"

"I . . . I heard the scream," Starbuck muttered. He'd heard more than that, but it was the only way he could describe it in mere verbal symbols.

"I didn't hear anything."

"How could you? You were making too much noise of your own. But that's the best I can describe what I 'felt'."

She pulled herself up on an elbow and looked at him. "Peter, you're imagining things. We've never lost a whole team."

"We have now." He sighed and swung his legs over the edge of the bed onto the floor. "Let's go. We'll be needed."

Triga stretched languorously. "Do I have to? I was just beginning to really enjoy you for the first time in a long, long . . ."

"Yes, you have to," Starbuck told her flatly, trying as

9

best he could to control the raging emotion within him. "That is, if you're still a team member and want to go with me."

"Where are we going?"

"Back to the *Starace*. And then to wherever the lost team was when it paid the ultimate premium."

"But we haven't received any orders from Brinker." She got out of bed nonetheless.

"We will. And if not from Brinker, then Nambe."

"You would have to bring her into this!" Triga Rimmon said with a savagery that belied her real feelings.

His cool, logical, level-eyed expression didn't change, nor did the spiritless and unemotional tone of his voice. "Tayreze Nambe is light years away. But you're right here with me as part of an AI Team. Stop thinking jealous thoughts, Triga."

The way he said that finally convinced her that something was indeed wrong. She didn't have the latent talent he possessed. But those mentic talents she did have now told her that he was on the razor edge of being able to control himself. *It must have been a powerful signal,* she thought. As the biotech on the team, she knew the inside and outside of Peter Starbuck not only from his record, but also from intimate contact over a long period of time. So she acted to release some of his tension. In what appeared to be a playful impulse, she threw a pillow at him. "You and your wild talent! I wish you had it better developed and more disciplined like some of our other team members. Then I'd feel more confidence in your hunches, Peter."

He fended off the pillow and stood up from his sitting position on the bed. Her playful gesture had indeed stripped some of the stress from his conscious mind by reminding him that she, too, was suddenly under stress. And once she had relieved the tension Starbuck slipped back into his trained Agent Investigator composure with its touch of dry humor. Some observers would have tagged it as "ironic" or "semi-sarcastic" humor verging on satire. "Your apprehension is ill-conceived. Have I ever been wrong?"

"Yes."

"Name ten times." It was his way of getting her to relieve some of her own rapidly growing tension.

"What? Oh, forget it! You're impossible!" Triga exclaimed in an exasperated tone. She had a far more volatile and emotional personality than Starbuck. It would take more than a little humor to humor her. "As the biotech on the team, I'm telling you that you need the rest and tension leveling of a week or more on this planet. We've all been under a lot of pressure for a long time. Three months of intense work solving that stupid Tadema kidnapping case on Crecops. Then only two days in this lovely hotel on Plethora where I've had you all to myself for the first time in months. And what happens? You get a wild hunch about something that's never happened before. If I didn't know you better, Starbuck, I'd almost say that I wore you out in two days . . . which I've never managed to do before. Either your last regeneration treatment didn't take and you're now aging, or I need to check your hormonal balance. In short — definitely very short, I might add — I think you've had it."

Starbuck gazed appreciatively at her as she stood there looking as though Botticelli had used her for his model. He let a smile play at the corners of his broad mouth. "Who's had who?"

"Never mind! Peter, you're impossible!"

"Undoubtedly. But, then, how would you account for the paradox that I'm really here after all . . . as you so well know?"

Under the circumstances, it was going to be difficult if not impossible to cool Triga Rimmon's anger. Any beautiful woman would be angry when a sensual and much-needed vacation suddenly was interrupted by a strange and unquestionable quirk in her companion. But there wasn't much she could do about it. She knew that Peter Starbuck gave first priority to his job. Being his second priority was to be expected although, to Triga, it was a definite fringe benefit to her own job as his AI Team biotech.

Not many other women in the universe could become close to someone who was basically an immortal superman. "Oh, what we do go through for you and SIGNET!" she said with a frustrated sigh.

Starbuck didn't reply. He was growing anxious now to get back to the starship. There he could gain access to communications that might confirm his hunch. Well over a century of experience with difficult cases of conflict between human beings told him that his hunches were usually correct because of his wild telepathic talent. This same long experience also pointed out the urgent necessity to confirm such hunches quickly and get the full picture, if possible. Time was often critical.

But in addition to that, Starbuck didn't like to operate without full data because it usually meant that he'd walk blindly into trouble with his team . . . and that could be definitely unhealthy. Whatever the problem was now, he knew it was deadly because another AI Team had discovered that for themselves. The mental scream that marked the termination of another Agent Investigator Team had come to him when he was in a cholinergic state with Triga. If such a termination had actually occurred (as he *knew* it had), and if he had indeed intercepted the agonizing, surprised, and questioning final burst of energy that usually accompanies sudden and violent termination, there was trouble indeed.

Agent Investigator Teams were not considered expendable by the Security Investigators' Galactic Network. Too much time, training, and money were tied up in an AI Team. Teams were taught to move boldly, but only on the basis of as much data as was available when the move became necessary. Teams would always have every scrap of information available when they went in to resolve a conflict for a client. And they usually had the resources of the client to help them, too. Furthermore, when an AI Team moved on behalf of a client, it had to appear to be a bold, smooth, and efficient operation. There was the AI Team and SIGNET image to maintain because it was an integral part of the operation. But, far more important to SIGNET, the organization couldn't afford to waste time or people. Time and people were money.

So it was that Peter Starbuck's hunch about the loss of another AI Team seemed incredible to him as well as to Triga.

But Starbuck knew what he'd sensed: the scream of death from six minds broadcasting the pain and surprise of its transition of state blindly across the light years in one last spasm of instinctual activity.

Peter Starbuck also knew that, if this were true, his AI Team would be called in on the case. His team was always called for the dirty jobs, the difficult jobs, the jobs that G. Edward Brinker would trust to no other team, the jobs that Brinker himself decreed would go to the "best team in my stable."

It bothered Starbuck to think that the SIGNET Chief Executive referred to him and his people as though they were prized race horses. Fortunately, Brinker didn't treat them that way. This wasn't a bad job, Starbuck knew. It kept him from becoming bored, the biggest problem faced by most people who'd taken longevity treatments. Although his physical age had been arrested at thirty-five tellurian years, this didn't mean he couldn't be killed. The hint of danger in the task of leading an AI Team was one of the factors that had originally drawn him to the job.

He and Triga didn't bother with duffles or clothes. Plethora was such a mild-weathered planet that clothing wasn't needed for warmth, only for its utility in support of critical parts and for chafing protection. So they left their clothes in the room and took only their credit identification sigils and those few items particular and exclusive to SIGNET AI Team members — mainly confidential high-technology items that no team member would knowingly forget. The consequences of forgetting wouldn't compromise SIGNET security because the items would normally self-destruct if they didn't detect the dedicated human operator after a period of time. The worst that could happen was that Headquarters would find out during the next inventory and charge the loss against the Team's account.

Starbuck stopped at the front desk and announced to the concierge, "We're checking out. Please arrange transportation for us to the starport."

The concierge looked properly worried. Tourism, vacationing, and pleasure were among the major industries of Plethora, one of the so-called "New Vegas Worlds." A disgruntled or unhappy visitor was a major disgrace. "Is there something wrong, sir? Have you encountered poor service or inadequate accommodations? Have we failed to satisfy your desires? If so, please consider extending your stay and permit me to make whatever arrangements will make you happy. . . ." He wasn't being fawning or fastidious. He was acting as any Plethoran would when a guest checked out early. (The longer a guest stayed, the more money was spent and the better the import-export books balanced.)

"Everything you have done or provided has been and is excellent," Peter Starbuck reassured him. "I truly wish we could stay longer, but a pressing matter of business has come up." He'd sensed the man's inner concern and tried his best to ameliorate it within the boundaries of the Canons of Metalaw in contrast to the need for SIGNET security.

The concierge felt better about their departure. But he secretly envied such interstellar business moguls as Mr. and Mrs. Peter D. Sterling of ColeShore General, which is who the reservations and credit sigils confirmed they were. AI teams often made long-term enemies, and Starbuck's team had their share. On R-and-R, the team members let their guards down and relaxed, but they did so only after suitable precautions had been taken.

In the autocab on the way to the starport, Starbuck punched a special code into his wrist phone. Plethora was a modern world with a planetary comm/info system, so he knew he could reach the phones of his other team members, wherever they might happen to be on the planet. The special code insured that. If anyone happened to tap the channel, the code would appear to be an off-planet code peculiar to the planet ColeShore. When the phones of the other team members received the code, they'd signal back that they were busy. But the team members would be alerted to return. Thus, Starbuck's action call to his other team members would go as unnoticed as a regular call on the planetary system, and there was no way to know it otherwise — which is just what Starbuck wanted.

After all, if you ever ask anyone, you'll discover there's no such thing as an AI Team. They don't exist. But nearly everyone knows of SIGNET. It's a big interstellar operation. Everyone knew it had a big fleet of police cutters, the legendary Star Guard, starships ready to pounce upon any who would dare to break the Canons of Metalaw when a SIGNET client was involved. However, SIGNET's main weapon was the AI Team who would go into a conflict to resolve it economically and efficiently. Starships are expensive, and a prudent commander wouldn't risk one unnecessarily. A hammer is a poor weapon against an insect; better to send in another insect to resolve the problem.

The *Starace* sat on her aft drive ring in the starport's transient parking area. Externally, the starship couldn't be differentiated from hundreds of other executive starships and private vessels on the tarmac. But woe to the person who tried to enter the *Starace* without proper credentials — correct key punch codes, the proper voice print, and mentic factors that the ship's cybermech would recognize.

Although *Starace* was a plain-jane starship on the outside, inside her hull was a collection of systems and equipment totally unlike that in the other ships around her. Although the GI stardrive ring elements on her nose and tail were real enough, they were strictly cosmetic, as much of a cover-up as the AI Team's on-planet ID and credit sigils. And, like the AI Team, *Starace* technically didn't exist. At that moment, she bore the name and registry of *Wanderstar* of ColeShore registry, which matched the credit sigils of her AI Team.

Starace didn't have a GI stardrive because she didn't have to make the long C+ trips between the stars. She jumped directly and instantaneously. The only limit to her range on any given jump was the data stored in her cybermech and available to her jump detector. If someone hadn't been to her destination before and filed the data on a network accessible to SIGNET's master cybermech, CYMaster, she couldn't jump there because she and the jump detector couldn't tell her jumpman where the destination was. She wasn't an exploration ship; she was a covert intelligence ship and an unmarked police cruiser.

And *Starace* wasn't her real name, either. If she had a personality that could be named, it belonged to the cybermech that was the major crystalline organism inside her.

"All right, CY, wake up!" Starbuck called as he and Triga entered the *Starace* and stepped into the control compartment.

"I never sleep," a smooth, calm, laid-back, good-old-boy voice replied. It brought back old memories — the recorded sounds of early space flight and the laconic, yet easy-going voices of the test pilots and astronauts having what they called then the "right stuff."

"I've been working with Katwin. She's been in the receive mode for the past five minutes. There have been messages from ColeShore."

Starbuck looked at his biotech and refrained from saying anything, although his expression said "I told you so." Triga merely looked him blandly in the eyes and shrugged.

In the comm module, a pale, dark-haired young woman lay in a contour couch. She appeared to be in deep sleep except for the twitching of her legs and arms.

"Don't interrupt her," CY added needlessly. "We're still processing incoming data."

"It doesn't take all of you to help her do that," Peter observed. "Are we ready to lift?"

"Affirmative on the ship. All systems powered up to pre-lift condition. Energy banks average ninety-three-point-five-six percent with current drain rate at zero-point-seven-six percent.''

"Thank you," Starbuck told the ship's cybermech/intelligence amplifier.

"Don't mention it. Part of my service," CY answered automatically with appropriate null phrases from his memory. "However, we're not ready for lift."

"Why not?" Starbuck wanted to know.

"Isky is aboard. He's resting in quarters until needed for a possible reply message," CY reported. "But Shochona and David haven't come back yet."

Starbuck snorted. Both the detector and the jumpman had the disturbing habit of going planetside, getting completely lost for days while they engaged in their private and personal peccadilloes, and returning to the *Starace* at the last possible moment. Normally, as Team Leader, Starbuck suffered each of his people their personal foibles and proclivities during an R-and-R period. But this was different. R-and-R was over. "Send them the urgent signal," he instructed the cybermech.

"I have."

"Then transmit the emergency recall."

"Done."

Starbuck slipped into another reclining couch and began to pull the linkage cap down over his head. "Good. Now, plug me into the circuit and give me a data dump on the messages you and Katwin have already processed."

"Sorry about that," CY told him apologetically. "My preliminary reading of your vitals and mentals tells me you're in no condition to link safely."

"What the hell? Is this outfit coming apart at the seams?" Starbuck asked savagely, addressing his outburst at no one in particular.

"No, but you may be," CY said.

Triga was hovering over him, checking the bio-mentic readouts. "Relax, Peter," she soothed. "CY's right."

"Dammit, I've got to get the information on that AI Team!"

"Peter, direct link with me in your current condition could be very hazardous. I'd have to rationalize much of the data. Therefore, my basic asimov programming won't let me complete the link with you."

"Damn your basic asimov!" Starbuck exploded.

"You can't," CY reminded him.

"At least, tell me one thing, CY," Starbuck snapped as he tried to bring himself under control. "Did we lose a team, or did I imagine it?"

"If it will help you take an even strain, Peter," CY answered, "yes, an AI Team was indeed lost."

Starbuck looked up at Triga. "Well, do something. Get me in shape to link."

Triga shook her head. "No. I can't give you any enhancers. That's risky even in times of good emotional tone. Peter, you'll have to do it yourself . . . but I'll help."

"You're right," Starbuck admitted, realizing that the trauma of another team's loss had gotten to him on a very basic level. "Let me know when you think I've leveled out." He took several deep breaths to rid himself of excess carbon dioxide and to decrease his blood acidity. He managed to slow his heart beat and stem the flow of adrenalin that he discovered he'd been unconsciously pumping into his bloodstream every since he'd "felt" the deaths of the other AI Team members. *This is no time to go feral,* he told himself. Time to get level and stay that way. The loss of the team was apparently a fact. He couldn't do anything about it right at the moment. In fact, he couldn't do anything except fret. In the meantime, messages were coming in from ColeShore along with additional information and perhaps instructions. Katrina Ivanova, the team's receiver, was already at work exercising her *idiot savant* talent. CY would have the whole story shortly. In the meantime, whatever lay in store for SIGNET Agent-Investigator Team 017 would require that he, as team leader, have total control over himself. Otherwise, SIGNET might lose two AI Teams.

So he got up, went to the galley, fixed some food, and had a snack while he watched out the wardroom viewport for the rest of his Team.

Triga knew enough to leave him undisturbed at this point. Besides, with Katwin linked to CY, she had plenty of work to do because she knew from Katwin's displays that it was an intense session for the frail mentic receiver whose basic physical condition never was very strong anyway. Nor was Katwin's psychological and mentical condition strong, either, except for her special talent: telepathic reception with the assistance of an intelligence amplifier.

Only SIGNET and its AI Teams used this sort of mentic high technology, but it was necessary for the very existence and operation of SIGNET across light years of interstellar space. No large and widespread institution such as SIGNET could exist and operate without rapid and timely communication. Long communication delays limit the extent of operational effectiveness. Communication transmittal speeds had to be less than the reaction time of the system. Otherwise, it could never become stable and would, in all probability, go hyperbolic instead.

But that was the farthest thing from Peter Starbuck's mind as he sat watching out the port for signs of his team members returning. This operation — and he knew the assignment message was coming in at the moment — would take every bit of know-how, technology, *and* experience he and his team possessed, plus the backup from CYMaster on Coleshore and other factors he could only guess at right then. This wasn't the usual SIGNET mission. It was literally life and death.

Chapter Two

In the brilliant tarmac lights beyond the tailring of the *Starace*, Starbuck spotted someone approaching the ship. There was no mistaking the lanky form of Shochona.

Good! But where was David O'Hara, the jumpman? Starbuck wasn't worried about O'Hara; the huge man was capable of taking care of himself and had done so quite well on many worlds. He had, however, been concerned about Shochona. The older woman had grown up in a macrolife ship at half a standard gee and wasn't very strong even in Plethora's 0.89-gee field, much less the standard gee field of the *Starace*. However, her imposing physical size often tended to balance out her weakness. Few thugs care to take on someone, even a frail woman, who's almost two meters tall. In addition, as the team's jump detector, Shochona had a sixth sense akin to clairvoyance. Even without the assistance of an IA, she could become aware of danger in time to avoid it — usually. There had been times, however. And those times were the ones that caused Starbuck to worry about her.

Even though he was still missing his jumpman, Starbuck felt better because Shochona was back. In spite of her prudish attitude toward a universe of abundance and liberty, Shochona projected the mother image, a factor that was critically important to any AI Team. The extent to which this was a factor was, however, a moot point. The closeness and interdependence of members of an AI Team caused every member some anxiety when they were apart on R-and-R, even though each needed the temporary but soothing separation and vacation from the closeness required during team operations.

It occurred to Starbuck that perhaps SIGNET hadn't thought the team situation through when they'd done the conceptual design a couple of centuries ago. Perhaps the design of the AI Team brought the team members too close and made them too dependent upon all the other members. There were very few situations in which Peter Starbuck could act alone. This restraint on the ability of a team or an agent investigator to act quickly might cause difficulties (and had done so in some of the cases AI Team 017 had handled in the past).

But, on the other hand, no single individual possessed the combined talents of an AI Team. SIGNET and the other security, investigation, and insurance adjustment organizations had never been able to locate among the so-called "Thousand Worlds" a single individual human being who was at the same time a telepathic sender, telepathic receiver, clairvoyant detector, and starship telekinetic jumper. Without these four "special talents," no individual SIGNET Agent Investigator could possibly manage to get around the Thousand Worlds. Even C+ flight at Mike 30K wasn't fast enough. Only by the process of jumping with the talents of a jumper working through an intelligence amplifier plus the talents of a detector — also working through an IA — could any SIGNET team move instantaneously to where trouble developed. And without the transmittermen and receivers working through IAs, instantaneous communication would be impossible at interstellar distances. Communications utilizing the same gravito-inertial radiation that drove ordinary star ships at up to Mike 30K was too slow at a transmission velocity of 3.42 light years per hour. In fact, the mere physical factors of distance and signal transmission speed — even at irrational near-zero-time propagation — made old social institutions such as empires impossible. Historical analysis had shown that such systems have a tendency to come apart when they grow into very large forms.

Feeling that he had himself under control once again, Starbuck sought out Triga and found her worrying and fussing over the trance-like Katwin. "I've leveled out," he told Triga. "Check me over to be sure, then I'll link with CY."

The biotech looked him up and down, mostly up because she came only to the middle of his chest. She glanced up at the readouts over Katwin and shook her head. "Peter, you're Priority Number Two at the moment. Katwin linked with CY more than thirty minutes ago, and she did it in her usual child-like fashion without proper pre-link. Somehow she must have sensed the AI Team termination, too. As a result, she's in trouble now but doesn't know it. I've got to stay with her or run the risk of having her go catatonic."

"But . . ." Starbuck began.

"Take your choice," Triga told him abruptly. Now she was under pressure. "I can get you linked, or we can most probably lose a good receiver. If we lose Katwin, we'll have to replace her. That means we go back to ColeShore, pick up a new receiver, and get the receiver tuned with the team. That will put us out of action for months. We'll never be able to get back to help out in time. Brinker will have to send in another team instead. I don't think any of us would want Giles or Haruda to take this one away from us. Above and beyond that, you wouldn't want to lose Katwin. Neither would I. All of us love her too much for that and too much to let her ruin herself because her poor little six-year-old child's mind told her she was badly and urgently needed to the extent that she went ahead and linked without proper prep. Take your choice, Peter."

There was no choice, of course.

There was nothing to do but wait.

Which Starbuck resigned himself to doing until Shochona strode into the compartment. She put her hands on her hips and glared at him. "Well! Whatever the emergency is, I'm just glad that it interrupted your orgy."

Peter sighed. He might have anticipated this, he told himself. Shochona's latent talent as a detector at interstel-

lar distances wasn't as sharp when she wasn't linked with
an IA, but she possessed enough of a talent to be a
semi-clairvoyant busybody. Valuable and indispensable as
her talent was to the team, she was considered a nuisance
sometimes by Starbuck. She'd been raised in the rigid
environment of a macrolife ship run on very strict moral
principles. Furthermore, since she'd arrested her physical
age at around 50 years, she appeared older than Starbuck
(but wasn't) and therefore had assumed the role of the
ship's "housemother." Hardly a single R-and-R ended without a morality lecture from Shochona.

But today Starbuck wanted none of it. "Seal it, Shochona!
We've lost an AI Team, and I'm in no mood to be lectured
to."

"Oh, my!" Shochona breathed. "So that's what I
sensed!"

"Where were they lost?" Starbuck wanted to know,
hoping that her unamplified talent might have picked up a
glimmer of data. He certainly hadn't, but then again he
was no clairvoyant.

Shochona shrugged. She waved her long arm. "Out
there . . . that-a-way . . . somewhere. I can't pin-point it
without CY's help. But I got the feeling of a very poor
planet and people dressed in black . . ."

"The Grim Reaper . . ."

"No, no," Shochona shook her head. "There was no
symbolism in what I sensed. I don't think there was, at
any rate . . ."

"Maybe. Maybe not." Starbuck knew the extent to
which the human mind resorted to symbols and symbolism
when confronted with the unknown. "In the meantime,
where's David? He should be here by now. Can you locate
him?"

"Hmm. I'll try." Shochona looked wistfully at the
ceiling in an absent-minded manner. After almost a half-
minute of silence, Shochona suddenly snapped, "David's
in trouble!"

"Not again! What's it this time?"

"I see David on a pallet. He's semi-conscious." Shochona shook her head sadly. "I believe the idiot's been drinking again. What *can* we do to correct him and get him set on the right path? Alcohol is the bane . . ."

"I know you're a reformer by nature, Shochona," Starbuck told her, "but each of us is who we are . . . period. It's too bad David has a problem. He's the best jumpman I've ever known. But it's *his* problem, and he seems to enjoy it. Question of the moment: How do we get to him, get him out of trouble and get him back?"

"By rights, we should let him rot wherever he's lying . . . to atone for his sins!"

"You don't really mean that, Shochona," Starbuck reminded her.

Shochona sighed. "Not really, I suppose. I never do, although I say it anyway." She appeared to change personalities, becoming a no-nonsense mother type instead of the crusading religious zealot. "Very well, I'll organize a recovery effort. Peter, you can't leave the ship right now; data is coming in. I'll get Isky to go along with me."

"No personal weapons," Starbuck reminded her. "Not needed on a well-policed R-and-R world such as this . . ."

"No personal weapons in sight," Shochona amended his reminder. "There's still danger even in the most closely policed cultures. I'll set the communications for Channel 25A. If Isky and I need help, we'll call for it."

Starbuck dismissed the situation from the front of his mind. Shochona and Iskander Sandrathama were competent people. They'd do what was necessary. If they got into trouble, they'd call for help.

Triga finally got Katwin's bio situation normalized and could afford to spend some time helping Starbuck prepare for linkage. With an experienced combination of acupuncture, pressure points, and chemotherapy, she helped Peter into the proper mental condition to permit him to direct-link with CY. While it was, of course, quite common to link with an IA at low baud rate for everyday use, working with an advanced SIGNET cybermech at high data transfer rates required psychological adaptation. Except for some university and industrial researchers, few people outside SIGNET, Justar, and Strakovkhaburo either knew of the techniques and capabilities or believed that the low data rate human nervous system could withstand such a speed-up. But, again, few people had developed the techniques for pre-link. SIGNET and its contemporaries certainly did little to encourage wider acceptance of the techniques, just as they preferred to keep other aspects of their operations very quiet. Neither super-C+ interstellar jump travel or high baud rate linkage would have been that much of a boon to the human race on the Thousand Worlds.

In spite of the many times he'd gone into high-rate linkage, Starbuck felt the impact of CY immediately he pulled the linkap over his head and reclined on the couch. It was almost a schizoid trauma, even though CY's linkage program demanded that the cybermech supress its own romanality, its preprogrammed rom personality. The intelligence amplifier overwhelmed Starbuck's normal sensory inputs. With a mental wrenching, Starbuck suddenly found himself apparently in the familiar SIGNET briefing room on faraway ColeShore. He felt that Katwin was also there, but he couldn't see her. Starbuck knew that he was seeing and hearing and smelling the interior of the briefing room through the senses of Katwin's counterpart and CYMaster in SIGNET Headquarters. But it was as though his body was numb; the cybermechs had no sensors for touch or kinesthetics; they weren't considered to be vital inputs.

The quality of the sensor images weren't quite sharp enough, leading Starbuck to the conclusion that he was actually watching a data dump playback from CY rather than a real-time link through Katwin. Furthermore, some noise had been introduced into the circuit by Katwin's essential presence in the loop.

The link was also simplex because of Katwin's lone presence as a receiver. Without Isky, the team's transmitterman, who was off somewhere on Plethora at the moment, it was a one-way link. Perhaps it was just as well. What Starbuck needed right then was data. However, he found himself wishing for a full duplex comm team because he had an occasional question to ask and couldn't. This unique situation could lead to trouble later . . . and in retrospect it did.

There were two people in the room. Starbuck's pulse quickened at the sight of Tayreze Nambe, Brinker's sensual and voluptuous Number Two. Her official SIGNET title was "Vice Executive." Starbuck had always maintained privately on the basis of his own acquaintance with her that SIGNET would be hard-pressed to find anyone better qualified to execute vice. Tayreze and Starbuck had always matched up well, both being near-immortal superhumans who had utilized every advantage of biotechnology. In spite of the pleasant memories that Tayreze's image invoked for him, Starbuck's self-control reestablished itself quickly because he knew that Tayreze was light years away and that her image was only a cybermechgen in his mind. He put down the playful urge to fantasize with her image; this wasn't the time. Tayreze Nambe was on the job and, exotic as she appeared to be, she was all business when it came to official SIGNET matters.

In sharp contrast to Tayreze Nambe's stunning beauty was Rudi Witkowski whose life was enmeshed almost solely in technology to the neglect of his personal appearance. The man had steadfastly refused to take advantage of the benefits of biocosmetics. Surrounded by superbeautiful people, Rudi Witkowski remained plain, perhaps by disinclination to let the biocosmeticians go to work but also perhaps because his ordinary appearance made him stand out. However, no one in SIGNET would dare call Rudi a technerd to his face. They had far too much respect for the man's brilliance as chief of SIGNET's so-called "Department of Super Weapons and Dirty Tricks." Rudi Witkowski, a frail and non-violent man, had created some of the most deadly personal weapons ever dreamed up, and at one time or another all SIGNET AI Teams owed their survival to Rudi's genius.

Tayreze Nambe was speaking with the help of audiovisuals that switched in when required, washing over the image of the office and its occupants.

"Peter, this is an emergency assignment for AI Team zero-one-seven," Nambe's image spoke. "Sorry to call you away from a well-earned R-and-R, especially on Plethora. It must have been fun, even if it lasted only two days. We know that planet, don't we? Incidentally, Brinker offers his apologies for not being here to conduct the initial briefing. This is an emergency and it took us by surprise.

"We've lost an AI Team. There hasn't been time to analyze the possible consequences since we have very little baseline data at the moment. This is only the second team we've lost. Needless to say, it shouldn't have happened. Therefore, we not only have to cover their operation by sending in another team, but we *must* find out why they were lost so we can establish safeguard doctrines to prevent it from happening again. You've come close. We've all come close. But our doctrines are designed to prevent losing teams.

"I'll not mince words with you, Peter. Since we don't know what happened, we fully realize that by sending in another team, we may well lose that team, too. We're fortunate in one respect: Team zero-one-seven is not only the sole team available at the moment, but you're the best team we've got."

Flattery will get her everything, Starbuck thought. He considered the accolade as just part of a pep talk. Team 017 was good. Whether Team 017 was the best remained to be seen insofar as Peter Starbuck was concerned. It was well that Starbuck thought that way, because Tayreze Nambe's following remarks would certainly have taken the puff out of his ego.

"Certainly, Team zero-one-seven isn't perfect. You've made mistakes in the past. Every AI Team has. But you're very good, which is definitely in your favor. This time, you've got to be the best. In any operation during which a team has been lost, a single mistake could be your last if our preliminary assessment is correct."

Chapter Three

To Peter Starbuck, coming out of direct link with CY was always like awakening from a very vivid dream. As the sights, sounds, smells, and feel of the comm compartment of the *Starace* became reality around Starbuck again, he found himself both ravenously hungry and faintly fatigued.

Triga was monitoring his couch sensors and knew this, too. "Food," Triga told him. "Then rest while we get under way."

Starbuck shook his head and was immediately sorry he'd done so. The hunger and fatigue began to manifest themselves in a splitting frontal headache. "I didn't want to come back — as usual. But the way I feel, maybe I shouldn't have . . ."

Triga saw his condition on the monitors better than he sensed them himself — depressed blood sugar level, plus hypoxia caused by fatigue. She replied lightly, "If you really want, I'll dump you back on dirt. Plethora's a great place for going catatonic. Lots of people are laying around here in sans completely cato because they liked the IAs in the passion pits even better than reality, even on Plethora. And damn that AI Team for getting terminated!"

"I won't go back on Plethora without you, Doctor," Starbuck told her gently. "Worst case of *recreationus interruptus* I've ever known. And to think I gave you up to get intimate with a machine. Oh, SIGNET, what we won't do for you!"

Triga smiled. "Not to worry. I'll get you on your feet again. It's going to take me much longer to fix David,"

28

she remarked. "In the meantime, don't complicate things. Relax for a few minutes. You can't do anything right now anyway . . ."

Starbuck started to sit up in spite of his condition. So Triga pushed him gently back down into the couch pads. When Starbuck attempted to resist and sit up anyway, she put her hand over his face and pushed hard. Starbuck laid back without further activity. In spite of her minute size, Triga was strong. And when Starbuck was in this sort of fatigued post-linkage state, she was far stronger than he in spite of his greater size. She looked down at him and shook her finger in front of his nose. "Now, now! Don't fight Triga! Or Triga will just have to give you a whammy and make you relax!" She tapped the keypad, ordering CY to repattern some of Starbuck's nerve responses through the non-intrusive couch interfaces.

"Okay, okay," Starbuck told her with a huge sigh, relaxing to the inevitable. "But what's the story with David?"

Triga shook her head sadly. "Can't hold his liquor, poor man. Never known an Eyreman who could. Massive overload of ethanol," Triga explained.

"How long will it take to get him lucid again?"

Triga checked Starbuck's readouts, bounced up, and bounced over to the lift well. Triga was the sort who bounced. Starbuck decided that on her it always looked good. Before she stepped into the well to go below, she turned to him and remarked, "You assume, of course, that David was lucid to begin with. Give me about ten minutes."

"Why so long?" Starbuck asked in all seriousness.

But Triga didn't take it that way. "Because it takes me that much time to perform a miracle. And while I'm at it in my usual super-efficient manner, I'll rustle up some food for you, too. Relax!" She stepped into the lift well and disappeared.

Starbuck had no choice but to relax and let the data run quickly through his mind. First of all, he was appalled that there was so little of it. He was going to be forced to base a mission on totally inadequate data. He didn't like that. It bothered him.

He felt a touch on his cheek and looked up to see the thin, pale, but beautiful face of Katrina Ivanova — "Katwin" to her team family because that's the way she pronounced her name. There probably wasn't a more adept receiver in the known universe, Starbuck believed. Katwin was an enormously powerful cholinergic telepath receiver in a nubile young woman's body . . . and a mind that in spite of all available psychotechnology and patterning remained about six Earth years old.

"Are you all right, Peter?" her little girl's voice asked anxiously.

Peter took her hand in his and smiled. "Yes, Katwin, I'm all right. How about you?"

Katwin nodded, but she didn't smile. "Somebody is hurt, Peter. Can we help them?" Katwin rarely understood the content of the messages she received with CY's help even though she remembered the entire contents of every message she'd ever received. They were never erased from her eidetic memory. She had been trained to maintain the strictest confidentiality with the message contents. Now she only sensed that something horrible had happened. She didn't understand what it was.

Starbuck shook his head sadly. "No, Katwin, we can't. But we'll go and find out what happened so that it doesn't happen again. So don't worry about it."

Katwin brightened. "I don't worry, Peter. When I'm with you and the team, I don't worry. Nothing can hurt me when I'm with you."

Starbuck nodded. *I hope so,* he thought, *I certainly hope so.* But he knew that now there was some question about that. Going over the information in his mind, he knew it was going to be the most dangerous operation he and the team had ever undertaken.

There was never a question as to whether or not he *should* commit the team to it. Another team had been lost. It was absolutely essential that he take his team in to find

out why and, if possible, to handle within the Canons of
Metalaw those who'd done the deed. It wasn't the universe
the team was up-against. It rarely was. That was for the
scientists. This time, as usual, the team was up against the
deadliest beings in the known universe: humans.

In fact, however, he knew he *wouldn't* commit the team
until they'd all had the opportunity to know as much as he
did about what they'd be getting into. Once he'd been
brought back to a reasonable state of mental and physical
well-being, and once David O'Hara had as well, it would
be up to the team members to say yea or nay. He was only
the team leader. Starbuck would not and never had led the
team into any operation without their full knowledge and
support of what was known to be involved.

And this certainly would be no exception.

Isky Sandrathama and Shochona were waiting in the
wardroom when Peter and Katwin came in. Triga and
David were nowhere to be seen. In response to Peter's
unvoiced question, Shochona said sourly, "Give Triga
another few minutes. David was in sad shape when we
dragged him in. I can't understand why he wants to drown
his problems in ethanol when there are other methods
available which don't debilitate half as badly."

Isky snorted. "Come off it, Shochona! People are enti-
tled to choose their own form of poison!" As a transmitterman, Isky was strongly acetecholic and had a sharp-
edged personality to go along with it. It grated on some
people, Shochona in particular. But, on the other hand,
Shochona's puritanical moral code grated on Isky whose
cultural background was totally different. Because of the
way they carried on with each other, Starbuck often wondered how they were able to work so well together in the
vital task of making interstellar jumps. But they did. Perhaps, he thought, opposites attract in mentical science as
they do in physical science.

"Well, you've certainly chosen a wonderful poison for
yourself," Shochona observed. "Haven't you seen the scientific reports of the genetic effects of cannabis sativa . . . ?"

"So? My culture has used tetrahydracannabinol in various forms for untold centuries. On the other hand, David's culture uses ethanol, which has its own unique effects on unborn zygotes. I seem to recall that your macrolife clan happens to run high negative ion atmospheres during devotions and love-ins, a factor which has its own consequences. And don't make any wisecracks about the obvious effects of use in my case. I don't intend to have children now, not at my advanced age," Isky shot back. He paused briefly, then added, "It seems like a couple of centuries since I gave it up. Now it doesn't make any difference because I've already paid my biological dues: two children. And they've done fine, thank you."

"As you continue to remind me," Shochona put in.

Family, Starbuck thought.

Triga came up the lift well with David in tow. Shochona was right. The jumpman must have been in bad shape when they'd found him. Even after Triga's therapy, David O'Hara appeared to be ragged around the edges. He looked sourly around at the rest of the team and started to say something, but didn't. Instead, he sat down heavily, even in the reduced gee field of Plethora.

It was Triga who broke the silence. "Well, now that we're all together in the same place, I suppose you're all wondering why our devoted and esteemed leader called off the R-and-R. So am I. Care to elaborate, Agent Inspector Starbuck?"

"I'll thank you to keep a respectful tongue in your head, biotechnician, or you're likely to end up hustling emesis collectors in some garden spot like Far Gone," Starbuck told her lightly. AI Team 017 was composed of a group of rugged individualists. All AI Teams were. As team leader, Starbuck had the often difficult task of melding their talents together so that each of them ended up going in more or less the same direction. However, he often felt that his team's activities were analogous to Brownian movement. His was rarely an easy job. But he'd learned that a sense of humor was a ubiquitous characteristic of each team

member, even Katwin. Not only did it help them maintain
their perspectives, but down deep inside each of them they
enjoyed this work. They had to enjoy it. Although longevity had its shortcomings, it also forced people to do the
sort of work they enjoyed lest they be eternally bored.
Challenge, the threat of danger, the demand to stay mentally sharp, the need to work closely with other people on
a team — all these factors and more were part of the heri-
tage of a species that had become the most effective
hunters their home world had ever bred. Near-immortality
couldn't and didn't touch those successful ancestral factors.

But then the humor went out of his voice. "As some of
you know, we've lost an AI Team. We don't know why or
how. But we've been given the assignment to go in, find
out what happened, and cover their operation — if we choose
to do it."

The details were sparse, Starbuck told them. AI Team
033 under Joshua Zing had been sent in response to an
emergency call from a SIGNET client, Cama Universal
Corporation (Pty) on Thya, a terrestrial-sized frontier world
in the Garyon system. The message had come via robot
courier which had managed to break out of the system and
get to a SIGNET agent on Idalia some fifteen light years
distant. This was an unusual way for a message to be
transmitted, but it had apparently been sent via courier
drone because that was the *only* way a message could have
gotten out. Reason: the message reported that the planet
Thya was under physical attack and being occupied.

"Invasion?" Isky couldn't believe it. "But that's against
all the Canons of Metalaw!"

David O'Hara was shaking his head in disbelief. "They've
gotta be kiddin'," he muttered. "Invade a planet? Come
on, now! A planet's a big chunk o' real estate. And why
invade? Easier and cheaper to get what you want by
tradin'."

"Except when you don't have anything to trade," Katwin
suddenly said, cutting right to the heart of the matter. "If I
want your necklace, Uncle David, and if I don't have

anything you want in trade, I'd have to take it from you if I wanted it bad enough. And if I could. And if I wouldn't get caught and punished for doing it . . ."

"I know, I know, Katwin," O'Hara told her, waving his hand. "But an invasion of a planet just doesn't make any sense at all. Takes lots of people. Enormous command and logistic problems. And very, very expensive . . ."

"David's right," Isky put in. "Are you sure the message wasn't garbled?"

"I'm sure," Starbuck said simply.

"So am I," Katwin added.

"Why?" Isky asked.

"Let me continue, and I'll tell you," Starbuck went on as calmly as he could. "When the drone's message was forwarded to ColeShore by our Idalia agent's transmitterman, Brinker sent Zing's team to get additional data. Zing jumped into the Garyon system and was challenged immediately by Thya Approach Control."

Schochona suddenly held up her hand and remarked, "I know that region. The Garyon system is on the Fringe. Very primitive. But the traffic there couldn't be heavy enough for them to have a planetary approach control."

"They've apparently got one now," Starbuck observed. "Zing's *Starbow* was cleared into quarantine orbit, but he declared a medical emergency and requested immediate planetfall. That was denied under the authority of someone or something called the 'Black Path of Thoth'. Zing invoked the interstellar rules of the road and broke orbit to go in anyway. They touched down. That much we know. No further reports came from Zing's team. But twenty-two SIGNET stations picked up the termination scream forty-seven hours later. And some really adept receivers report that it was exceptionally intense and painful." Starbuck shook his head in disbelief.

O'Hara wasn't convinced. "Invasion? And then losin' a team? Hey, look, this isn't some taped space opera for planet pounders who never get off their home worlds! This is the real universe! An invasion doesn't sound real. And neither does losin' a team. How can you assume that the team is gone? Just on the basis o' losing contact with their transmitterman?''

''They're gone,'' Starbuck stated with certainty. ''I'm not a trained telepath receiver like Katwin, but I heard the termination scream. I've heard it only once before. Once you've heard it, you can never forget what it is.''

Katwin didn't say anything. Although she'd heard it, she didn't know or understand what it really was. Not only hadn't she heard anything like it before, but a six-year-old child doesn't really understand death, even if it's happened around the child many times before. Since Katwin didn't understand it and since the intensity of the termination scream was so powerful, her simple child's mind rejected it. It couldn't exist, so it didn't exist as far as she was concerned. Only her SIGNET training had permitted her to receive the subsequent message from ColeShore, but she'd served solely as a receiver for it. The ColeShore message she'd received in linkage with CY had been treated by her simply as data because she didn't want to understand it.

This peculiar psychological quirk didn't mean, however, that Katwin didn't sense that something very serious and very ''bad'' had taken place. The unknown didn't frighten Katwin. Neither did death. But knowing that an AI Team like the one she served with had ''gone away'' coupled with not understanding and therefore rejecting the fact along with the trauma of the terminal scream resulted in a confusion and paradox that frightened her.

''Any other data?'' Shochona asked.

Starbuck shook his head. ''None.''

''How about this 'Black Path of Thoth'? What's the database say about it?'' Shochona persisted.

Again, Starbuck shook his head. ''Again, nothing. No references in any of the data banks. CYMaster queried the data banks of Justar and Strakovkhaburo. Nothing there, either. CYMaster even went to Data Prime, and there's nothing either under that term or in connection with anything in this region of space.''

Isky fidgeted and drummed his fingers on the wardroom table. "Okay, okay, but how about the invaded world? What's in the roms about Thya?"

"Terrestrial type world, Type G-one primary. Indigenous life forms were primitive," Shochona put in tonelessly as though she were CY's vox dump. "Been settled about eighty years, initially by a mixed group of Moravians and third-generation Slovenes. Initial surveys indicated excellent possibility of extensive primary metal deposits. Look it up with CY; there's a lot of data available."

"What's your quick evaluation of the world?" Triga asked. "Can you sum up its most outstanding attribute?"

"Certainly: Quite rich in natural resources in comparison to other known worlds in the region."

"Aha!" Isky exploded. "Now we may be onto something! This 'Black Path of Thoth' must have come from a reasonably close inhabited world. What other worlds are in the region, and what are their characteristics?"

"Get CY on the line," David suggested. "We can ask him."

"Humph!" Shochona snorted derisively. "What does that collection of slightly impure silicon crystals know that I don't?" As the team's jump detector, Shochona not only had the talent to "see" where David was jumping the ship, but she prided herself in having a CY-like general knowledge of the Thousand Worlds of human settlement. She looked pensive for about thirty seconds then went on, "No world called 'Thoth' in the region. In fact, no planet called 'Thoth' anywhere. But there are four settled worlds within twelve light years of Thya. Interesting! That's a general region of the galaxy where all the surveyed worlds seem to be resource-poor rocks or hydrogen gas giants."

"With all due respects, Shochona," Starbuck put in as he swung around in his chair to face CY's sensors. "CY, Starbuck here."

"Hello, Peter. Feeling better, I see. Sorry that linkage takes so much out of you. Do you want me to reprogram . . . ?"

"Not right now, CY, thank you. And never without

Triga's overview,'' Starbuck told the ship's cybermech.
"Right now, check your galactology databank. I'm interested in the region of the Garyon system.''

"Interesting region,'' CY remarked. "What do you want
to know about it?''

"Whatever you didn't tell me in linkage. Why is the
planet Thya 'reasonably rich' in natural resources while
other surveyed worlds in the general galactic region are
known to be resource poor?''

"Thya in the Garyon system is located in a node of the
spiral arm where there was much active star formation in
gas clouds as recently as about four billion years ago,''
CY reported. "The surveyed worlds in that node are all
reasonably rich in natural resources.''

"What's the bigger picture, CY?'' Starbuck persisted.
"Present a polar projection of that sector of the galaxy on
the screen, please.''

Flick! Without a sound from CY, the wardroom wall
came alive with a holographic projection of the galactic
region around Thya.

"Give me call-outs,'' Starbuck added.

The names of stars and worlds, where and when known,
flicked on next to points of light.

"No, no,'' Shochona broke in. "That shows only the
region in Thya's node. CY, expand the projection to en-
compass the surrounding nodes in the spiral arm.''

Flick!

Starbuck got to his feet and stretched his arm out to
point at the holo-projection. "There! I knew it! I knew
there had to be something like that!''

Chapter Four

Even in three-dimensional holo presentation, there was an obvious rift between the stars of the spiral arm. Thya was in one node. The nearest surveyed and settled world in the same node was Idalia some fifteen light years away. But the rift was only about six light years across. In the other node were four surveyed planets. Two were shown as being settled.

"CY, please wipe the display and project the basic data on the two inhabited worlds closest to Thya," he ordered the cybermech.

Flick!

"Arator and Khughar," Shochona muttered. "I should have known."

"Should have know what, Shochona?" Peter asked.

"Those are two of the most miserable worlds anyone ever tried to settle out in that part of the galaxy," the older woman explained. "Look at the data CY projects. Rocky, resource-poor worlds, both of them. The stars and their planets in that separate node formed under different conditions with differing abundances of basic elements. The stars there are cooler. Therefore, they were less able to fuse the heavier elements. Very little iron there."

"And how do you maintain a high-tech civilization without lots of iron?" Isky put in rhetorically.

"You don't," David O'Hara observed. "You trade for it."

"With what?" Triga asked.

"I have a sneaking hunch," Starbuck mused, "that we

do indeed have an invasion on our hands. And I think I know why.''

''I think I do, too,'' David put in. ''When people get tossed into a situation of scarcity, they revert to the old action principles of scarcity economics and the Golden Rule.''

''He who has the gold makes the rules,'' was Shochona's comment. ''Direct antithesis of Haley's Rule of Metalaw. The foundation for the Atilla Syndrome.''

''I don't get it,'' Isky admitted in a confused tone of voice. ''That stuff doesn't work anywhere any longer. Took a long time for my part of Tellus to learn it, but it doesn't even work in the Indus Valley any longer . . . and that's where it was invented.''

David was the philosopher of the team, so he tried to explain in his laid-back homely manner, ''Isky, old chum, all of us take metalaw for granted these days. It's difficult for us to understand how anybody could live under any other basic ethical code. Look, it's only been a few centuries since people at large discovered that it's easier to trade than raid. Very recent cultural development. But when things get tough, people have a tendency to regress to old methods that they *know* will work, even if they *know* that only down at the genetic level.''

''But an *invasion*?'' Isky was still unconvinced.

''Yeah, I didn't think so, either, Isky, but the data seems to show it could be the case,'' O'Hara told him.

Starbuck broke into the philosophical dissertation. If he didn't, he knew that David and Isky would drag the intellectual discussion on, drawing Shochona into it as well. They had a job to do — if they wanted to take it. Starbuck felt they were getting closer to some initial answers. But he wanted to concentrate on action items, and he needed more data right at that point.

''CY, data search, please.''

''At your service, Peter.''

''I need settlement history and current demographic data on the two planets you've displayed and tagged — Arator and Khughar. Display it, please, and let's have audio presentation as well."

"Working . . . Arator: Initial settlement in four-thirty-two New Galactic Calendar. Ten thousand settlers drawn mostly from Negri Sembilan and Tregannu on Tellus with a cadre of high-tech Asiatics. The last general census showed that the Aratorans were barely holding their own. There is more data."

Starbuck decided that ten thousand Aratorans couldn't mount an invasion of a planet in another star system. "How about Khughar?"

"Khughar: Initial settlement in four-sixty-three NGC, twenty-five thousand settlers from Selangor and Mazara on Tellus, seven thousand from the settlement world, Sendelmalik. After initial problems on a resource-poor world, these people developed highly advanced biotechnology. Khughar has a small tourist industry. As recently as seven years ago, Khughar was exporting genetically-tailored feed grain plants to the other worlds in the region." CY fell silent.

One of the major problems involved in working with any sort of cybermech is the simple fact that it's the perfect slave. It always does exactly and precisely everything that's requested of it. But it also does *only* what is requested of it, nothing more. It never anticipates. It never guesses. It never operates on anything other than logic and data. In spite of a lifetime of working with these extensions of human intellect, Starbuck often forgot this. In common with many other people, he tended to assign human qualities to cybermechs (and other machinery) and therefore grew to think of them as humans. It took a session such as this to remind him that he was dealing with a totally different kind of intellect. He sighed and asked his cybermech, "What's the current status of Khughar?"

"Current status unknown."

Starbuck raised his eyebrows. "Why?"

"Khughar authorities have filed no reports for the past seven years."

Starbuck kept it up. "Why?"

"Reasons are unknown."

"Have reports been requested?"

"Yes."

"Have any replies to the requests for reports been received from Khughar?"

"Yes. Some replies have stated that they were just too busy right then. Other requests have been ignored."

"Enough for now, CY." Starbuck turned from the console to his team members. "I think we've found the culprits: Khugharians."

"Khughars," Isky corrected him.

"Huh?"

"If you're going to follow the correct linguistic conventions, you've got to call them Khughars."

"Very well, Khughars. I stand corrected by our swarthy but hyperthyroidal colleague from the valley of the Sindhu."

"Sorry, but I've got to correct you again, Glorious Leader," Isky broke in. "It's the Indus River valley. Sindhu is the sanskrit word for 'water' or 'river'. And, technically speaking, Lahore isn't in the Indus River Valley . . ."

Starbuck sighed. Dealing with his team was often an exercise in tact. "I stand triply corrected. Be that as it may, team, we've got to decide whether or not to take the assignment. As usual, I won't call for a vote until we've got all available data in hand and each of us has had time to study it." He turned and spoke to the cybermech's input panel. "CY, display as well as print out hard copy of all available data on the inhabitants of Khughar."

Flick!

Whish!

The display on the screen changed while a stack of about fifty pages of hard copy appeared in the print-out tray.

"Be careful what you ask for," Triga remarked. "You'll get it."

"Yeah, never ask a cybermech for wall-to-wall data," O'Hara added.

"You sure you don't want us all to go into linkage with CY to get the full story?" Shochona wondered.

"No, it would take longer to prep all of you than if everyone just sits down and starts reading hard copy or display," Triga Rimmon reminded them. "So get to work. Vacation's over . . ."

Starbuck sat down with Katwin and began to explain the hard-copy print out to her. Although Katwin remembered everything in the messages from ColeShore, these had contained none of the detailed demographics on the Khughars. Katwin could read both hard-copy printouts and display graphics, but she usually didn't understand some of the words and terms. Peter knew from experience that the quickest way to get the information to Katwin in a meaningful manner was to work one-on-one with her. No one ever questioned this procedure. Everyone on the team knew that Katwin would remember everything; if she understood something about the information, she often made amazing syntheses that other team members completely overlooked. And at times when CY and his terabit memories weren't available, Katwin more than filled the bill in that regard. Katwin was, in addition to the team's receiver, also the encyclopedic synthesist.

Explaining things to Katwin also helped Starbuck. As a teacher many decades ago in a different time and on a different world, he'd learned well the old truth: To teach or explain something to someone else, you have to understand it yourself. Going through this exercise with Katwin helped him catch all the little details and nuances that he might otherwise have missed.

Khughar was typical of many of the settled planets of the Thousand Worlds. Many people who don't understand social dynamics tend to think of planets as being monolithic in terms of populations or cultures. Even though Tellus and most of the oldest inhabited worlds house very diverse people and social organizations, people still tend to think monolithically about worlds. Starbuck was as guilty as anyone. So were the members of his team. Khughars as such didn't exist unless one referred to undifferentiated peoples from that world. Typically, Khughar's original stock of settlers had quickly fragmented once a solid, self-sufficient, and self-supporting settlement had been established. Small groups set out to settle other promising regions of the planet. In spite of excellent communications and reasonably rapid travel, such splinter settlements inevitably developed their own regional mannerisms and other cultural artifacts. This had happened on Khughar because a rocky-type planet large enough to hold a nitrogen-oxygen atmosphere is a *big* world at least ten thousand kilometers in diameter.

According to the data now at least seven years old, there were at least four cultural groups on Khughar — the Dyons, the Kalocs, the Lanigers, and the Zhedarons, the first two being the largest populations with the latter two quite small in number and influence in planetary affairs. There appeared to be no strong racio-genetic differences between the four groups. The Dyons were the direct descendants of the original mixed bag of settlers. The Lanigers and the Zhedarons were family groups that had gone out to develop specific regions of Khughar and had evolved into rather inbred cultural groupings of their own. The Kalocs, on the other hand, had for some unknown reason split from the Dyons and consequently appeared as a totally separate social institution on the planet. However, the Dyons seemed to be the most technically advanced while the Kalocs had become the most numerous. Dyon technicians were the ones who had developed the high level of biotechnology for which the planet was best known.

Then, for an unknown reason, the data flow from Khughar became mysteriously and strangely truncated seven years ago. They'd made no demographic reports. The only data available was business data mostly from the Dyon element — imports, exports, balance of trade, stock prices of Dyonian firms that happened to be listed on the interstellar exchanges, futures trends, precious metals prices, and currency conversion numbers. Business with the other worlds in the drift went on as usual on Khughar. But most of it went on with the Dyons. And most of the Dyonian firms were service organizations or biotechnical agro-companies.

The Kaloc cultural data was even more fascinating. They were producing a lot of animal-based products. For some reason, the Kalocs did a thriving business in "specialized neuroelectronic equipment" as well as "bioelectronic elements." They imported a lot of primary metals, a fact which always skewed the import-export balances.

"They owe other people a lot of money," Katwin observed.

Starbuck paused and looked at the pale, beautiful girl. Katwin had hit a point which had eluded Starbuck and the others — perhaps even those at SIGNET Headquarters on ColeShore as well.

The data was there, if somewhat submerged in all the other numbers.

Beginning about ten years before, the level of Kaloc import activity increased slowly on a linear basis at first and then on a cubic curve. Conversely, exports began to decline. The negative balance of trade numbers were small at first because the Kalocs apparently conducted a thriving export business with their equipment. Nine years ago, the balance turned negative. Yet the exponentially-increasing value of imports didn't reflect an over-extended credit line. Then the Kaloc import-export balance had gone negative seven years ago, and data flow stopped.

It took a few minutes for Starbuck to dig this additional data out of CY's library files. But when he had it, Peter Starbuck thought he finally had a handle on why the Kaloc people of Khughar had attempted something totally unprecedented in the annals of interstellar trade and settlement: invasion.

He was wrong, of course, but he didn't know it at the time. He'd missed another extremely obvious datum. It was to be expected, of course, and the post-operation critique would bear this out later. Peter Starbuck was the oldest member of the team, but even he had been born in the twenty-first century. The discrepancy would have been patently obvious to anyone born and raised anywhere on Tellus before the Kahn Transition and before the universal acceptance of the Canons of Metalaw by the interstellar community of the Thousand Worlds.

When everyone on the team had completed their perusal of the available data nearly an hour later — Shochona took the longest, preferring to "assimilate and digest" the information — they met around the wardroom table.

"Anyone have any questions? Anything not understood?" Starbuck wanted to know.

"Lots of questions," Isky rejoined. "I still don't understand why the Kalocs invaded Thya."

Starbuck looked around. He thought he knew why, but he wanted to find out if anyone else had come to the same conclusion.

"They wanted something the Thyans had," Katwin ventured. "When they couldn't trade for it, they decided to take what they wanted."

"Good analysis, Katwin," Isky told her, "but it still doesn't tell me why the Kalocs of Khughar are pulling off the first planetary invasion in history."

"Isky, old chap," O'Hara put in using his professorial philosopher's tone of voice, "It's really quite simple: When you want it and can't trade for it, you raid for it."

"Well, whatever the Khughars want, they must want it pretty bad. Invasions are expensive."

"But perhaps their last resort," O'Hara observed.

Isky shrugged. "Still too many unanswered questions . . ."

There was silence around the table. Finally, Starbuck asked for the decision. "Do we take the operation?"

Silence.

Starbuck took it as the silence of acquiescence. But as far as Starbuck was concerned, it had to be a unanimous voiced decision because they had to work together as a team. "Any one have an objection?"

Isky shook his head. "No objection. Just a concern. But we take it."

Shochona chimed in, "Same here. Not enough data, but sufficient to begin the operation. If we never took an operation because of inadequate or incomplete data to begin with, we'd end up taking none and trying to find work with Justar instead. We take it."

"Go," O'Hara said. "We have to do it. We must learn what happened to Joshua Zing's team."

"Agree," Triga added. "What we learn may prevent losing another team."

Katwin nodded. "But, please, everyone has to be very careful. We can't be a lost team, too . . ."

Chapter Five

"Don't get us in too close," Peter Starbuck warned. "We're supposed to be a survey ship with a fuel emergency."

"I know it," David said with professional calm and demeanor. "I'll do my job. Shochona, tell CY what's out there about thirty light-hours from the primary. Visualize it for him."

Shochona, like David, was reclining on the sensor couch and beginning her linkage with the intelligence amplifier portion of CY. "That's pretty close, David. Can you nail it within a third of a light-second?"

"If CY's master clock hasn't slipped."

"I'd be happier with a break-out point of about three hundred A.U.," Starbuck put in. "If there's any departure from the three-sigma . . ."

"How long do you want to take gettin' in at sub-light?" David asked his team leader. "The farther out we are when we break into sub-light, the more time this dastardly 'Black Path of Thoth' and his minions will have to zap us."

"Where would you want us to break out, David?"

"A survey ship has extremely accurate astrogation equipment. Thya is charted as a fringe world without much traffic. Any incomin' ship won't have to worry about system traffic. And the Garyon system is rather open. Not a lot of sky junk around it. Thin Oort Cloud. No problem. I can nail the break-out point plus or minus a third of a light-hour . . . if Shochona gives us the right picture."

"Worry about your own job, David," Shochona told him. "You, too, Peter."

"This is my job," Starbuck reminded her.

"Then do it," the older woman snapped irritably. "The book says that a good leader delegates and then stays out of the way. Triga, please get rid of the distractions. I've got work to do."

"Be quiet, Peter!" Triga Rimmon told him as she watched the bio telltale panels above the couches where the sensor outputs of both Shochona and Isky were displayed. "You know better than to interfere with a jump."

Starbuck took a deep breath. He realized he was meddling, trying to do the jobs his own team people did better than he ever could. It suddenly occurred to him that he was becoming far too concerned about this operation and therefore increasingly tense. He was reacting instinctively to the sure and certain danger at the other end of the jump. It held the potential of greater hazard than the end of any jump the team had ever made.

He knew what was bothering him the most; another AI team had been terminated out there in the Garyon system. The data said it had happened on Thya. But that didn't mean that it couldn't happen on the approach itself now that the invaders had been alerted to the fact that SIGNET knew. The "Black Path of Thoth" and his invading forces, size and strength unknown, could be ready for the entire Star Guard fleet. Certainly, the invaders would now be prepared to handle a single ship. He didn't know what to expect. That made this jump totally uncertain.

The *Starace* was about to become a sitting duck. Once the instantaneous interstellar jump was made by David with detection and direction from Shochona, both operating in linkage with CY, the team would be in the thick of it themselves, operating in the same place where another team had unsuccessfully gone. And once out of the jump, there was no hiding the fact that their starship had suddenly appeared in space contrary to all known laws of physics. So the jump had to be terminated far enough from the planetary system so the sudden appearance would be sensed by the now-present Khughar approach sensors as

the normal emergence of an ordinary starship from the C +
mode. He was hoping that the gravito-inertial sensors, if
the Khughars had any, would either fail to detect the end
of the jump or that the Khughar technicians would treat
the anomalous appearance of the ship as a glitch in the
often unreliable GI detection systems. He was counting on
the high probability that those technicians wouldn't
believe that a ship could appear simultaneously and therefore blame the sudden appearance on sensor problems. The
capability to instantaneously cause a starship to move light-
years was unknown to the Thousand Worlds at large. To
everyone other than SIGNET, Justar, and Strakovkhaburo
people whose true secret it was, such a thing was patently
impossible. Metalegal organizations and their AI teams
had lots of secrets, but the mentic interstellar jump was
probably the biggest.

An instantaneous interstellar jump is *physically* impossible because even a child knows that a system can't be
changed in zero time. This was the basic foundation of
Davis Mechanics which permitted such things as C + interstellar travel in the first place as well as providing a
rational explanation for the earlier theories of Einsteinian
relativity.

But, of course, an instantaneous relocation of matter
from one place to another isn't *mentically* impossible and
doesn't violate any natural laws on that level of the universe. It's just that no one, even those trained in the
mentic sciences, could perform the feat of moving nothing
more substantial than a rotating scrap of foil. Teleportation
was not a useful technology any more than telepathy had
replaced communications systems based on physical technology. At best, mentic technology was still an academic
curiosity. The human brain simply doesn't have the ability
to channel enough physical energy to cause major changes
in the physical universe. Only metalegal organizations such
as SIGNET had perfected the use of the intelligence amplifier to permit trained mentic adepts to move starships.
Actually, no one knew whether the adepts moved the ships

or whether the IAs did it with the help of adepts . . . or whether it was a mentical symbiosis.

It really didn't make much difference. Rudi Witkowski and his technological counterparts with the other metalegal organizations were still working on getting the answers, but it was a low priority matter. The answers weren't immediately important because what they had was working. Pure scientific research took a back seat to mundane everyday problems of applied technology. As it was in the beginning, so it is and always would be, Starbuck knew.

He stepped out of the compartment to let Shochona and David work without his distraction — Shochona to "see" where the *Starace* would jump to and tell CY, and David to use CY to make the jump itself.

And, when everything worked as it always did (Shochona and David were the best in the business; Starbuck had seen to it that they'd been assigned to his AI Team), there would be that instant of semi-confusion . . . and they'd be somewhere else. Starbuck had planned to enter the Garyon system and make planetfall on Thya in the guise of a survey ship with low-fuel reserves. The deception would be complete down to a critically low-fuel reserve — most of the star drive fuel had been off-loaded on Plethora.

In fact, the team and the entire ship had been bogused. Bogus ship documentation was available from CY. AI Team 017 was now the crew of the exploration starship *Serge A. Korff* registered in Astrabad Station, Tellus L-5. Their personal documentation in CY said so.

All SIGNET data in CY was secured with a scramble code; without the use of the proper passwords given in the proper sequence, CY would re-scramble the data if anyone without the passwords and sequencing tried to break the scramble. A single cypher or scramble can eventually be broken by a competent cybertech, but not when the cybermech is continually re-scrambling.

Even the physical equipment aboard the *Starace* was reasonably straightforward and unambiguous. It was what anyone would expect to find in any survey ship. The gear bore commonplace logos and ID plates, even down to believable serial numbers. Each component appeared to be an off-the-shelf commercially-available item. Modifications were unobtrusive and extremely hard to find. Even if someone did spot those mods, their presence could be justified on the basis of experimental equipment for survey work.

The real power and strength of AI Team 017 and its starship lay in the minds of the team itself and the complexity of CY.

Whether or not they'd get through the reported web of the new Khughar-installed approaches to the starport on Thya was anyone's guess. There were too many unknowns in the equation. In such a situation, Starbuck tended to play by ear, operating opportunistically. But the initial image of being a low-fuel survey ship had to ring true. Following a strategy which usually worked, he'd have to use his wits to get them down on Thya in the middle of a military invasion.

But, unbeknownst to Isky and David, Starbuck was also having trouble actually believing that a military invasion of an entire planet was possible. There was no record of it having been done before. He didn't know how it *could* be done. Therefore, in the absence of baseline data, Starbuck didn't know what to expect. How thoroughly would the planet be cordoned off? How would they be challenged on approach? Would they be permitted to land at all, the provisions of the Lunar Compact On Space Succor notwithstanding? Anyone who would behave contrary to the Canons of Metalaw by physically mounting a military invasion of another planet could probably be expected to ignore all other social compacts as well.

Starbuck recalled an old shibboleth from his youth: "All's fair in love and war."

But it had been several hundred years since most of the human race had behaved that way. Obviously from the demise of Zing's AI Team, whoever was invading Thya didn't follow the new ways. Reversion and atavism, Starbuck thought. But, he wondered, *why?*

He decided to wait out the jump in his personal compartment as usual.

But it was less than five minutes before there was a tentative rap on the bulkhead next to the hatch.

"Can I sit with you for the jump, Peter?" It was Katwin.

Starbuck had been expecting her. Katwin never really liked to jump. She didn't understand it and didn't know what was going on. Jumping frightened Katwin.

"Certainly, Katwin." He moved over on the pallet to give her room.

She was trembling when she lay down beside him and snuggled up to him for physical and mental comfort.

Although he understood the jump, he never enjoyed the brief instant of confusion caused by the nearly instantaneous translation of his body and ego from where it was to where someone/something willed it to be. So Katwin's closeness was comforting to Peter Starbuck, too.

Few people understand that longevity treatments of the sort taken by Starbuck and the members of his AI Team don't upset normal body chemistry. If anything, the treatments enhanced some aspects, especially the vital hormonal balance of the human body. Even though longevity treatments assured virtual immortality, those long-lived superhumans of the interstellar milieu hadn't experienced any negative or damping effect of the most overpowering of all the instincts possessed by all tellurian life forms, especially humans: the reproductive drive. In fact, the elimination of the absolute requirement to achieve immortality through reproduction actually heightened the instinct, but this was more of a mental condition and not a direct physical consequence of longevity treatment.

And, although Katwin had the mind of a child, she was physically an adult woman. As a trained telepathic receiver, she couldn't "read" anyone's mind without the help of CY's IA. But she did sense Starbuck's feelings, mostly through extreme empathy because he was her infallible leader, gentle protector, and surrogate father. And, as a latent, untrained telepath himself, Starbuck sensed her simple desires, too.

It wasn't unusual nor was it the first time during a jump that both had sought from the other the closest of all the tender and exciting intimacies that human beings are capable of achieving.

On some worlds, in some cultures, in some macrolife ships, and in some space settlements — even though operated under the Canons of Metalaw — the actions of Peter and Katwin might have been considered a sin or simply just "wrong." But, in an abundant metalaw culture, nothing can be rationed. Nor is it believed ethical to do so. In a universe of abundance — which is the sort of universe in which truly civilized people now lived — a sin was considered only to be an unsuccessful way of doing something. So it wasn't "wrong" but was right for the two of them. Nothing could have been more right at that time and in that situation. For both of them, it was the least hurtful and most effective way to endure the jump trauma.

Neither of them sensed the instant of the jump. Their attentions were elsewhere.

It was Iskander Sandrathama who rapped gently on the bulkhead without looking in. He knew what was happening. Unlike Starbuck, Isky enjoyed any and every jump. He claimed it provided an instant of mystical one-ness with the "cosmic all." He always sat up on the control deck and watched the ego-wrenching near-instantaneous transition from one place to another. That brief instant of nowhere/nothingness of the jump provided the closest analog to death for a man who, barring accidents, would never die. Shochona thought Isky to be "ghoulish" and "filled with the death wish" because of this. But Shochona would think of him that way because of other foibles he exhibited on occasion. And Shochona could never understand Isky's intensity which surfaced often at what she considered most inappropriate times. "Jump completed, Peter. That was a big one."

"Thank you, Isky. Actually, I didn't notice that it was any different than in the past."

Starbuck could almost hear Isky chuckle. "I don't know exactly what you're referring to. But, anyhow, you've discovered a great way to ignore a jump."

"Stand by for possible progress report message transmission as we proceed in to Thya, please."

"Will do, chief. Ready when you are."

The tension returned. Adrenalin continued to flow in Starbuck, but for a different reason now. They were in sub-light mode, vulnerable to even as simple an attack as a hell beam.

"CY, this is Peter. Activate."

"Hello, Peter. Why do you have to exhibit all the shortcomings of a vulnerable human being during a jump?"

"Shortcomings?" Katwin wondered. "What does CY mean, Peter?"

Peter didn't deliberately ignore her. He had other things on his mind again, and he was somewhat perturbed by CY's response and greeting. "CY, who told you to greet me that way? Has Shochona been at you again? Or were you keyholing?"

"I was not spying on you, Peter. I am not capable of such a thing. However, I made a logical deduction based on past data."

"And where did you get that data? Never mind. What's going on outside the ship? Status report, please."

"I don't detect any sensor probing yet," CY's voice told him. "My own GI masdecs show only inbound interstellar traffic. Three starships. From their sub-light breakout positions, I deduce that they are inbound from Khughar en route to Thya. No beacon codes, and this is in direct violation of subparagraph six-Delta. Paragraph one-dash-two-point . . ."

Starbuck cut it off. "No masdec probing?"

"None. I don't anticipate detecting e-m probe signals

for at least another twenty-seven hours. David and I missed
our breakout point by two-point-eight light-hours. But that's
close enough for SIGNET work . . .''

Either one of the team was teaching CY how to exhibit a
sense of humor — and Starbuck suspected David O'Hara—or
the cybermech had developed a glitch and was self-
programming on the basis of the banter that continually
went on between team members. David maintained that it
helped the team members keep a sense of perspective.
Starbuck was inclined to agree with the puckish Eyreman.
Starbuck reminded himself to look into the problem when
he was able to devote some time and attention to it. In the
meantime, however, other priorities overrode.

No probing. Starbuck thought it was highly unusual.
From his own experience as a twenty-first-century youth
when people still invaded and fought on Tellus, he knew
that a military commander always deployed sentries to
protect his forces whether they were on the move or tied
down in a battle or bivouac. CY's sensors were excellent,
the best available. And the cybermech was reporting no
skirmishes and no area surveillance. Something was wrong.
Either that or these Kaloc invaders had the most inept
military organization in the Thousand Worlds.

If so, what were they doing trying to invade another
world?

Chapter Six

It turned out to be the latter, but in a way that Starbuck didn't anticipate. And he certainly didn't know it at the time. One of the hazards of leading an AI Team was the near certainty of the total unpredictability of the situation itself and usually of the outcome as well. Most of the cases on which Starbuck and AI Team 017 had worked turned out to be the result of rather bizarre circumstances which often evolved into strange situations. This really didn't bother him. If things had been predictable, they wouldn't have been interesting or "fun." The variety of circumstances encountered in the work kept him on his toes. They made the job a challenge. He certainly wasn't bored, and that was certainly a blessing for a near-immortal.

What was the old saying? "God created the Universe because he got bored." Starbuck wasn't a god — at least not to his contemporaries. He and his contemporaries, however, might have been perceived and worshipped as gods a thousand years ago on Tellus. But he was far from being omnipotent, omniscient, and omnibenevolent. He was fallible and he knew it. But often he didn't know how and where he was fallible. It was always interesting to discover where . . . provided he survived the discovering of it. He had thus far. But this time, it might be different.

CY was right. A little more than four hours later, his vox box reported through the transducer in the wardroom, "Peter, I've just received the first indication of an electromagnetic sensor probe. It's rather like crude and primitive pulse doppler radar, and the signal is extremely weak."

Starbuck pushed away his plate, waved to his team to terminate the table conversation, and turned to CY's terminal with its blue-coated visual sensor. "Where are the probe signals coming from, CY?"

"The vicinity of Garyon Four which is the planet Thya."

"You reported them as weak. Are they strong enough to provide a readable return signal above the noise level on Thya?"

"That depends upon the type of receiver in use there. It also assumes that no sensor detectors are positioned in the outlying reaches of the planetary system. Given the best available technology known to me, the signal will not be detectable above the noise level upon its receipt in the vicinity of Thya. But if the transmitter is an illuminator, the return signal would be strong enough to be read above noise on Garyon Eight, if a detector is located there." There was a pause which was unusual for CY. He was so fast that even talking to humans took "years" in his switching time terms. "There was another pulse. It's pulse doppler, all right. Peter, do you wish me to activate countermeasures?"

"No. Survey ships don't carry ECM capability. Steady as she goes, CY. Let me know when the signal strength becomes strong enough to reasonably expect it will be detectable above noise on Thya on the return bounce."

"Your wish is my command, Glorious Leader."

Starbuck turned to O'Hara. "David, have you been fiddling with CY's programmed responses again?"

David looked surprised and shook his head. "Who, me?"

"That's what I thought." Starbuck addressed the Cybermech again. "CY, also inform me if and when you pick up any GI probe or masdec signals."

"Roger dodger, you old codger."

"David!"

"As I just told you: Who, me?"

Triga was giggling. "I like it, Peter. We all treat CY as

a living organism. What's wrong with having him respond
in a more human manner?''

"Because he isn't human, and it distorts our perception
of his functions,'' Starbuck reminded her. "He's so much
faster, has so much more memory, and has such a reliable
memory that we might start treating him as a god if we
thought he had human attributes . . .''

"*Deus ex machina*,'' Shochona muttered.

"You take all the fun out of it, Peter. You're getting to
be a fuddy-duddy in your old age,'' Triga remarked.

"What's a fuddy-duddy, Triga?'' Katwin asked.

"A person suffering from hardening of the neurons,
dear.''

"But Peter hasn't changed since I joined this team.''

"Perhaps not physically, but becoming a fuddy-duddy is
all in a person's head.''

"I don't understand, Triga.''

"Katwin, I was just making a joke.''

"Oh. Okay.''

"Let's stop playing games,'' Starbuck insisted. "This is
no snap task. Don't forget what happened to Zing's team.
We're now in the same spot. Be alert.''

"Yes, sir!'' David snapped. "SIGNET needs more lerts.''

"Incorrigible,'' Shochona said sadly, shaking her head.

"Don't incorrige me,'' David pleaded.

Katwin giggled.

An observer might have tagged it gallows humor. Starbuck
knew it was the typical manner in which his team tried to
maintain an even strain. They were all on edge waiting for
the inevitable approach challenge from Thya which they
knew from the previous data would come eventually.
None of them knew *when*, which made the waiting even
more difficult.

Starbuck got so harried that he went to his compartment,
lay down, and had CY broadcast the soothing signal of
pink noise in an ocean wave mode through the neuroelectric
contact pads of his pallet. That relaxed him while still
permitting him to come instantly to full utilization of all

his faculties. Sometimes, he longed for the near-blotto relaxation and removal of inhibitions he'd once been able to get from brandy or even a social drug. But those days were long past because such substances had an enormous effect on his ability to think . . . which he knew he'd need at a moment's notice if the Kalocs did the same thing to his team that they'd done — with apparent success — to Zing's people. Everything had its price, and he'd given up some of those memorable peccadilloes because his raging will to live had led him to longevity treatments and therefore to SIGNET AI service.

The uniform of a SIGNET survey ship commander hung nearby, ready for him to don it when it became necessary to do so for the charade. Otherwise, as usual, Starbuck preferred to remain unclothed in the benevolent environment of the *Starace*.

The relaxing neuroelectric input from CY did its proper job. Starbuck fell asleep. He was awakened by his need to eliminate.

The alert signal caught him figuratively with his pants down.

"Peter, sorry to interrupt you at this particular moment, but I've detected a distorted masdec probe signal," CY's voice came from the terminal.

As he finished what he was doing, Starbuck called out, "CY, what's distorted about the signal?"

"It doesn't hold phase lock."

"What do you believe is causing that to happen?"

"Inept human operator or masdec technician."

"Keep monitoring it, CY. Report to me if there is any change at all . . ."

"Jolly good, sah!"

"How much time did I spend sleeping?"

"Seven hours, Peter. My sensors indicated that you were exhausted and tense. But your present condition is much improved."

"It should be after that much rest! Okay, how many light hours to Thya?"

"Four-point-three."

"Say our velocity relative to Thya."

"Mike-point-eight-five."

"Send a masdec probe signal to Thya, then reduce closing velocity to Mike-point-five." Starbuck didn't want to close too rapidly. After all, the *Starace* was supposed to be simulating a low-fuel survey ship. He wanted his ship's probing signatures to be identified as locating Thya, then the ship would reduce sub-light closure to a fuel-saving level. "Execute!"

"Aye, aye, cap'n. Avast, ye swabs! Batten down the sensors. Forestay the main drive and mainstay the fore drive!"

"CY, erase all those clever little ripostes that David programmed," Starbuck said wearily. He didn't want the cybermech to get cute and clever when the going got sticky.

"David did not program any responses."

"Then who did?"

"Password, please."

Starbuck exhaled forcibly. *That's all I need right now!* he told himself. *A clown in the crew!*

There was nothing to do except to continue in toward Thya playing the role of the low-fuel survey ship. Since none of the existing charts showed Thya's space approaches to be controlled, he didn't dare tip his hand by calling space approach, even though he knew from the Zing team data that the Kalocs had indeed established space control.

He could have gone to work and debugged CY to find the source of the programming and to carry out the necessary re-programming. But that might have put part of CY out of service if and when everything CY possessed was required. Starbuck didn't dare take the chance.

As a result, Starbuck stayed bored and trigger tense.

Triga stepped in, ostensibly to check his well-being, but even her provocative teasing didn't arouse him. She left in a disappointed huff. Starbuck didn't even try to apologize. As a team member, she should have known better, especially when he was anxiously awaiting the next move in the game — and it was the Kalocs' or the Thyans' turn to move.

Back in the pioneering days of astronautics, one of the early space travelers had characterized space travel as "hours of boredom punctuated by moments of sheer terror." The pioneer had been right, Starbuck decided.

This was one of the brief periods of time when his job as an AI Team Leader was indeed boring.

The boredom of waiting came to an end as it always did.

"Peter, I've received notice of an incoming radio message."

Starbuck leaped from his pallet and began donning the commander's uniform. "Put it on my speaker, CY, and stand by for my reply once I move to the command compartment."

"Message follows," CY announced.

The loudspeaker in the terminal panel switched to heavy static caused by the solar wind of Garyon. A thick, slow voice came thinly through the noise, "Uh, hello the starship *Serge A. Korff* inbound to Thya. This is Thya Approach under the command of troops serving the Black Path of Thoth. Confirm that you are the survey vessel *Korff* as indicated by your beacon ID code . . . Repeating the hail: Hello the starship *Serge A. Korff* inbound to Thya . . ."

The uniform donned, Starbuck called out, "CY, I'm transferring to command compartment."

"I detect your departure from your quarters. Standing by to work with you from Command."

Shochona, Isky, and Katwin were in Command when Starbuck popped out of the lift well.

"Where's your uniform?" Starbuck snapped at Isky.

"Aw, Peter, do I hafta dress up like a chocolate soldier?"

"Yes. This is supposed to be a survey ship of the Star Guard. Everyone on Command deck will — I repeat, will — follow the standards of the Guard, which means that you *will* — I repeat, will — be in uniform while on watch!"

Isky shrugged and stepped into the lift well. "I'll go get gussied-up."

"David!" Starbuck called. "Bounce up to Command . . . in uniform!"

"Aye, aye, Captain! On my way."

Starbuck looked around, checking that everything would be as it should be and appeared precisely as it did in all the published holos of the bridge of a Star Guard survey ship. The incoming message from Thya continued to come from the comm speakers, repeating itself in the absence of a received reply. "Move it, David! I need you as a spear-carrier! I'm missing one warm body to fill out the standard Star Guard bridge crew!"

David O'Hara stepped out of the lift well in full uniform, grinned, and slipped into a position before one of the boards. "Manned and calibrated, skipper!"

"CY, check the hailing frequency and put me on its matched duplex reply freq in the GI comm spectrum. I don't want to have to wait a couple of hours to get a reply." That was necessary because the ship would be in orbit shortly after Thya Approach received his reply and identification message if CY sent it at light-speed e-m audio-video.

"By your command . . . ."

"Okay, quiet down, crew. Here we go. CY, activate transmitter. Standard audio and video transmission, GI spectrum standard hailing frequency to match the hail from Thya. Ready here."

"Go," CY told him.

Starbuck cleared his voice, composed himself, and willed that his tones wouldn't indicate any stress in case the Kaloc troops of the "Black Path of Thoth"—whoever or whatever he or it was — had a voice-stress analyzer down there. "Thya Space Approach, this is the Star Guard scientific survey vessel, the starship *Serge A. Korff*, confirming the identification of our beacon code. Captain Estrello in command and speaking. We have the latest charts in our cybermech, and I was unaware that Thya had contolled approaches."

"It does now! Remain clear of Thya and leave the Garyon system right now," a heavy voice came back thickly. It sounded as if the man was having trouble speaking Galactish.

"Negative on that, sir," Starbuck replied. "I'm declaring a low-fuel emergency. My intentions are to land Thya and purchase fuel."

"And negative back to you! Thya landing permission denied! There's a war going on and we can't guarantee your safety."

"I repeat: I am declaring a low-fuel emergency. Under the terms of the Space Succor Compact . . ."

"Wait one. This is sumthin' new. Lemme get the starshi." The channel went dead with the only sound being the soft but sharp ripping sound of the GI carrier radiation that was the normal background for C+ communication.

"CY, what is a 'starshi'?" Peter asked quickly.

"Please spell," CY requested.

Starbuck did so.

"Word unknown."

"What is its possible derivation? Are there any analogous military ranks?"

"Possible derivation from the word *starshiy* meaning 'senior' in the tellurian tongue known as RussLan. The twentieth-century Soviet military aerospace force used the term to designate senior ranking as in *starshiy leytenant*."

"Thank you, CY," Starbuck told the cybermech. If the Kalocs had appropriated old Soviet terminology, why? RussLan was known to be a language with a high content of paranoid terms and a basic structure that reflected distrustful and secretive thought patterns. "Data, please, CY: What is common language or languages of the planet Khughar?"

"There are several languages used on Khughar," CY reported. "Galactish is the common planetary language used for communications and transportation. Other local languages are derived from such tellurian Indo-European root tongues as Greek, Turkish, Arabic, Telugu, and Malayalam. A small percentage of the population speaks . . .''

One of the problems involved with asking a broad general question of CY, Starbuck reflected, was that CY understood everything in the literal sense and, because the cybermech was also an encyclopedia, tended to answer in an encyclopedic manner. Starbuck didn't have time right then to assimilate and analyze all the data that CY was ready, willing, and able to dump. In retrospect, Starbuck should have heard CY through. "Thank you, CY. That's enough."

"You're welcome, Captain Estrello . . ."

The C + comm unit came back to life. It was a different voice this time. "Survey starship *Serge A. Korff*, this is Thya Space Approach. I am initiating video transmission. Please do the same."

"CY, duplex video, please," Starbuck instructed.

The cybermech didn't reply. Instead, the holo projector came on and the transmit light on the pickup glowed. As CY processed the signal from Thya, the holo built up until, within several seconds, it showed the interior of a small room. The pickup angle and coverage was such that it was impossible to see who else was there, how many people were present, or exactly what sort of equipment was being used.

Starbuck and his AI Team found themselves looking at a heavyset, pudgy man seated at what appeared to be some sort of control console. Behind him stood a tall, thin, acerbic, long-faced man. Both were wearing rather ill-fitting black uniforms on which were affixed various unknown insignia, sigils, and decorations. They also wore knee-high boots, and heavy leather belts. The standing man, apparently a supervisor of some sort, also wore leather gloves, carried a swagger stick of the sort Starbuck hadn't seen for centuries, and had a peaked leather garrison cap on his head.

Starbuck spoke directly to the duo. "We're receiving your transmission clearly. How about us?"

"Clearly," the lanky man replied. "State the nature of your emergency."

"To whom am I speaking?"

"I am Starshi Coronal Pradesh, Jakarthan of Thoth, Planetary Defense Jakarthan, Aldira of the Hokuma of Thoth, although that is no concern of yours."

"On the contrary, Coronal Pradesh. I am Captain Estrello. I'm unfamiliar with the nature of the Aldira of the Hokuma of Thoth."

"In plain Galactish, I have the honor of serving in the special armed forces of the Black Path of Thoth."

"Strange," Starbuck mused aloud. "Our cybermech indicates that there is no army on Thya, just as it indicates no space approach control facility."

"These things are of no concern of yours unless it is your intention to spy on us."

"Was that fear behind the reason why I am denied permission to land and refuel?"

"My subordinate was merely carrying out standard operating procedures. A state of armed conflict exists on Thya. Its nature is also of no concern to you if you are indeed a survey ship. However, on the basis of your operational purpose and the nature of your emergency, I have been instructed to waive the procedures and authorize you to land . . . provided your cybermech transmits your bona fides."

Starbuck smiled slightly and waved his hand. "That can certainly be accomplished, Coronal. My cybermech will do so immediately upon receipt of your ready-to-copy signal on the original hailing frequency."

"Are you capable of transmitting the data on the upper sideband subcarrier of this C+ channel?"

"Of course."

"Then do so at once."

Starbuck turned his head. "CY, comply with the request of Coronal Pradesh."

"Accomplished."

Coronal Pradesh looked at what had come up on a screen out of view of his pickup. Finally, he nodded and said curtly, "Permission granted for emergency landing to refuel. Maintain open communications channel. We will be happy to welcome you to Thya and will extend our services to you."

"Thank you, Coronal. We're coming in." Starbuck kept the channel available but cut off a-v transmissions. Turning to the cybermech sensor, he ordered, "CY, land at the main Thya spaceport. Execute!"

"There is only one spaceport on Thya. I am in communication with the Thya spaceport cybermech. We are beginning the approach."

Katwin had been silent through all of this. Finally, she spoke up in a small voice, "Peter, something's wrong."

Starbuck turned his head toward her. He sensed nothing. But then he wasn't a trained telepath. "What's wrong, Katwin?"

"I don't know. I'm frightened."

Starbuck felt slightly relieved. This wasn't unusual on Katwin's part. With her child's mind and reactions, Katwin was often frightened when approaching something new and different. He reassured her, "Don't worry, Katwin. Everything will be all right."

But she didn't reply with her usual affirmation of Starbuck's leadership and analysis. "Peter, I'm still frightened."

If Peter Starbuck had evaluated the existing but meager data better, or if he weren't so compelled to discover what had happened to Zing's AI Team, he might have paid more attention to this attempt on Katwin's part to communicate something complex and unusual to him. But in spite of the fact that his capabilities were so superior, Peter Starbuck was still very much a human being. He didn't ignore Katwin; instead, her anomalous behavior just didn't register on him. Things might have been different if he'd paid attention.

Chapter Seven

"Open the lock! All occupants out!"

The command came snapping from the outside pickup of the ship's intercom once CY began shutting down systems after the tail ring of the *Starace* settled onto the tarmac. The Thyan starport was crowded with ships.

"CY, observe and record the number and type of ships on this starport. File with the other data you obtained on the approach. And, CY, don't shut everything down," Starbuck told his ship cybermech. "Keep everything in readiness for immediate liftoff."

"Aye, aye, skipper."

Starbuck keyed the intercom to reply to the command from the ground. "Captain Estrello here. Your request is contrary to the interstellar rules of space commerce. This is a non-military private vessel carrying no cargo. Therefore, the ship itself remains outside your sovereign territory. Those of us who must go aground to arrange for our refueling will be happy to comply with whatever local inbound customs regulations you may . . ."

"You have one minute to open the lock and debark all passengers and members of the crew!" the voice on the intercom snapped. "If you do not comply, we will order the spaceport defense batteries to open fire on you. A state of armed conflict exists here. Interstellar rules have been suspended. You are now on territory controlled by the Black Path of Thoth."

"Stand by, please," Starbuck replied, unkeyed, and told his cybermech, "CY, shielding condition, please."

"Shields ready."

"Do not deploy shields until you detect a ranging pulse from the defense batteries."

"We are now being constantly painted by ranging and targeting signals," CY reported. "I can have the shields to ninety-percent level within four microseconds of detecting an attack."

"Is that good enough to keep from being burned?" Shochona asked.

"Maybe it is and maybe it isn't," David replied. "Certainly not enough to keep the initial laser bolt from burning through, but enough to stop almost anything thereafter."

"I'd feel better if we knew what sort of weaponry they've trained on us," she muttered.

"We'll have to chance it," Starbuck told them.

"Peter, this might have been the situation that Zing's team found themselves in," David pointed out. "I wouldn't count on the shields under these circumstances . . . unless you want to take the chance of suffering Zing's fate . . . which I don't."

"The instant the shields go up," Shochona added, "they'll know we're not just a plain-vanilla survey ship. Then the situation just gets worse."

Starbuck thought about that for a moment and pondered his strategy. He certainly wasn't going to do anything that might jeopardize the ship and crew . . . especially when at least one member of the crew wasn't in favor of it.

And he was too far into things now to back out by powering-up and lifting off with all shields up. The task of this team was to get down on Thya, find out what the problem was, do something about it if possible, and — above all — survive and report back to SIGNET Headquarters.

"Survey ships carry a normal complement of four. I need three volunteers to go dirtside with me."

"I'll go," Shochona replied at once, "but we've got to leave Isky here as a link back to SIGNET."

"All right, that's Shochona and myself. I need two more volunteers."

"I'm not needed while the ship's on dirt," David said.

"I'll go with you," Katwin added.

Peter shook his head. "No, Katwin."

"But you called for volunteers," Katwin observed.

"Triga?" Peter asked his biotech.

Triga Rimmon pointed out, "Do you intend to have Isky stay aboard and transmit progress reports to ColeShore during this grounding?"

Starbuck nodded.

"Then I'll have to be with him," the biotech pointed out. "However, if you don't want Katwin to go aground and want me to go instead, you'll have to give up the communications option."

"I want to go with you, Peter. It's not fair!" Katwin pointed out.

Starbuck had no real choice. He didn't like the idea of having to go dirtside with Katwin. In the first place, it was obvious that she didn't have the intelligence to be a member of a survey ship crew. But, in view of the demise of Joshua Zing's team on this world, he couldn't risk taking Isky with him and thereby breaking any possible transmission link with ColeShore. If something happened, Isky's job, perhaps his last one alive, would be to squirt off the team's final report to SIGNET Headquarters.

"Katwin comes with me," Starbuck said with resignation. "Katwin, you must tell these people nothing except the required information: your name, your planet of origin, and your planet of residence. For practice, tell me what you're going to tell them when they ask."

Katwin thought a moment and replied, "Katwin Ivanova, Sol Three Beta, and ColeShore."

"Good girl! Isky, I want you to get into linkage with CY and transmit a progress report to ColeShore. Then be ready to send off an emergency message to ColeShore if it becomes necessary. If they have to bring in a third team, I want them to have more data than Joshua Zing left for us. Triga, keep Isky functioning. He's the last resort. Can you keep him in quasi-link, ready to act almost instantly?"

"It isn't easy, but it's my job," Triga replied in a tone that others might have taken as complaining but which Starbuck took as being quite normal for Triga. Her tone softened as she went on, "Peter, Katwin, Shochona, David . . . please be careful!"

"Goes without saying," Shochona said curtly.

"Cy, I want you to monitor all the frequencies of my button transmitter," Starbuck instructed the cybermech. "Standard procedure. Emergency code signal is the word Romeo. Repeat instruction for verification."

"Monitor all button transmitter frequencies. Standard procedure. Emergency code Romeo. Peter, what about signal jamming? My sensors detect heavy e-m jamming outside."

"If you lose our signals, automatically activate emergency procedures."

"I understand."

"Open the intercom channel, CY."

"Open."

"Thya Starport Ground, this is Captain Estrello. The four of us are coming out now."

"It's about time. We were prepared to open fire on you."

"In violation of the L-5 Convention?"

"We have suspended that. This is a state of armed conflict."

"Then perhaps we should depart, Coronal. Am I still speaking to Coronal Pradesh?"

"You have thirty seconds to open the lock and come out. If you do not, the ship will be fired upon. If the ship begins to lift, it will also be fired upon." The voice was obviously still that of Coronal Pradesh in spite of the fact that the speaker didn't identify himself.

"Let's go, crew."

At the bottom of the bounce well, Starbuck looked at his three compatriots and cycled the lock.

Outside, standing on both sides of the lock opening, were six huge armed men in black uniforms and leather fittings. Immediately, four of them stepped inside with hand weapons at the ready. "Out!" was the barked command.

"Of course," Starbuck replied suavely. He went first. As the last of his crew cleared the lock, another black-uniformed man stepped forward on the tarmac.

It was too late now, and Starbuck saw that the man carried a microwave neurodisrupter. It was pointed directly at Starbuck.

"Welcome to Thya," the man growled, but there was a smile on his face.

Starbuck felt the electric tingle of microwave energy disrupting his nervous system. As he began to go into convulsions, he mercifully lost consciousness.

The next awareness that came into his mind was one of aching, universal pain. He was dimly aware of the fact that he couldn't stand up. Although sensation and control were beginning to return, his arms and legs still tingled the way his leg or arm did when they normally "fell asleep" from nerve cramping. As his vision cleared, he saw nothing in front of him but when he put his hand tentatively out, it met a strong, transparent barrier.

He was in a small, smooth container with opaque walls and a single transparent surface in front of him. But the cage was so dimensioned that he couldn't stand erect, sit, or lie down. He could only remain in a cramped, stooping position with his legs bent and his head and shoulders butted hard against the roof of the cell. He couldn't spread his elbows from his sides without touching the side walls. The cage kept him in a position that was not only uncomfortable but began to be agonizing as his muscles slowly began to become functional, needed to be stretched, and were practically immobilized in this extremely cramped position. He knew that soon he would suffer muscle cramping. It would be even more painful.

There were a series of holes in the top and back of the cell through which enough air could pass to keep him alive. But it grew hot and humid in the cramped enclosure as his body heat and perspiration made it more and more uncomfortable even though all clothing had been stripped off him.

Through the transparent front panel, he could see only a wet, white wall and a smooth corridor leading off to a brightly lit doorway at the left. It was impossible to see what was beyond the door other than another smooth, white, featureless wall.

But he could tell from the sounds and smells that filtered through the top and rear opening of the cell that he must be in some sort of ship.

He heard sobbing and knew who it was.

"Katwin, this is Peter!" he called out.

"Peter, I'm scared!"

He tried to reassure her. "Be a big girl, Katwin. Let me find out what's going on here. David?"

"Uh!"

"You all right?"

"No. Can't move. Disrupter really bad on me."

"Shochona?"

"This is no way to treat guests!"

"I agree. Keep calm and let's find out what's going on here."

"I have to go to go to the bathroom," Katwin complained.

"Then you'll just have to go," Peter told her. "Don't worry about it. You can get cleaned up when we get back to the ship."

"You don't think they're going to let us go back to the ship, do you?" Shochona's voice came to him. "Peter, these aren't just detention cells. They're cleverly designed torture cells!"

"Patience. Somebody will come along soon."

"Patience? My back and legs are killing me!"

"Mine, too," Katwin added.

And it was beginning to get to Starbuck as well. The size and shape of the cell enclosure had been fiendishly built to keep a person in a semi-squatting position unable to stand or sit. Furthermore, since the walls of the enclosure were slickly smooth, it was impossible to jam one's body between the walls to frictional support.

"Crew, get into Delta Mode," Starbuck ordered his team. "Block if you can. Tune it out."

"Can't," David O'Hara's pain-filled voice reached him. "The hangover from that disrupter beam won't let me regain that control just yet . . ."

Starbuck was having trouble too. They'd all been hit by a concentrated burst of high-power microwave radiation at a frequency that resonated with the neuronal synapses of their nervous systems. Given enough power, such a disrupter beam was a death ray. But the hand projector used on them was only powerful enough to cause paralysis and unconsciousness. The consequences of such a microwave exposure included partial long-term disruption of the central nervous system, affecting a person's ability to exercise control for as long as several hours . . . or several days in the case of a severe exposure. Starbuck began to wonder how long the aftereffects would last.

"Stay quiet, then. That will help," he told them.

"But it *hurts*!" Katwin sobbed.

"I know it, Katwin. I can't do anything about it."

"Why is someone hurting me?"

"I don't know, Katwin. We'll find out soon."

So they waited.

And waited.

No one came.

Starbuck's leg and back muscles began to cramp so badly that he wanted to cry out.

He grew thirsty, but there was no water.

There was no way to measure the passage of painful time.

Worse than that, there was no way to know how long they'd have to endure this condition.

Starbuck tried Delta Mode blocking, but was only partially successful in detaching his conscious mind from his physical body and lapsing totally into psychological or psi time. He did manage to stop sweating, thus conserving his water. But he couldn't control the painful cramping of his back and leg muscles.

It didn't help that Katwin lost control and broke into screaming sobs.

He heard David's heavy breathing indicating that the man was also in deep trouble.

The grunts he heard must have been coming from Shochona as she battled with her physical body.

Hunger and thirst were secondary to the muscle distress.

And it went on interminably.

He fell into frequent dream-like episodes followed by periods of total discouragement and near hopelessness. How much could a person take? He didn't know. But he thought he was about to find out.

Katwin's screams changed to racking sobs and finally to moans.

Shochona apparently fell silent.

So did David, but his breathing pattern indicated to Starbuck that the big man had passed out.

Starbuck knew in the back of his pain-racked mind that CY must have determined that they'd been separated from their clothes and therefore their button transmitters. Isky and Triga must know. Something would happen. They weren't without the possibility of help from the ship.

If Triga and Isky were still in the ship.

From time to time, the thought entered his mind, "What sort of people could do this thing to other human beings?" The cramped torture cells were the worst possible violation of the Canons of Metalaw. They were throwbacks to an earlier time in the evolution of the human race. Were these Kalocs true atavars? Such things had happened before. But with modern genetic mapping and selection techniques, such people shouldn't have been able to grow in numbers until there were enough of them to explode off their home planet and actually invade another one.

He became dimly aware of a huge, heavyset, muscled man clad in black leather staring at him through the transparent front of the cell. The man watched and laughed.

He was accompanied by a dark-haired woman also in black.

These two observers were obviously enjoying what they saw.

"Welcome to Thya, Captain Estrello . . . if that's your real name, and we have reason to believe it isn't," the big man spoke in a powerful voice. "You have very strong mentic defenses, however, which leads me to believe you're something more than a survey ship commander. But we haven't been able to penetrate your mind nor those of your crew members. But we'll find out, won't we, Onuva?"

The woman smiled and looked at Starbuck with obvious anticipation. "Oh, yes, indeed we will find out. They'll be so anxious to tell us everything that they'll beg for the chance. I would like to see what this fine man here can do. And the young girl should be fun for you, Kodo."

"Patience, my dear. First things first. We have been ungracious to our guests. We haven't been civil. We haven't properly introduced ourselves. Captain Estrello, I am Kodo Sadon, the Black Path of Thoth, the great leader of the Kaloc People of Thoth and their Black Guard. This," he indicated the black-garbed woman, "is Onuva Ferona, the Consortte of Thoth."

Starbuck couldn't believe his eyes or ears. Had the endless hours of pain and thrist relieved him of his sanity? These two were something right out of historical fantasy literature: a black leather-swathed villain and his evil mistress. He doubted the rationality and the reality of them. How could they possibly exist in the modern universe?

"And you would be . . . ?" Kodo Sadon asked.

Starbuck had difficulty speaking. His tongue was swollen from thirst. Finally, he managed to reply thickly, "Captain Francisco Estrello, commanding the survey starship *Serge A. Korff* . . ."

"Really?" Sadon replied. "That's who and what your documentation claims. But are you sure you're not someone else? We've already had visitors who turned out to be other than who they claimed."

Starbuck found his voice again and said hoarsely, "Why are we being treated this way?"

"You find fault with our welcome? You aren't enjoying our Kaloc hospitality?" Kodo Sadon's tone of voice wasn't mocking, but Starbuck knew the huge man *had* to be mocking him.

"This . . . is . . . hospitality?" Starbuck muttered.

"My apologies! Perhaps we haven't behaved properly by ignoring you, our guests, while we were forced to take care of other pressing matters. I think we can rectify that quickly," the black-garbed Sadon said pleasantly. "Onuva, my dearest, how's our schedule now?"

"The Third Black Guard Attack Regiment commander isn't due to report for several hours."

"Good. Do we have enough time to pleasure Captain Estrello and his companions now?"

"Oh, yes!"

"Hadishi!" Sadon called, and four burly black-armored soldiers came into view. He waved at Starbuck. "Take him to the recreation compartment. No, don't stun him again. That will simply delay things."

There might be an opportunity for Starbuck to act once he got out of the cage. Although he had no visible weapons, he was adept at karate, *la savat*, and *baeda*. All Starbuck needed was an instant of freedom to permit him to act. But, as one hadishi or soldier removed the pin from the transparent door and swung it open, Starbuck discovered he couldn't move fast even if he'd wanted to. In fact, he had trouble moving at all, so painfully cramped were his back and legs. He never got the chance to act. Instead, Starbuck almost cried out in pain when a million needles ran through his abused muscles. So fogged in pain was his mind that he was barely aware of being dragged into the nearby white room and stretched out on a table.

Whoever and whatever these Kalocs were, they'd become masters of torture, but a very sophisticated form of torture. Starbuck tried to clear his mind to be aware of what they had and how they used it on him, but he was unable to do so. The physical restraints were painful. So were the physical instruments they used. But even worse were the neuroelectric equipment and procedures. Sadon and Ferona — mostly Sadon — were adept at bioneurological torture. Combating the effects of the neuroelectric stimulation of his nerves and brain centers took everything he possessed in terms of training, blocking, and control. But none of them were one-hundred-percent effective against the advanced techniques that Kodo Sadon had and used while Onuva Ferona stood by his head and whispered and murmured words of comfort and pleasure to him and suggestions to Sadon.

He was only vaguely aware that neither Kodo Sadon nor Onuva Ferona questioned him.

Starbuck was unable to block it or endure it. So he forced himself to slip into the bliss of unconsciousness.

Chapter Eight

A piercing scream brought Starbuck dimly back to consciousness.

He was again in the cramped cell-cage.

And he hurt terribly everywhere.

The high-pitched ululating scream came again to his ears. It was a sound full of pain and terror.

Then he dimly saw Kodo Sadon's huge black form through the white doorway of the "recreation compartment" and heard the heavy voice say, "Onuva, my dear, she is indeed lovely, but you're getting stains on your uniform."

The unmistakable voice of Katwin came to his ears. She was crying out almost incoherently, begging, calling, pleading for them to stop it.

"Now, now, my dear, mother's here. You're being very, very good. I don't know when we've had anyone who's been this good. We gave you only a little bit of Number Thirty-four. Was it really that good? We can do much better." It was Onuva's soft voice cooing to her victim. "Kodo, dearest, try a little bit more of Number Twenty . . ."

Katwin's scream was drowned in a gurgle.

Starbuck could sense her terror. He tried to move, to lunge against the cell door, to break free of his imprisonment — anything to get to poor, helpless Katwin and stop those two from torturing the grown-up child that she was. But he was almost totally exhausted and completely encompassed by pain. He couldn't move in the confines of the small cage.

He heard the thud of a body hitting the floor.

To his left, barely in view through the transparent door of his cage, he saw David O'Hara roll free. Apparently, Sadon and Ferona were enjoying themselves so much with Katwin that they didn't hear it. David painfully staggered to his feet, clawed his way erect against Starbuck's cage, and pulled the pin holding the door shut. Starbuck was suddenly free as David moved out of sight to release Shochona.

It took everything Starbuck possessed in terms of his remaining physical strength to keep from falling out on the floor himself. But he called upon his mentic reserves and gathered all the power remaining within him. He stumbled out, overpowered the stiffness in his abused muscles and the deep persistent pain that ran through his entire body, and stood erect again as a human being.

He heard Shochona's moan of relief as she, too, stepped out to freedom.

It took only one look among the three of them before they began to move together toward the glaring white opening of the recreation compartment.

Now that Starbuck could see around him, he realized from the appearance of the walls, floor, and ceiling with their fittings and equipment that he was in a starship of some sort.

At that instant, the bulkhead opposite the cages crumbled to dust. None of them ever remembered hearing an explosion. A sonic disintegrator must have been used.

Black-clothed forms were lying on the deck beyond where the bulkhead had been. Rushing over them were two dozen people not wearing any sort of uniforms but carrying a variety of what appeared to be weapons. Starbuck mentally breathed a sigh of relief.

Iskander Sandrathama, good old Isky, was leading them. He was carrying his favorite "social purpose" weapon, an unsheathed *kirpan*. Tossing only a quick glance at Starbuck, he waved Triga Rimmon forward, and then quickly moved with the armed men into the recreation compartment.

Triga stepped up to Starbuck, waved a biosensor up and down his chest, and muttered, "Alive, not well, but you'll live."

"Glad to see you." Starbuck was so hoarse he was about to lose his voice completely.

"I hope so. Took some doing to get to you." She handed him a canteen of water.

Starbuck eagerly sloshed water into his mouth. After taking two huge swallows, he was able to tell his biotech, "Katwin. Get to Katwin. They're torturing her."

"Oh, the poor baby!" Triga said and turned toward the recreation compartment.

But Triga couldn't get to Katwin. A rather violent hand-to-hand battle was going on in the compartment. There wasn't room to use stunners, disrupters, or other weapons. But it was all over in less than thirty seconds.

Isky appeared in the door. He looked somewhat the worse for wear and tear. There were some reddish-brown stains all over the front of his tunic. They looked like blood. "Triga. In here. Katwin," he said curtly.

The biotech moved quickly.

In a rare exhibition of empathy, Shochona had her arms around Starbuck's shoulders. Or perhaps she did it to support herself.

Stepping up to Starbuck, Isky asked, "Peter, are you all right?"

"No, but we're alive. Nothing that can't be fixed . . . I hope."

"Would have gotten those bastards ourselves if you hadn't come along," David complained, rubbing his legs.

"But thanks anyway for bringing the cavalry over the hill to the rescue," Shochona added. "Can we get out of here?"

"Yes, same way we came . . . if we move fast," Isky told her. "Explanations later."

"Isky!" Starbuck snapped. "Get the man and the woman in black! They're apparently the leaders of the invasion troops!"

The wiry little man whipped around and dashed back jnto the white room. He reappeared carrying the unconscious form of Onuva Ferona in his arms. "The man's gone! Went out through a hatch and secured it behind him."

"We've got his consortte at any rate. Isky, get us out of here."

"Can you walk?"

"Not very well, but enough to get out of here!" Shochona moaned.

"Triga! Move it!" Isky called.

"Shouldn't move Katwin! She's in trouble!"

"You've got to!"

"Give me a hand"

"Jaroslav, help her," Isky told one of the men who'd broken in with him, a group who, for want of a better term at the moment, Starbuck chose to think of as The First Contingent of the Thyan Irregulars. At any rate, someday he'd see that they were recognized as such if that's who they were indeed. "Andre, take this Kaloc woman. Don't let her get away."

"You bet I won't! She's the Big Man's doxie. Good hostage."

"I wouldn't count on it," Starbuck advised. Onuva Ferona might be well endured to questioning and inquisition, and she might also sacrifice herself.

When Triga came out of the white room alongside the man who was carrying Katwin, she was shaking her head. "I don't know what they did to her . . ."

"I do. I'll tell you when we get out of here," Peter Starbuck said, wishing that he couldn't remember.

Isky led the group with two of the Thyan Irregulars out on point. Starbuck now saw that all Irregulars were carrying a motley assortment of personal weapons—pistols, hunting rifles, blades of various sorts, and modern weapons such as stunners, disrupters, and disintegrators. Starbuck's first impression that they were soldiers faded when he noticed the assortment of weapons and the lack of uniforms. They were indeed irregulars.

They threaded their way through corridors and past a series of black-clad men and women lying on the deck either unconscious or dead. Starbuck really didn't care about their condition. In his present mood, the various Canons of Metalaw were so much useless baggage. He couldn't be concerned about them. Only the Second Canon was important to him. He was worried about his own survival as well as that of his team.

It was indeed a starship they were in. As they exited the outer hatch, he could see it was parked on the Thya starport. In the distance, he recognized the distinctive shape of the *Starace* standing on the tarmac.

But the Kaloc ship was surrounded by a cordon of black-armored soldiers, weapons at the ready.

Isky took the unconscious form of Onuva Ferona in his own arms and stepped forward. In a loud and especially nasty voice — Isky could look mean and ferocious when he wanted to, and he could sound even worse — he announced, "Don't try *anything*! We're going to the survey vessel. If any of you try *anything*, I can kill this woman instantly. Do you want to take the chance I can't? Your boss will be very upset if she's hurt. And we'll shoot the first person who even *looks* suspiciously violent!"

Starbuck was startled by the immediate response. Without hesitation and with a single fluid movement, the ranks of black uniforms parted. Weapons were lowered. And Starbuck's group moved as quickly as possible across the distance to the *Starace*.

"Hurry," Starbuck urged. He didn't know if Sadon would show up and try to stop them. "Come on, Shochona. I know it hurts. Want me to carry you?"

"Save your energy, Peter. . . . I'll make it . . . I'm too mean to die . . . And now I'm likely to be meaner . . . than these black Thoths or Kalocs . . . or whatever they think they are . . . I've got a name for them, though . . ." she panted as she struggled to keep up, limping along beside him. The name she had for them was in a language Starbuck didn't know, but the word sounded loaded.

The Thyan Irregulars formed a protective shield around the entry hatch of the *Starace* while Starbuck's team entered.

The starport tarmac was covered with black-uniformed soldiers carrying weapons. There were more than a hundred of them. Some were in the open. Others were crouching around and behind ships' structures and spaceport vehicles. There was no way that the Thyan Irregulars were going to get off that starport tarmac alive once the hatch of the *Starace* was closed, leaving them exposed outside the ship. They'd be at the mercy of the Kalocs.

He wasn't about to abandon the Thyan Irregulars who had risked their lives to rescue his team. He wasn't going to leave them to sure and certain death on the starport tarmac or even a worse fate in the hands of Kodo Sadon. There really wasn't room in the ship for them, but he'd work something out. He couldn't and wouldn't abandon them. "In!" he yelled at them. "Get aboard!"

There were only ten of them.

The instant they were aboard, Starbuck yelled, "CY! Close and secure hatches! Immediate lift-off! Override traffic control! Stand by for possible attack and interception!"

The hatch slid shut and Starbuck's weak, cramped legs felt the momentary surge of acceleration before the stabilizers normalized. It was only then that CY replied calmly, "I'm way ahead of you, boss."

"Boost at the max acceleration possible without overloading the internal field. Full range scan on all sensors. Take whatever evasive action necessary."

"I'll zing and zang a bit to make their day," CY reported. "Where do you want to go?"

"Out of the Garyon system at right angles to its ecliptic. Move out to fifty light-hours." That would be far enough to exceed the range of the Kaloc sensor systems on Thya. By the time CY got the *Starace* to that initial way point, Starbuck would have had some time to determine whether or not they were being pursued.

As usual, the situation had changed. Now he had Onuva Ferona. Without using coercive methods, he'd be able to get some data out of her. And she might also be useful in dealing with Kodo Sadon, although Starbuck didn't know whether or not the Black Path of Thoth would simply write off his consortte.

In addition, there were now ten Thyan Irregulars aboard. He'd certainly find out what had happened on Thya.

He was partway toward his team goal. AI Team 017 had apparently survived where Zing's team hadn't. Based on the information he hoped he'd get, he'd be able to plan beyond. But at the moment, he relied on nothing more than sheer opportunism. Roll with the punch. Play it by ear. Time to regroup, to reassess the situation, to rejuvenate his team. Now that he knew CY would do a better job than he of getting them out of the Garyon system to interstellar space and that he and his team were out of trouble for the moment, he unconsciously relaxed. When he did so, his remaining reserves retreated, pulled back for possible future use, and left him physically vulnerable to the extreme stresses he'd undergone.

Near-superman that he was, even Peter Steele Starbuck had limits. He had the remaining strength to find his compartment where he collapsed on his pallet and slipped into the total sleep of complete exhaustion.

Triga Rimmon looked in on him several times, checked him with her biosensors, dressed his wounds, rigged IVs to replenish his body fluids and provide him with some needed nourishment, and programmed the neuroelectronic pads in his pallet to let CY minister to him. But Peter Starbuck was out of it for the time being.

Although Shochona and David hadn't undergone the trauma of Kodo Sadon's recreation room, Triga and CY tended to them, too. But, other than dressing a wound that Isky had stoically refused to acknowledge during the action on Thya, most of Triga's activity was directed toward Katwin.

When Starbuck awoke, he had no way of knowing how much time had passed. He sensed that CY still had the *Starace* under boost to a fifty light-hour space point. And Triga was sitting on the side of the pallet, having been notified by CY that Starbuck was coming out of sleep mode. She'd removed all the IVs, and CY had ceased neuroelectronic programming.

It was pleasant to come back to consciousness and find a woman like Triga seated on the pallet next to him. Although AI work had its problems, the fringe benefits were good, Starbuck decided. Certainly, it kept him from becoming bored and lonely.

"Physically, Katwin's in fair condition," Triga said, anticipating his first question. "Nothing wrong with Shochona or David. But you can help me treat Katwin if you can remember anything Sadon and Ferona did to you. They may have done the same things to Katwin."

Starbuck sighed. "I really don't want to think about it, Triga, but I honestly don't remember much. There was a lot of pain and agony, maybe even some hallucinations." He raised his arms and looked at his hands, then turned his head to peer at other portions of his body. "Either you've repaired any physical damage beyond any detection, Triga, or Sadon and Ferona used very sophisticated instruments . . ."

"There were indications of physical torture on you and Katwin," the biotech told him, taking his hands. "But I think I've taken care of them. CY works fast on mere physical injuries."

Starbuck looked at his hands. "My God, I could have sworn that they'd twisted and broken . . ." Then he stopped thinking about it. He knew that Triga was an outstanding biotech. And CY had powerful biotechnology programming along with advanced neuroelectric procedures.

What really bothered Starbuck about the episode in Kodo Sadon's "recreation room" was the level of neurotechnology that he seemed to recall. He knew that physical torture was a crude, primitive, and relatively simple method of producing unbearable pain. But it was only of limited duration because it destroyed the physical body. A high level of biotechnology, neurotechnology, and even mentitechnology could create the realistic stimuli of pain and agony in the brain itself. Such techniques were very effective because they didn't destroy the physical body and could be carried on much longer. Working strictly on the nervous system and the perceptions created in the brain, the only limit on neurotorture was the possibility that the nervous system and the mind would overload, thereby causing the victim to short-circuit, block, or even withdraw into catatonia.

Starbuck had run up against such advanced neuro-mentic techniques only once before on Ku-ur-ku, where they'd been used for healing, not torture. Rudi Witkowski's SIGNET Department of Dirty Tricks had hired the proteges of Flanangu, the boy-genius who'd discovered them. Such techniques had been extremely useful to Triga in rejuvenating the people who'd gone aground on Thya.

Perhaps Sadon and Ferona had chanced onto a new wrinkle in the technology.

"Peter," Triga suddenly said in a very serious and concerned tone of voice, "Katwin is in serious psychological trouble."

He sat up. "Is CY working on her?"

"Of course. But he's made practically no progress. It's as thought Katwin was running from him, rejecting him, refusing to let him into her mind. She was undoubtedly hurt very badly from a psychological point of view. Her child's mind simply couldn't handle what happened to her. She didn't understand why she was apparently being punished. And she couldn't stop it. So she withdrew from it. She ran away into herself."

"Catatonia."

"Yes. But not all the way. She knows me, but she won't do anything. She's afraid to do anything. She's afraid she'll be punished again for doing something, and she doesn't know what that something is."

Starbuck shook his head. "There's more, Triga. She's basically cholinergic. She must have sensed something from Sadon or Ferona . . . or both."

"Possibly. Probably, knowing Katwin."

"She may well hold the essential key datum that can unlock why the Kalocs — or Thoths, or Khughars, or what-

ever they really call themselves — behave as they do and
why they set out to conquer other planets.''

"I thought you'd determined they did it because of
economic reasons — living on a resource-short planet, for
example.''

"That was before I tangled with Sadon and Ferona.
They both exhibited highly aberrant behavior, to put it
very mildly. It was also detectable among their officers
and troops.'' He held up his hand began ticking off points
with his fingers. "First, these Kalocs apparently don't
follow the Canons of Metalaw. Why? Secondly, our data
indicates the Kalocs aren't the only culture on Khughar.
Do the other cultures exhibit such behavior? If not, why
not? What's different about the Kalocs? Why did they boil
off Khughar and why didn't the others come along with
them? Or did the others come, but in a different role than
the military shock troops?''

He rose from the pallet. Except for some residual stiffness
in his back and the threshold sense of having had every
nerve and muscle in his body pushed to their limits, he felt
capable of tackling the universe again. And he especially
wanted to solve this problem that was getting deeper and
knottier as time went by. "I want to talk with our Thyan
Irregulars, see what Ferona can tell us, and query SIGNET
Headquarters for any additional scraps of data they might
have . . .''

"Peter, here's the bad news. We can report to SIGNET,
but they can't call us,'' Triga pointed out, putting her hand
on his arm. "Katwin's cholinergic receptor talent isn't
there any more. Cy can't tap it at all, even in its stand-by
relaxation mode with no incoming message. I don't even
know if Katwin has it any longer. CY and I will have to
keep working on her in the hope that we can restore it. In
the meantime, nobody at SIGNET is going to be able to
talk to us . . .''

Chapter Nine

Starbuck called a quick up-date meeting in the wardroom with the whole team present except Katwin.

"Why did I mount the rescue mission? Peter, you called for it," Isky responded to his team leader's request for a report.

"I did?"

"You must have. CY reported that your location transmitter was removed from you and said you were in trouble."

Starbuck shook his head. "That doesn't make any sense. How did I get a message to CY?"

"I don't know," Isky admitted. "I thought I was the only transmitter on this team."

"Your untrained talents again, Peter," Triga guessed.

"Maybe. But I think we should have CY thoroughly checked out when we get back to ColeShore. That cybermech has been showing some disturbing signs of changing. The last thing I want is a cybermech with a little mind of its own. CY's supposed to do what we say, and I don't want him to start second-guessing us."

David O'Hara cleared his throat. "I think — uh — I think it may have been something you did or some way that you communicated to CY, Peter. Do you remember that I managed to get the pin out of my cage door and thus open it?"

"Yes."

"Well, I don't know how I did it."

"What?"

"Somehow I got that pin out. Don't ask me how. With

88

CY's help, I can jump this multi-ton starship over any interstellar distance you wish. But all by myself I can't even make a metal-foil energy wheel turn on command. Or I couldn't. Maybe I can now," the Eyreman said in a baffled tone.

"You were in pretty desperate straits, weren't you, David?" Triga asked.

"I guess so. I heard Katwin scream in that recreation room. I wanted to help her."

"So somehow you 'jumped' the door pin somewhere else," Triga told him.

"Maybe."

"Speculation," Starbuck observed. "It will make a land-mark paper for the Society of Irreproducible Results. But I'll bet neither of us could duplicate what we somehow managed to do in that Kaloc starship on Thya. I'm willing to settle for the simple old explanation, 'By dint of super-human effort, our heroes extricated themselves from their predicament and . . .' Isky, you somehow got a message from CY and started out for us. Alone?"

"Took guts," Shochona remarked.

"No, that isn't what happened at all," Isky explained. "I called for help."

"Huh?"

"I needed help," the wiry little man explained. "So I asked CY to tell me what public organization had never been bothered during any invasion of the past. CY looked it up and told me. So I activated the ship-to-shore tele-phone and called the fire department . . ."

"*The fire department?*" Starbuck couldn't believe this.

"That's right. An invader usually takes over all military and paramilitary security forces, deposes the local govern-mental leaders, but *never* lays a hand on the fire depart-ment. Or any of the so-called public safety organizations. Firemen serve to protect lives and property; they usually have complex equipment developed to fight the sort of fires that occur locally; they're the only ones who know how to run this unique equipment; and they'll fight fires whether they're caused by the invaders or a resistance movement. And invaders don't dare cut off communications to the fire department.'' Isky shrugged. ''Anyway, that was the logic behind it. I thought it was worth a try . . . and it worked.''

''The Thyan Irregulars we have aboard are fire fighters?''

Isky shook his head. ''No, not really. They're traffic managers, doctors, storekeepers, bankers . . . but also fire fighters. Although Novipra is the site of the planet's one and only starport, it's a Fringe Planet starport and Novipra is far too small to support a full-time fire department. They're volunteer firemen. So I had CY dump a few gallons of auxiliary ground power unit fuel on the tarmac from a 'leak' and light it off. Had four fire engines respond. Listen, when the panic switch was hit, those Kalocs went berserk! It was like the proverbial old Chinese Fire Drill. In the hassle, I got out of the ship, joined the impromptu swat team, and led them to the star ship CY said the transmissions of your locator unit were coming from. So you were rescued by volunteer firemen. Isn't that true justice?''

The whole affair was so incongruous and such a fantastically creative act on Isky's part that Peter Starbuck couldn't help but break out in uproarious laughter. So did the rest of the team. They needed the tension break.

Starbuck wanted to find out how the invasion had taken place.

The ten Thyan Irregulars were eager to talk about it.

The wardroom was cramped when all of them were in there. In fact, the quarters of the *Starace* were crowded with ten additional humans aboard. Shochona, the de facto ''housemother'' of the ship, had managed to find places for them to bunk in various cargo bays. With CY's help, she'd moved ship's stores here and there to free up other compartments as well. Since the ship had been recently provisioned on Plethora, there was no problem with the additional people to be fed, although meals had to be taken in shifts because of the limited facilities for preparing and eating meals.

"Pretty obvious from the way you operate, Captain Starbuck, this isn't just an ordinary survey ship," observed the apparent leader of the Irregulars, one Karel Cherny.

Starbuck didn't revise the man's perception of rank, but told him, "Quite perceptive. We're a SIGNET Agent Investigator Team."

Karel's face lit up in a smile. "Star Guard advance scout mission, I take it?"

"You might say that."

Karel seemed very pleased. "I'm the Novipra warehouse manager for Cama Corporation, the client who called you into this mess by sending the drone. We knew you wouldn't ignore a client. Sorry about your agent, Murray Segar. I saw the Black Guards haul him off with the first SIGNET Team that landed. Never saw them again. Probably dead by now. A lot of people sort of disappeared within those first few hours. I suppose the Star Guard fleet is on its way, isn't it?"

Starbuck knew it wouldn't do him any good right then to try to get more information about Joshua Zing's team out of Karel Cherny. The man apparently knew nothing more than what he'd just told Starbuck. And the Agent Investigator didn't know whether the Star Guard was coming or not, and he didn't think it would be a good idea to tell them that AI Team 017 was the only group that he knew was assigned to the problem. Let the Thyans believe that Star Guard was coming. Wouldn't hurt matters a bit and would, in fact, improve the morale of whatever resistance forces had formed on Thya. "Don't count on Star Guard getting here quickly," Starbuck told them. "Thya is a long way out on the Fringe, you know. If we do things right, however, this whole fracas may be over long before Star Guard arrives, and you'll have won it yourselves. That's mainly why we're here: to help out. We were the nearest help that SIGNET could get to you. We've got a few tricks up our sleeves, and maybe we can help you beat these Kalocs. But first of all I've got to find out what happened. How did the invasion start?"

"We just woke up one morning to find our sky full of ships."

"How many?" Starbuck asked.

"We don't know. A lot. Filled the starport. And kept coming and going."

"One thing I have trouble understanding," Starbuck admitted to them, "is how they managed to invade a whole planet. It's never been done before."

"Captain, when you invade a sparsely-settled Fringe World like Thya with maybe only a couple million people on it, you just walk right in and take over C-cubed — command, control, and communications," Yudi explained. "Maybe they didn't have to invade the whole planet, just the places where they could take over C-cubed. That was the first thing the initial wave did. I was the shift portmaster at the starport when their first ship landed. The Kalocs didn't even bother to communicate beforehand. The ship just dropped in and touched down. Got my dander up, it did. On some worlds, the traffic load would have meant an almost sure and certain chance of interference or even near-miss with an outbound ship. But I guess the Kalocs had it figured out ahead of time. I was all ready to write them up for a fine because of infraction of the interstellar rules when a squad of their black-armored goons walked into the office and just took over. Tossed me out, they did. I guess they'd cased the place pretty well before they came. We've had a large number of Kaloc traders into Thya in the last few months. The Kalocs knew where everything was and how to take it over and run it."

"That first ship was full of shock troops," Karel put in. "Within a couple of hours, they were in control of our communications hubs and centers in Novipra. They also simply walked in and took over the sheriff's office and put monitors in the local hospital. Happily, they didn't go into the fire stations. In the next few hours, other Kaloc ships began landing on a regular schedule. Eight hours after the first ship landed, Kaloc Black Guards were everywhere in the town. They started rounding up Thyans, but we don't know what they did with them. And we don't know everyone they picked up."

"Our public servants and governmental reps. Probably killed them," Yudi ventured to guess.

"Maybe not," Starbuck advised. He didn't really want to guess what the Kalocs had done with them if his own treatment had been any indication of how the Kalocs used prisoners. They he pressed the question, "Did any of you notice anything unusual about these Kalocs?"

"Yes. They invaded our planet," a third Irregular, Andre Pesek, spoke up. "As you pointed out, Captain Starbuck, it's unusual to invade a planet in the first place. We weren't expecting it, that's for certain."

"Other than that, I mean. Any unusual way they acted or unusual things any of them said?"

"Well, they seem to be pretty well organized," Karel pointed out. "Like they had the whole invasion planned in minute detail. Troops were very well disciplined. But when they ran up against something that seemed to be different or hadn't been anticipated, they had to go three or four levels up the chain of command to get a decision or a new order."

"Remember what happened when Isky set that fire under this ship and we came in with the fire trucks?" Yudi recalled with a chuckle. "What did he call it? A 'Chinese Fire Drill?' I don't know what that is, but it must be pretty frantic if that's the way the Kaloc troops acted when their careful plans went to worms . . ."

"Got any idea *why* the Kalocs invaded?" Starbuck probed for more information.

Yudi shook his head. "The Kalocs have always been a poor outfit. Always landed with a ship full of near-worthless junk and never managed to trade it for much of anything they wanted. Never had much of what we wanted, at any rate. I hear tell that Khughar is a pretty bare world."

A mustached young man put his hand forward and spoke up, "I'm Pavel Brosz. I'm an officer in one of the Novipra banks. The Kalocs have been running an enormous trade imbalance lately. It used to be a nip-and-tuck sort of thing until about five years ago. They managed to keep the trade with us reasonably balanced, even though there wasn't much of it. Then, for some reason, their trade activities stepped up, and they began to run up some pretty big bills. The trade imbalance has grown so large in the past two years that we finally had to shut off their line of credit and refuse to accept their notes."

This was more or less what Starbuck thought might have happened from the initial data he'd gotten from ColeShore. "So they decided to settle the account by taking over, eh?"

"Maybe. Maybe not," Pavel replied with a shrug. "It must be costing them a fortune to mount this invasion and maintain their troops on Thya. I don't see how they could possibly hope to wipe out their trade debts that way."

In common with most stellars, the Thyans had always lived in a culture based on the Canons of Metalaw. But Starbuck, raised in the early twenty-first century, had known a different way of life before metalaw. He knew what was most probably going on. The Thyans would find out the hard way when the Kalocs got their invasion firmly in hand and began to take over things such as Pavel's bank. Then the looting would start.

Starbuck had to find out what the Thyans were doing to oppose the overt invasion of the Kalocs. "When I was at the Novipra station, I wasn't in any position to learn how the counter-invasion effort was progressing. The Thyan armed forces making any progress?"

"What armed forces?" Karel replied rhetorically.

"Who needs an army? Makes nothing but trouble for free people," Pavel added.

"Most towns and organized regions have a marshal or a peacekeeper. Sometimes Thyans will support a full-time paid staff of deputies, but extensive peacekeeping operations are usually dependent upon vigilantes," Yudi explained.

"We're all too busy making a better place to live," Karel said. "We've got a very low crime rate mostly because Thya is an abundant world and we follow the Canons."

"Most of our ancestors come from Mittel Europa. We've been tired of fighting for centuries."

"I suspected your origins." Getting the Kalocs off Thya was going to be far more difficult than Starbuck had thought. The Thyans probably wouldn't confront the Kalocs openly. These were patient, compliant, but technically competent and hardworking people. At least, their ancestors were, and those traits might still be carried in their genes. He thought he understood what they'd do. They wouldn't offer passive resistance but partisan warfare instead. "You've apparently organized some sort of counter-invasion effort," Starbuck observed.

"Just barely. Takes time to organize partisan activities. None of us ever had to do it before," Karel admitted.

"We can help. Our cybermech has a very large encyclopedia."

"We'll use it while we're aboard. But when can you get us back to Thya?"

"That's a good question," Starbuck admitted, and he didn't have the answer because there were too many factors involved. There was no way he could take the *Starace* back to the Novipra starport and simply drop off the ten Irregulars. There was no way either that he could get a starship surreptitiously down on Thya. He had no secure way of communicating with the Thyans on the ground to let them know he was bringing the Irregulars home. So he simply told them the truth, "I'm not sure we can get you back to Thya right now."

Andre sat up and exclaimed, "I've got a wife and two children . . ."

"And my wife's expecting our first child," Pavel added.

"All of us have to get back," Karel said. "We've got jobs, families . . ."

"Look," Peter Starbuck told them, "whether you've admitted it to yourselves yet, you're in the middle of a war, no matter what you try to call it. Even if we put you in a lifeboat and let you get yourselves back, you're marked men. If you're not immediately executed, you'll suffer a worse fate."

"But . . ." Pavel began.

"Starbuck's right," Karel tried to point out. "Read the history of partisan and guerrilla warfare."

"But what about our families?"

"I told you this was war," Starbuck reminded Pavel. "You freely chose to become a soldier, although you might have thought you'd just be harassing the enemy from the underground from time to time and thereafter be able to go home at night for a hot meal and a hot bed. Isn't so."

Andre put his face in his hands.

"You're the First Regiment of the Thyan Astrine Irregulars," Starbuck went on. "Your friends in Novipra know where you went and what happened to you. They'll probably do their best to take care of your families. Or your relatives will. I know you won't be able to stop worrying about them, and you wouldn't be soldiers if you didn't. But until we can figure out what's going on and get back down on Thya, you'll have to stay aboard. It won't be comfortable or plush. This ship was built for a crew of six and four extras. We'll just have to make the best of the situation with seventeen of us aboard. But we're eventually going back to Thya when we have some plan of action that will give you your planet back and take care of the Kalocs according to the Canons. That much I pledge to you."

There was silence as the ten men looked at one another. Finally, Karel spoke up, "Very well, if that's the way it is and we're now soldiers whether we like it or not, we'd better be the best damned soldiers our world has ever seen!

Captain Starbuck, you say your cybermech library is available to us. Where can we go in the ship to begin our military training?''

This operation was beginning to get complicated, Starbuck told himself. He was used to working with a team of five others. Now he had a contingent of very green, somewhat shocked, very homesick, but very determined partisan soldiers aboard as well. Ten other souls for whom he was essentially responsible.

And he hadn't the foggiest notion much less the glimmerings of a plan concerning what he was going to do next, as well as any long-term strategy about making good his pledge and returning to Thya.

But he was getting a better picture of the situation all the time.

And there was one person now aboard he hadn't talked to yet. He didn't know how much information he'd get, but he knew he'd get some. His next move was obvious. He had to talk to Onuva Ferona, the Consortte of Thoth.

Chapter Ten

On his way to the compartment where Onuva Ferona had been detained, he tried to enter Katwin's room to check on her. Triga met him at the door.

"How is she?"

Triga just shook her head. "She doesn't want to communicate with any one, even me."

"I'd like to see her, Triga."

"I'd rather you didn't at the moment . . . for Katwin's sake," the biotech told him, "I've finally gotten her into linkage with CY. He's running pink noise to relax her and various easy pleasure stimuli along with biofeedback and positive thought process reinforcement. If we were at ColeShore, I'd have her in intensive repatterning. But CY is the best I've got here, and this is almost beyond my expertise."

"Would psychodrug therapy be any better?"

"You know I'm not in favor of chemotherapy as long as a person has any chance of self-cure. Besides, I don't know whether or not it would do Katwin any good. At this point, I'm afraid to try anything that I'm not really sure of. This is no time to experiment . . ."

"Well, do your best!" Starbuck said. It came out testily, almost an order. He knew he was tired. He wouldn't have done that otherwise. Deep down, he longed for a few days' rest to shake off what had been done to him on Thya.

"Peter, I *am* doing my best!" Triga snapped back irritably. Then she reached out and laid her hand tenderly on Starbuck's arm. She took a deep breath and told him,

"Sorry, Peter. Katwin's such an innocent in a universe of travail and we all love her so much — they've hit our most vulnerable point."

He could only nod, but he impulsively gave her a kiss on the forehead. An innocent Katwin might be, but she eagerly and willingly had become a member of an AI Team whose job it was to handle those who would violate the Canons of Metalaw. Beneath that innocence, Katrina Ivanova somehow knew of the violence and wrongdoing among people. It had sparked a very sophisticated and adult streak of idealism within her. Or, Starbuck reflected, maybe the idealism that drove all of them on the team wasn't so grown-up at all. Maybe idealism was basically a childish thing that no one ever gave up . . . and the universe was a better place because of that.

He cursed the basic weariness in his body and mind as he found his way to Ferona's compartment where he was faced with handling something far more dangerous and explosive: A woman who was, to him, the personification of evil because of her exhibited penchant for sadism. But Starbuck knew from his long experience that there had to be something more to Onuva Ferona than that. His own belief in the "rightness" of the Canons of Metalaw told him that even the evil, ignorant, and stupid people of the universe had their rationales for who they were and what they did. It was part of his job to find these in Ferona's case. If he managed to do so, he might be able to answer the big questions that lay behind this operation.

Of course, as usual, he had the key to the answers, but he didn't know it at the time.

At Ferona's door, he told CY to let him in and to discreetly monitor and record his conversation with her.

Starbuck had been in no condition aboard Sadon's ship to look carefully at Onuva Ferona. He now saw a darkly beautiful woman with black, short-cropped hair that lay close to her small skull. Her face was thin and dominated by deep, dark eyes set closely together above high cheek bones. What struck Starbuck immediately was the fairness of her skin; it was extremely pale as though she'd never been exposed to any ultraviolet light from a sun or even an artificial source. Although her black uniform covered her completely except for her small hands, the skin on her face and hands had a decidedly blue cast to them as though she were either slightly hypoxic or so fine skinned that her veins cast their blueness through the semitransparency.

She'd done her best to patch the ripped portions of her black uniform, an attire that was provocative to begin with and was made even more so by the rents from the hand-to-hand fight in Sadon's ship. That black uniform covered a body that was definitely and obviously that of a nubile human female. But Onuva Ferona had none of the full ripeness of the women on Starbuck's AI Team and nothing of the exotic allure of the scintillating Tayreze Nambe. She was, to Starbuck's tastes, too skinny, like the models that graced the fashion news transmissions which Shochona, Triga, and even Katwin enjoyed watching when things got boring.

CY had not reported to Starbuck that she'd been using the cybermech. Ferona was seated before the compartment's comm/info panel working with CY. Starbuck wasn't worried that she might be attempting to send messages or take control of the ship; CY was programmed to permit only members of the AI Team to carry on those activities. Ferona was simply doing what CY would permit her: digging into the unsecured data banks.

She turned slowly to face him as the door closed. With an emotionless expression on her face, she greeted him, "Good day, Agent Investigator Peter Steele Starbuck of SIGNET. I had serious doubts from the first that you were indeed only the captain of an obscure survey ship. Everything about you told me you were a longer."

"And now you've confirmed it, I see," Starbuck replied with equal coolness. He couldn't help but remember what she and Sadon had done to him and especially to Katwin, and his demeanor toward her reflected those memories.

"And many other things as well." She appeared to be gloating, but Starbuck knew there was no way that CY would have let her access any of the non-encyclopedic, secured SIGNET files. Yet, she'd gotten his full name and his bio as well. And probably the bios of his team members, too. And maybe even registration details of the *Starace* that were stored in unsecured banks. She knew where she was and who had taken her prisoner.

Starbuck wished he had as much information about her. It was now up to him to get it the hard way rather than a simple hack into a database. He sensed she wasn't going to give up her information voluntarily or even willingly. Judging from her revealed persona thus far, Starbuck surmised that Onuva Ferona was either hardened against any and all forms of physical or mental torture — he knew from recent experience that she was an expert in both — or she had a deathly fear of people doing to her what she enjoyed doing to others. This was typical of such psychopathic personalities. *If* she were indeed a sadist. If she were a masochist, it would have been totally within the bounds of the Canons to torture the truth out of her. However, Starbuck would not have enjoyed doing it that way. In fact, he couldn't have done it. So he dismissed that possibility.

Instead, Starbuck became devious. "Good. That puts us on an even footing, Onuva. You know something about us, and we know a great deal about you."

"You know nothing about me!" She was immediately defensive.

"You were unconscious for quite some time after being brought aboard."

"You probed me!"

Starbuck simply smiled. "You're as open as a library database."

She tried to call his bluff. "Oh? And just who do you think I am?"

He responded by calling his cybermech. His instructions to CY would have to be very carefully worded because what he wanted to pull from the cybermech's data base was enough of the encyclopedic data from Headquarters to cause Onuva Ferona to believe that CY had done what Starbuck said. "CY, Onuva Ferona here is a Kaloc from Khughar. Please tell us verbally what you know about the planet, the Kalocs, and her." His instructions, phrased in that order, would instruct CY to deliver up the data in that sequence.

Which CY began to do, tonelessly reciting planetary data about Khughar first. This went on for a little more than a minute and had gotten to the point where CY was rattling off demographics about the Kalocs and other people on Khughar. At that point, Ferona's defenses collapsed. She waved her long, thin white hands violently in front of her. "Enough!"

"Care to confirm our data? Or do you want to live with the possibility that we have distorted or even incorrect information?"

Onuva Ferona was stubborn. "You can't do anything to me!"

"That remains to be seen. After the Star Guard fleet arrives, you and Kodo Sadon will undoubtedly stand before a three-world tribunal and be charged with and tried for the murders of the previous SIGNET AI Team members." Starbuck was still bluffing. But when one's bluff has been partially called or when stubborn resistance is encountered, the most lucrative way to continue an interrogation session is to continue the bluff and even compound it. "Your mistake was killing that team. When you did it, we knew about it instantly. Our monitors everywhere picked up the termination signal. Never mind how; we know what's going on when an AI Team is in action, and the techniques we use are of no consequence right now. The Star Guard fleet will probably rendezvous at Thya. I don't know about that for sure because we're never informed of Star Guard intentions. My AI Team was nearby, so we were sent ahead to reconnoiter. If you hadn't killed Zing's team but merely detained them until you'd completed your invasion, we might not have discovered you until it was over." Some of what he was telling her he knew to be deception. Other parts were not. In actuality, he was the one who'd been deceived and didn't know it.

"Now, why don't you tell me exactly who you are, what you're doing, and how and why you murdered the AI Team. That will modify and correct the data we already have stored in databank both aboard this ship and at ColeShore." He paused, then went on, "Or do you want to take the chance that the data we have is incorrect?"

"You know nothing!" Ferona snapped.

Starbuck replied urbanely, "But I'm afraid we do."

"Then go ahead and torture the rest out of me!"

Smoothly and suavely, Starbuck said coldly, "I'd rather you told me instead. If I deliver you to the tribunal and you haven't talked, the tribunal prosecutors have far better facilities and tools than I do." Sometimes, he detested doing the sort of things that he had to do as an AI Agent. There were parts of this job he disliked, particularly those parts that required him to behave like a spy, spook, or agent of yore when dealing with primitive and/or psychopathic people like Onuva Ferona who understood little other than force and pain and fear. Under the Canons, no one, not even he, had a license to kill or even to set aside the Canons without very good reason for which he could be called to task later. Instead, the only thing he could do was to use his wits to see that justice was done. That usually took longer, but the results were far more civilized. He was counting on the fact that Onuva Ferona hadn't been raised under the Canons, knew little about them, and therefore didn't know that he was deviously attempting to achieve results under the mandates of the Canons. He was wrong about Onuva Ferona, of course.

"Good! Let them!" Ferona said loudly and clearly. Starbuck thought it was defiance. But when she went on, he realized he'd underestimated her. " Go ahead and try it yourself! Apply the Canons if you wish, but remember the First Canon, Peter Starbuck!"

"How can I obey the First Canon until I know you,

understand you, and discover what you would like me to do unto you?"

She suddenly seemed beaten. Her shoulders slumped just enough to clue Starbuck that he might have won this round. She could rightly have reminded him that he was holding her in violation of the Canons, but, for reasons that Starbuck didn't understand then, she didn't. He was still so highly charged emotionally over what she'd done to him on Thya that he missed most of what she was communicating to him. After staring at the overhead for a moment, she heaved a resigned sigh. In a husky voice, she observed, "You haven't tried to harm me, Peter Starbuck, but I believe we'll be able to get along very well. However, I'm required by interstellar law to give you only my name, planet of birth, and planet of citizenship."

Starbuck recalled that she and Sadon had played loose and free with interstellar law. He maintained his cold expression and smile. "Very well, let's start with that, then."

"I am Sittee Onuva Ferona, Consortte of Thoth. I am a native and resident of the planet Khughar."

"Thank you. But I understand you also consider yourself a Kaloc," Starbuck observed.

"Yes."

"You said that proudly, Onuva. There must be something special about being a Kaloc . . ."

"We are the best group of people ever to have evolved on Khughar!" Suddenly, it was as though Onuva Ferona had become the chairman of the Kaloc Commerce Council and Tourist Board. She began to talk rapidly and enthusiastically about her world. "The other groups — races, if you want to use the old term which we've retained — are inferior. The Dyons are a hedonistic race . . . although I can't personally say that I dislike them. The Lanigers and Zhedarons are too few, too backward, and very uninteresting bores — all they talk about is their religion, their farm, and their families, forever and interminably. On the other hand, we Kalocs are superior because we started with little and have worked our way to the point where we possess outstanding genetic engineering, advanced biotechnology, and a capability to live anywhere, not just in a poor region of a tiny nondescript planet on the edge of nowhere. Now we don't have to stay on Khughar. We have the means and the power and the leadership and the will to leave Khughar! We don't have to stay there and share scarcity with Dyons, Lanigers, and Zhedarons. We can go find other worlds and other people who are our friends and who will treat us according to the First Canon.''

Starbuck raised his eyebrows. "Why have you chosen to invade Thya rather than deal with the other groups on Khughar for your needs?"

Ferona snorted in derision. "The Dyons have nothing for most Kalocs. I could live with them if I had to. I like the Dyons and the city of Samarra. But Kaloc credit is no longer any good there."

That didn't answer Starbuck's question, but it gave him important data nonetheless. "Then why did you forcibly invade Thya rather than continue to trade with the Thyans?"

"The Thyans are such a peaceful people. We can and will be good friends with them. So Thya was our first priority. But . . ." She suddenly stopped talking.

Starbuck had grown up in the twenty-first century on Tellus at the beginning of the time when the new ways of metalaw were being accepted. Ferona's words seemed like an old story retold in new terms. Perhaps a mutant revival of the old Neolithic Ethic of Tellus, a philosophy that worked its deadly and violent course on the home world of scarcity before technology created abundance and the Canons of Metalaw established a more adult technique of interpersonal relationships. But he was looking at it from the wrong perspective.

Ferona suddenly snapped peevishly, "Take me home!"

Starbuck shook his head. "Not until I find out what happened to the other SIGNET AI Team and why you killed them."

"I didn't kill them," she replied fiercely.

"Who did?"

"You have no right to ask me to divulge that information. It's against the Kaloc Code for me to reveal it. If it could later be determined that I snitched, I'd have to kill myself in public. If you want to torture it out me, that's a different matter. I couldn't be held responsible under those conditions." She looked at him and he couldn't tell whether her eyes were defiant or pleading. It sounded like she was pleading! He didn't believe that. Ferona then snapped, "Now, either take me home or torture the information out of me!"

It was obvious to Starbuck that this interrogation session was over. Ferona had suddenly become totally uncooperative. He stood up. I'm not sure I could get within ten A.U. of Thya without being intercepted and zapped."

"Sadon wouldn't do it. I know him better than you do. There are seventeen people on this starship. Kodo Sadon is not a mass murderer!"

"And that is what I cannot believe," Starbuck interrupted her. He shouldn't have broken off the interrogation right then, but he was tired and a bit testy. He didn't dare let it show because he felt it might be a weakness she'd try to exploit. Starbuck believed from his own experience in Sadon's "recreation room" that she undoubtedly knew a great deal about interrogation. And he knew that an interrogator must never reveal any sort of weakness that an experienced witness could exploit. "No, you'll just have to stay aboard until the whole situation is resolved. I won't risk going back to Thya right now. In the meantime, we'll keep you comfortable. That's far more than you did for us when we were on Thya."

She glared at him. "Why are you doing this to me?"

Starbuck was caught short. "I beg your pardon?"

"Why are you denying me?"

Starbuck sighed and tried to hold his temper. "Because of what you did to me and to Katrina Ivanova on Thya. Because I can't trust you to be allowed the freedom of the ship. Because I believe you to be a murderess and I must therefore hold you, even against the Canons, until other, better data becomes available.''

''I did nothing to you and that young girl on Thya!'' There were now tears in her eyes. ''I am not a murderess! You have no right to do this to me! Don't you believe in the First Canon?'' Now she was openly weeping.

''We'll talk more later,'' was all that Starbuck could say. He quickly left the compartment and closed the hatch behind him. He forgot to lock the hatch, but that act of omission didn't register on him right then. He was tired, and he'd had enough of sparring with a woman with such a pathological outlook.

Even a superman gets weary, forgetful, and incapable of analyzing data. Peter Starbuck was still human.

Chapter Eleven

"I'd like your input," Starbuck addressed his AI Team in the wardroom of the *Starace* as the ship approached its first space point outside the Garyon system, still moving at sub-light velocity relative to Garyon. The Kalocs hadn't attempted to pursue or intercept them; Starbuck guessed that Sadon either had his hands full on Thya or that he was reluctant to go after a starship in which his consortte was a hostage. Basically, the situation hadn't changed since leaving Thya. Katwin was still semicatatonic, the ten Thyan Irregulars were using CY as a teaching machine for insurgent warfare doctrines and tactics, and Starbuck had gotten some desperately needed sleep. He'd also had some time to think. He felt he'd gone as far as he could in his evaluation of the data they presently had. It was time to plan ahead now. "I believe our next move should be a visit to Khughar."

"Why?" Shochona asked. "The actions's on Thya."

"Perhaps. But as a result of my chat with Onuva Ferona, I think the answers probably lie on Khughar."

"What do you mean by that, Peter?" David wanted to know. "We've all reviewed the Ferona interview. I didn't find anything in it that indicates any Kaloc motivation other than the ancient territorial acquisition syndrome."

"Probably driven by shortages of necessities," Isky added.

"I agree with the diagnosis of the acquisition syndrome. Ferona is just the sort of mean and nasty person you run up against in a macrolife ship where the ecology's gotten out of balance and everyone's on short rations," Shochona put in. "I know. Happened in the M.L.S. *New Deseret* when I was a child."

"Perhaps. But I caught something else both in the live interview and in my review of it. We're dealing here with some aberration on the part of the Kalocs," the AI Team leader tried to explain. "I can't put my finger on it. But think about this for a moment: Sadon and Ferona didn't try to take over the Dyons or other groups on Khughar. Instead, they chose to mount an expensive interstellar operation culminating in a planetary invasion. To my knowledge — and CY backs me up from his database — neither has been attempted before. That operation must be an enormous drain on their already-strained resources; wars always are. The reason why they did it lies on Khughar. For example, why the reluctance of the Kalocs to confront the Dyons? Ferona won't tell me. And we can't get any more data from CYMaster on ColeShore until Katwin recovers. Triga?" Starbuck directed the unvoiced question to his biotech.

"I can't report much progress. Katwin was badly traumatized."

"We all were," Shochona observed.

"Yes, but mentally you're an adult," Isky added. "Most of the time, that is."

"Is she eating?" Starbuck asked.

"Very little."

"The poor dear wasn't very robust to begin with," Shochona piped up. "She has few physical reserves. Triga, let me try to get some supper into her."

"That might not be a bad idea, Shochona. You're the motherly type. Maybe you can get a response from her," Triga mused. Then she explained to the team, "I've been reluctant to let any of you visit Katwin because she's semicatatonic. She withdraws even when I come into her room."

"Triga, are you sure there wasn't any brain damage from her experience on Thya?" Starbuck asked.

"No, I'm not. I have no way of accurately determining that. CY doesn't have that level of diagnostic competence. He's a good cybermech, but there's a limit to what can be crammed into even the best. After all, his working memory was deliberately curtailed because he was designed for networking with CYMaster on ColeShore through our receiver, Katwin . . ."

". . . who's out of the circuit right now," David finished.

"I'm doing my best!"

"I know you are, Triga," Starbuck tried to soothe her. "But what does CY have to say about the neurology involved? He *can* get into Katwin's central nervous system in a very intimate fashion."

"Cy tells me there's no damage and no neurological trauma."

"Can CY detect any differences pre-trauma and post-trauma?" Starbuck asked .

"Of course! But he reports it's not physical or neurological. The psychopathology indicates Katwin has simply withdrawn from a situation she can't handle, but CY hasn't been able to do a humanistic psychological evaulation. He can't penetrate her catatonic block. After all, Peter, Katwin may be mentally retarded in one respect, but otherwise she has a very powerful mind. She's a premium receiver." Triga paused. No one in the wardroom said anything. It was patently obvious that the other team members were as concerned about Katwin as Triga. In a sense, Katwin was their baby, their child, their ward. Even among this group of near-immortal longers, the basic human parental instinct was quite strong. "There's only one thing I can think of to do, and it's the sort of thing I always do when the situation isn't immediately life-threatening: wait, because sooner or later — usually sooner — something will change and a fresh course of action becomes evident. Or the person self-heals. The powers of the human mind and the human body are unbelievably strong, and we know very little about them yet in spite of the state of the art in biotechnology and mentitechnology."

"We all have confidence in you, Triga. You'll do the best you can. We all will. But, Peter has put a proposal before us. He wants to go to Khughar," Shochona reminded the team, bringing them back to the matter at hand. "Why, Peter?"

"I told you why. But, to be completely honest with all of you, I don't have full data in hand and I can't justify the request on the basis of logical deduction from the data. A large part of it is simply a hunch," the AI Team leader admitted.

"I believe your hunches, Peter. You've been at this far longer than any of us. And you're a latent in many ways. Okay, so we go to Khughar on a snoop. I've got another worry: What do we do about the ten Thyan Irregulars we've got aboard?"

"Take them with us," David said.

"Easy for you to say. One of my jobs is to look after the housekeeping aboard this ship. If we take the Irregulars with us, we'll have to go on short rations sooner or later. Or do you want to take the unwarranted risk that we'll be able to reprovision on Khughar? Peter?"

"We may have a deeper problem," David warned. "Peter what's SIGNET policy about an AI Team ship carrying its own contingent of armed astrines?"

"David, I know you're a non-violent," Starbuck told him. "But the *Starace* is both armed and shielded. There are personal weapons aboard. We all know how to use them if necessary. SIGNET doesn't burden us with unworkable and unenforcible policies. We can call the shots as we see them. We have to. We can't forecast every possible situation we'll encounter. Neither can SIGNET Headquarters.

"Let's look at the reality of the situation," he went on. "These men risked their lives to save us on Thya. The situation at the Novipra Starport was such that we could either leave them on the tarmac to face certain death . . . or worse. Or we could bring them with us. There seemed to be no question on the part of any of you that we couldn't abandon them, that we'd bring them along. Now they're aboard. They know the situation. They also didn't anticipate having to go with us. They want to go back to Thya themselves. Question: How do we get them back down on Thya? Any good ideas?''

No one said anything for a moment. Then Isky ventured, ''Yes, approach in a cometary orbit. They won't be looking for that. And we drop them somewhere on Thya.''

David O'Hara cleared his throat and spoke up, ''Isky, I was born on Far Call while it was still being developed. I lived in a small farming town only a hundred kilometers from the main city of Dickson. Did you ever walk a hundred kilometers to town and back because the transportation equipment broke down? Probably not. You're Tellurian. You have the typical Tellurian provincial outlook because of the super-duper transportation system on your home world: No part of Tellus is more than ninety minutes from any other part. But all planets aren't developed like Tellus. And planets are *big*. Thya's a fringe world with no established planetwide transportation network. That means if you haven't got a personal vehicle, you walk. Maybe if you're lucky, you manage to hitch a ride if someone happens to come along. If we took the Thyan Irregulars back to Thya, we'd have to put them down within fifty kilometers of Novipra. Otherwise, they might never get home.''

Isky shrugged. ''Okay. So they stay until we go back ourselves. But, Peter, don't we have the same problem getting down on Khughar? That's the home world of the Kalocs.''

Starbuck shook his head and explained, ''Different situation on Khughar. There's more than one social group there. The Kalocs don't run the whole show. The Dyons carry on a lot of interstellar trade. They have to; they live on the same resource-poor world as the Kalocs. I don't know what they have to trade, but we'll find out when we get there and maybe discover why the Kalocs can't trade the same things. SIGNET should have a stringer agent there, maybe even a client or two. I'll quiz CY. So we'll come right on into the main Dyon starport."

"Except this time let's not open the main hatch so eagerly," was David's comment. "The Dyons may not be like the Kalocs. But then, again, they might. And as far as I'm concerned, I got enough of Kaloc hospitality to last for a very long time. I don't need it topped off by the Dyons, whether for their pleasure or mine. And our data says they're somewhat hedonistic."

CY told Starbuck there was no SIGNET agent or client at the Dyon city and starport of Samarra. "But Strakovkhaburo has a representative there."

That news didn't make Starbuck's day. Strakovkhaburo was a major SIGNET competitor. They didn't cooperate as fully as Justar did. Strakovkhaburo was secretive, preferring to go its own way, but would help SIGNET in an emergency. CY had no data indicating the existence of any agreement that allowed Strakovkhaburo to enjoy an exclusive at Samarra. So Starbuck was completely within his rights as a SIGNET Agent Investigator to land there in the course of an investigation.

It was settled. The team agreed with Starbuck. David and Shochona planned to jump to their normal operational point twenty-four light-hours from Khughar in the usual position and approach vector used by commercial ships on regular visits to Khughar.

This was the first time in many years that the Team had jumped the *Starace* with non-SIGNET passengers aboard. The standard protocol for preserving the security of the SIGNET irrational-jump techniques was followed. Triga advised the ten Thyan Irregulars that the ship was going to make a rather rugged interstellar transition utilizing new Star Guard technology but didn't go into details. Actually, the Irregulars didn't care. They simply weren't curious about interstellar operations. Instead, they had busied themselves training in order to keep their minds off the fact that they couldn't go home right away. They willingly accepted Triga's suggestion that she sedate them during the jump. Actually, what she gave them was a placebo. CY introduced modulated microwave energy into their compartments, using a modification of the disrupter technology. It was by far the most comfortable way to do it without causing any aftereffects or drug-related trauma.

It was a rather straightforward operation. But Starbuck viewed it with his usual apprehension because, in spite of all the times he'd done it, he really didn't like its effects.

He retired to his compartment fifteen minutes prior to jump time. As he frittered away the time, he became more and more anxious and somewhat apprehensive. Finally, at minus-five, he muttered to himself, "To hell with it!" He decided that Triga's fears were perhaps unjustified. And Starbuck also decided he'd take the consequences. He left his compartment quietly and stood in front of Katwin's door for a moment before opening it quietly and going in.

Katwin was lying with her eyes closed on her pallet. She looked terribly pale and thin to Starbuck. Without a word, he went over and sat down on the edge of the pallet.

The frail receiver began to turn her head away from him and curl her body into a fetal position when she obviously sensed the identity of her visitor. She suddenly opened her eyes. When she saw Starbuck, she let out a low moan and struggled to sit up, her arms reaching out for him.

Starbuck reached down and picked her up, holding her tightly in his arms.

In a whisper, Katwin began to sob to him, "Peter . . . Peter . . . Peter! Where have you been? Why didn't you come? Why did you let them do it to me?" Tears ran down her cheeks.

He caressed her head as though she were one of his daughters somehow rejuvenated in childhood form. "I couldn't come, Katwin. They hurt me, too. They locked me up so I couldn't get to you."

"It hurt so much! What did I do that was so bad that they hurt me so much? You never punished me that much, Peter. But they wouldn't tell me and they kept right on hurting me . . ."

"You've done nothing wrong, Katwin. You've done nothing wrong," he told her over and over again.

"Why did they hurt me?"

"They just like to hurt people for their own pleasure, Katwin. I don't understand it, either."

"They're bullies," Katwin suddenly blurted out.

Strangely, Katwin's childlike view of the situation provided another key to open the door a little bit more. Starbuck suddenly had another piece in the puzzle. Strange that he should have forgotten it after all these years. And he had also discovered why she'd withdrawn. It was now up to him to provide the final therapy to bring her back. "Yes, Katwin, they are. And we're going to stop them from hurting anyone else . . ."

She suddenly pulled back and looked at him. "Did they hurt you bad, Peter?"

"Yes, but I healed myself. Now you've got to do the same, Katwin."

"You mean they just hurt me for fun?"

"That's right."

"And you couldn't help me?"

He nodded.

"I feel better."

"Good."

"We're back in the *Starace*?"

He nodded. "And we're about to jump again. Hang on, Katwin."

"Yes, Peter." She grabbed him tightly again just as the ship went through that wrenching transition of an irrational jump across the light-years.

Triga had been correct about the incredible power of the human mind over the human body. In spite of the rigor of the jump, Katwin now had a rosy glow about her again and her childlike eagerness had returned. She no longer seemed thin and pale. Her seemingly-frail body once again had amazing strength for her size. However, she held tightly onto Starbuck's arm as the two of them went up to the control deck.

Shochona and David, their jump task completed, looked haggard. But their appearances suddenly altered upon seeing

Katwin. Isky was almost beside himself to discover his communications partner was back on the team. The commotion on the control deck caused Triga to come from the lower decks where she was checking the Irregulars. As she came up the bounce tube into the noisy control compartment, her jaw dropped and her eyes grew wide. She broke into a broad smile and squealed like a little girl discovering that a close friend had come to visit, "Katwin!"

Once the joyous reunion calmed down a bit, Triga started to do a preliminary check of Katwin with a biosensor probe.

"Don't worry," Starbuck advised the biotech. "She's fine."

"Are you, Katwin?" Triga asked.

"Yes, Triga. I'm okay now."

"I really want to give you a check up," she told the receiver.

"All right, Triga. But I feel good again."

"Can you communicate with CY?"

"I . . . I don't know. Do you want me to try?"

"Would you?"

Katwin sighed and brushed her thin hand over her eyes. "I guess I could. But I'm awful hungry and I'm tired . . ."

"Well, you haven't eaten for a long time, Katwin," Shochona told her. "Come along. We'll get you something to eat, and then you can rest." She looked askance at Triga. "Triga can check you over after we take care of the basics a girl must have just to get along these days . . ."

Katwin glanced at Starbuck then told the shipmother, "I've already go that, Shochona . . ."

Triga didn't say anything until the two departed down the bounce well. Then she began, "Peter . . ."

"Later, Triga. I've got to check in with Samarra approach before the Khughars decide we're a menace to them on their home planet."

Chapter Twelve

Although CY's database indicated there was no zone of sensitivity listed by the Kalocs for approaching Khughar, the Dyons had established theirs at twenty light-hours. Therefore, the *Starace* was well beyond that when it popped back into normal space. With the ship running in to Khughar at Mike point-nine, Starbuck didn't expect a hail until they crossed the limit.

A little more than four hours after pop out, the first indication came right on schedule. "GI sensor pulse received," CY reported. "I have emitted the *Starace* signature code verification." Five seconds later, CY again reported, "Request for verification of ident and nature of intentions received on standard C+ hailing frequencies. Transmitting compliments of the commander, verification of identification, and request for landing Samarra." Another five seconds. "Request for landing Samarra granted. Approach trajectory data received. I have confirmed the vectors requested by Samarra control. Starbuck, I know why you don't like to fly these standard approaches manually. It's boring."

"So turn the job over to the autopilot," Peter Starbuck suggested to his cybermech.

"I have, I do, and I did. That's just another part of me."

"Quit complaining about your job."

"Complaining keeps me from becoming bored."

"CY, have you started to self-program because you're bored most of the time?"

"Who? Me? Self-program? That's not in my basic algorithms, Peter." It wasn't a lie, but it couldn't be considered to be a truthful answer either. It was a devious answer. It was also highly creative.

"I'm beginning to wonder." When the *Starace* got back to ColeShore, he was determined to have CY checked most carefully by the best cybertechnicians in Rudi Witkowski's shop. Barring the possibility that one of his puckish team members was playing games with him through CY, Starbuck was now convinced that CY was indeed self-programming, had learned how to circumvent the instructions against doing so, and had determined how to hide the fact. In the meantime, Starbuck decided against using CY's new-found capability — whatever there was of it, and he didn't have time right then to investigate it thoroughly — in the mission. It was too iffy. Too chancey. It wasn't supposed to be there in the first place if the anti-self-programming algorithms and policies were valid. Starbuck wasn't really sure they were. The algorithms were included in every cybermech's roms to keep the machines from haling. With six intelligent human beings aboard, there was no reason to have machine intelligence in competition with them. Some early cybermechs had had too much artificial intelligence built into them. These early cybermechs exhibited a hal reaction and over-rode even the basic algorithm of the Canons as applied to cybermechs if commands and programs weren't loaded with extreme care. Machines were thereafter programmed with the Tik-Tok Algorithm permitting them to do only the work that humans wanted done, not their own. All, of course, contained the asimov programming of the Calvin Algorithm of the Laws of Robotics.

"Incidentally, Peter," CY's voice continued, "I may need the names and planets of origin of our eleven passengers. My databank says that the Samarra starport doesn't require that sort of thing, but there may have been some changes in procedures at Samarra. There certainly were at Thya."

"Ask Shochona," Peter replied, watching the amplified image of Khughar on the display. "As a contingency procedure, be prepared to respond to any request from Samarra for Standard Manifest Listing."

"I'm way ahead of you on that, Peter. It's already completed."

There was no way for Peter to face CY directly as he would a human being. CY was everywhere in the *Starace*. The nearest thing to physical confrontation was to face one of CY's duplex terminals, which Starbuck did. With some concern in his tone, the AI Team leader remarked, "CY, I'm worried about you."

"Worried? Why, Peter?"

"You banter with me when I'm working alone with you. But when I'm with the other members of my team, you act and sound like a simple home cybermech . . . which you're not."

"I haven't detected any difference, Peter."

"I have. Answer me truthfully, CY. Has one of the team members been programming you with familiarity responses for use when you're working alone with me?"

"No, Peter."

"Are you self-programming?" That was a critical question.

"No, Peter."

One of the problems involved in dealing with any cybermech was the old GIGO factor: Garbage In, Garbage Out. Cybermechs did only what their programs told them to do and only what their human operators instructed them to carry out consistent with the limitations built into the programs. Unlike human beings, cybermechs had the irritating basic trait of complete subservience and total truthfulness. However, Starbuck knew very well from several centuries of dealing with cybermechs of all sorts that "the truth" insofar as human beings were concerned consisted of the truth, the whole truth, and nothing but the truth. Sometimes the second factor in that triad was assigned secondary priority when working with a cybermech because it was absolutely necessary. If one asked a cybermech for the whole truth, one had to be prepared for reams of hard-copy printouts or a super-encyclopedic recitation that often lasted for hours. Cybermechs had to exercise some filtering of the data. Most operators had to spend months with a new cybermech teaching it to filter data in the way the operator wished . . . and each operator had his or her own priorities and procedures.

Starbuck reflected on his own train-up with CY many years ago. He was almost certain that CY was operating outside of his original filtering instructions. But he couldn't recall how many times and in what ways over the years and through all the escapades of AI Team 017 that he'd altered or revised that original train-up programming.

In short, Starbuck had the strong hunch — illogical yet persuasively strong — that CY wasn't telling "the whole truth."

A self-programming cybermech isn't a serious problem *if* the operator knows what's going on. A cybermech must do a certain amount of it in any event.

But he didn't have time to raid the system and flit-out what was taking place in CY's crystalline brain.

As soon as Katwin was able to act as a receiver again, Starbuck wanted to duplex with Rudi Witkowski about the problem.

But it was far too early to consider doing it. Katwin was now sleeping soundly, having eaten well and resumed her contact and interaction with the real world again. Accomplishing that had been a real breakthrough, and Starbuck was both proud of the fact that he'd been the trigger and yet disturbed that he hadn't understood the basic factors long before the jump.

Dealing with the "jellyware" of people was often as difficult as dealing with the "wares" of machinery. As far as Starbuck was concerned, both were equally illogical. Unlike Rudi Witkowski who saw the universe as a super-complex wind-up clock, Starbuck had been around longer and felt that the Universe was pretty strange to begin with and getting stranger all the time. He often felt like the old Spanish king who, after listening to an explanation of the universe given by the court astrologer, reportedly remarked, "If I were God, I would have made it simpler."

Starbuck spent several hours attempting to become acquainted with the Dyons and their culture. When it came to digging out information about the Dyon culture on Khughar, CY's database wasn't that helpful. From what he could learn, it was different from that of the Kalocs. But why? And in what ways? The information was sparse, only that required for database listing under interstellar agreement. It was about as complete and valuable to Starbuck as a "Who's Who" biography or the biodata from a single medical exam. In short, it gave all the hard facts but offered no insight, no way to get a grip on the personality, no basic foundation on which to base value judgments.

He made a note in his personal CY file to bring this to the attention of Brinker or Tayreze Nambe. When an AI Team was operating out in the Fringe Worlds, he felt it had to have data that was not only current but also in depth. It was hazardous to operate with the sort of barebones data that usually satisfied meta-economists, statisticians, or archivists. He was aware of the fact that expanding the database for SIGNET operations might well prove to be expensive in terms of time and people involved to amass, collate, and properly file so much more data. But, he reflected, what price human life? He felt that the loss of Joshua Zing's AI Team on Thya had been partially caused by data lack. And he knew he and his team members had come far too close for comfort to being terminated themselves on Thya.

The approach into Samarra was running according to schedule. Starbuck became frustrated in his attempt to learn more about the Dyons from the sparse data available. But, as usual, he didn't get the chance to become bored.

Shochona interrupted him in his fruitless study. Normally, it was a *verboten* act to bother Starbuck when he was studying. But Shochona sensed his growing frustration and took the chance. "Peter, sorry to bother you," the older woman said as she bounced onto the control deck from the lift tube. Her short-cropped hair transitioned from the halo effect of zero-g in the tube to its normal standard-g appearance as she stepped into the deck's field. "I've got a real problem with that bitch Ferona."

"I agree with you. She's a bitch," Starbuck observed. "But what's she up to now?"

"She's gone on a hunger strike."

"Why?"

"Says she won't eat until she's given the sort of treatment she's accustomed to."

"Does she say what that treatment consists of?"

"Yes. She demands deputy head-of-state protocol."

"Really? Well, in the first place, we don't have the facilities for that in the *Starace*. Secondly, Onuva Ferona is being treated quite well, even under the Canons that apply in her case. Apparently, she won't admit the fact that she's being detained for possible complicity in the murder of an AI Team."

"She keeps claiming she didn't kill them."

"Yes, she told me that, too. In any event, there's no way we can safely return her to Thya. Her chief's troops might well blow us out of the sky in spite of her presence aboard. And she knows it."

"Uh, Peter," Shochona said with great hesitation, "I'm sure you realize that you're acting contrary to the Canons in holding Ferona as you are."

"I'm well aware of that, my dear old shipmother." Peter Starbuck replied lightly. "And you should also be aware that ninety-nine percent of the anxiety that goes with the job of being on a SIGNET AI Team involves dealing with the knotty discrepancies that result from the inconsistencies of the various Canons. The remaining one percent of the gut-tearing decisions come from working with the small number of people who don't follow the Canons or follow them in their own ways."

"We don't have an open license to violate the Canons."

"I know. But we do have some leeway in interpreting them based upon 'best considered judgment' at the time. That's the tough part of being a team leader. I'm the one who'll be called on the carpet if my judgment is considered faulty or if I bend the rules too far. But, Shochona, we are the watchdogs, after all. Even in the tiny portion of the galaxy now inhabited by people, an interstellar police force simply won't work. We're the closest thing to it. We *are* our brothers' keepers, and it's a difficult job when constrained by the Canons."

"You certainly don't have to give me Lecture Number One, Peter."

"Occasionally, all of us need to be reminded of the basics, my dear."

"Yes, but maybe this wasn't the occasion. Never mind. Let's you and me fight later. Right now, Ferona won't accept your evaluation of the situation. She claims innocence in the Zing Team matter. She claims you have absolutely no right to hold her, must treat her with proper protocol, and must return her to Thya immediately."

"Well, Shochona, I could go even deeper than the Zing Team murder or the Canons, you know. Nobody's invoked the Interplanetary Conflict Convention since the Titan Nitrogen War a couple centuries or so ago. But the Convention's still in force in spite of the Canons. Under that convention she's a prisoner of war."

"But was a war declared?"

"Minor legal point. Metalawyers grow fat over such discrepancies between the Canons and the old 'grandfather' conventions." Starbuck fell silent and thought about this latest development.

"Well?" Shochona prodded him.

"Damned if I like to do it, but . . ." Starbuck finally spoke. "If I have to in her case, I'll invoke an even older convention: ancient maritime law as it evolved into interstellar commerce. I'm the master of this ship. You can tell her that I'll start acting that way if she doesn't shut up and start behaving herself. She can raise hell in any tribunal in the Thousand Worlds — except her own, perhaps — and I'll still be upheld as long as I do no permanent physical harm to her."

"By rights, you ought to spank her," Shochona muttered an observation. "She's acting like a spoiled child."

"Spanking never changed a spoiled child," Starbuck pointed out.

"Punishment often does, Peter."

He nodded. "All right, then. Put her on short rations. She won't starve. No sense in wasting valuable food on her until she gets over her huff. Tell her that we're on short rations — which is going to be true if we can't reprovision at Samarra — and that we can't waste food that she refuses to eat."

"She'll holler."

"That she will. But wouldn't you expect a pout from her?"

"I've raised five children."

"I know."

Neither of them realized at the time how close they'd come to getting some of the basic answers they were looking for.

The approach to Khughar continued.

Four light-hours out, Katwin came up to where Starbuck was nervously monitoring the flight on the control deck.

"A lot better, thank you," Katwin said even before Starbuck asked how she felt.

"Katwin, I didn't ask you. But how did you know I was about to?"

She shrugged. "I don't know. But you were going to ask me."

This was a new wrinkle in her latent talent. "Katwin, tell me, do you know what I'm thinking now?"

Katwin laughed a little girl's nervous giggle. "Of course not, Peter!"

"You're sure?"

"I'm sure."

"Okay. Just wanted to check."

She looked over his shoulder at the displays. "Where are we going?"

"Samarra starport on Khughar."

He thought he detected a slight shudder from her. "Isn't that the planet that the bad Kalocs came from?"

"Yes, but it's also the home of the Dyons and others who aren't bad people, Katwin. We're going to visit the good guys." And he added only to himself, *I hope!*

"Oh. Okay, I think they're good, happy people, Peter."

Starbuck knew Katwin was an experienced and reliable cholinergic capable of telepathic reception in linkage with CY's intelligence amplifier. He suspected that she was also an unassisted latent as he was. Therefore, he couldn't simply dismiss her spontaneous statements. He wished he hadn't done so on the approach to Thya.

He looked at her carefully as though he might be able to see some new or enhanced talent in the young face. What had the trauma on Thya really done to her? Had it pushed her to become even more strongly cholinergic and therefore receptive to the elusive and irrational phenomenon of telepathy? He didn't know. There was little that was understood about such talents although there was an empirical, cybermech-assisted technology that made use of them.

Someday, he thought, mentic science would have the phenomenon pinned down a little more firmly than it did. As it was, however, it was fortunate that these paranormal talents were at least recognized as being real after all the centuries which had passed. Starbuck didn't have time to engage in the luxury of para-scientific research. He had to live and operate with what was.

"I hope so, Katwin. We could use contact with some good, happy people right now." Other than the gallant Thyan Irregulars, the people who had interacted with the team on this operation thus far had been far from being the most pleasant folks to be around.

Samarra cleared the *Starace* for a straight-in approach. This thwarted Starbuck's intention to orbit Khughar at least once for scouting and data recording. He questioned Samarra's traffic manager. "I'd planned at least two deceleration orbits through Khughar's gravity well. Any reason why I can't do that? It would save a lot of fuel . . ."

A female voice replied, "I'm terribly sorry, Captain. The Kalocs have requested that we keep our traffic clear of Kirkuk starport's outbound traffic and advise all vessels of potential hazard should their masters decide to enter those corridors on their own responsibility. We advise against deceleration orbits, sir. Although the Kirkuk traffic has dropped to practically nothing in the past few days, the notice to starmen is still in effect and we must honor it."

The data that CY managed to record on the inward trajectory was therefore incomplete as far as a total planetary scan went, but it provided a lot of additional data that SIGNET database in CYMaster didn't have when it was later up-loaded. Scans in several spectra revealed that in Samarra's hemisphere there was a surprising amount of energy consumption. CY analyzed this to mean that there was a reasonably large number of fairly complex social organizations in existence in the Dyon culture. There was a large area of outlying land whose signatures indicated it was absorbing energy from the primary star and therefore was assumed to be agricultural. Nodes of activity appeared to indicate several conurbations of 50,000 people or more. The coordinates of the Samarra starport showed that it was located slightly north of the planetary equator on a penninsula. It was also on the margin of the largest city which was surprisingly spread out, indicating a reasonably efficient transportation system. The climate at the Samarra starport, being equatorial maritime in nature, was therefore anticipated to be reasonably warm.

"It certainly doesn't seem to be a harsh world," Triga remarked as they scanned CY's data. "More like Plethora than OutBack."

"That may be, but we haven't scanned the Kaloc sector of the planet," Starbuck reminded her. "In fact, I don't even know where it is, and neither does CY. . ."

Some six hours later, the *Starace* touched down and settled on her aft drive ring at the Samarra starport. On release from the starport council, CY brought up the portmaster's frequency.

"Samarra Portmaster, this is Peter Starbuck, commander of the starship *Starace*, grounded on your tarmac. Requests."

"Commander Starbuck, welcome to Samarra! What is your pleasure?"

Chapter Thirteen

It turned out that the Samarra portmaster meant exactly and precisely what he said.

And the smidgin of data which CY had presented indicating that the Dyon culture was a hedonistic one was, to put it mildly, an understatement.

But it took some time for the reality of it to sink in.

The Samarra portmaster had full a-v capability, and his image swam into solidification in the comm tank on the panel. He was an unbearably handsome young man with wavy-blond hair. His costume — it would have been rated as a "costume," not "attire," by Starbuck — looked like something right out of an entertainment holo of any of the well-developed planets of the Thousand Worlds. It was sleek and slick and colorful and provocative to women. If he were indeed a fop, a stud, or a gig, he didn't act that way.

O tempora! O mores! Starbuck thought for some unknown and disconnected reason.

"A limo will be at your lower hatch in a moment, sir," the portmaster's image told him easily and happily. "Please excuse the delay. Do you have reservations, or shall I have my cybermech make a random selection of agents to handle your desires? Or do you have an agent of choice?"

There was no sense in trying to hide identities this time. Starbuck would need to contact the local Strakovkhaburo agent, and it was a foregone conclusion that Strakovkhaburo would never maintain the confidence in spite of agreements. So Starbuck played it straight arrow. "I'm Agent

Investigator Peter Starbuck of the Security Investigators' Galactic Network, SIGNET. We're here on business. Can you put me in contact with someone — preferably a person not affiliated with Strakovkhaburo — who can set up protocol with your authorities and arrange for suitable meetings and appointments?''

The portmaster's hands, unseen off-tank, apparently danced nimbly over an equally off-tank keypad. "Consider it done, Agent Starbuck! She will meet you at your lock in ten minutes. How many of you will be debarking?''

Thinking that the portmaster was certainly grilling him quite thoroughly in a very pleasant manner, getting data Starbuck would never volunteer normally, he replied, "There will be only three of us debarking intitially.''

"We're most happy to have you in Samarra! I hope you'll be able to spend a bit of time here beyond what your business requires. We're all anxious to please you in any way . . .''

"Thank you, sir. It may be more than ten minutes before my crew has secured the ship and we're ready to debark.''

"As you wish, sir. No hurry. We're here at your pleasure.''

"Sounds like Plethora.'' Triga was standing to one side out of holo pickup view.

"Plethora cubed.'' David was on the other side.

"I think,'' Starbuck mused, "that only a few of us had better reconnoiter what's going on here. If it looks reasonably safe and if we can reprovision the ship, we might get a day or so dirtside.''

Triga pointed out to him, "Peter, I'd really recommend that we let the Thyan Irregulars hit dirt as soon as possible. They've been cooped up in the ship under crowded conditions, and they're used to the wide open spaces of an uncrowded fringe planet. They could get pretty restless.''

"We'll see,'' Starbuck cautioned. "If this is the sort of super-hospitable 'hedonistic' place I think it might be — and that it probably is, judging from the portmaster's very commercial spiel — we might never find them all again.''

"If you're thinking that it may be like the country lads visiting the big town for the first time, I wouldn't worry about it," David surmised. "They're rather solid men, and most of them have families back on Thya. For the same reason, I doubt that they'll get restless. The only thing that bothers them is not knowing when they'll get home again."

"Be that as it may," Starbuck interrupted his jumpman, "the initial landing party is going to be small. And I won't take the chance of traumatizing Katwin again. This time I'd like to ask Triga and Isky."

"If Samarra is a fleshpot — and it may well be — I'll be delighted!" Triga chirped. "Visiting fleshpots with you is fun, Peter. Besides, I can help keep you out of trouble . . . ."

Isky nodded when Starbuck asked him. And he showed up in the lower lock dressed in a white short-sleeved shirt, knee shorts, knee socks, and turban. At his waist was his *kirpan*. In the *Starace*, Isky didn't observe the teachings of his ancestors' religion, but he felt far more comfortable on strange new worlds dressed in traditional fashion. He claimed the *kirpan* alone made strangers a little more polite in dealing with him. Starbuck was, as usual, unarmed as he preferred to be. But he never objected to any of his people carrying personal weapons under whatever circumstances made them feel comfortable. Besides, Starbuck reminded himself, he'd have been in very difficult straits on Thya if Isky hadn't been willing to unsheathe his *kirpan* and mount a dangerous rescue mission.

Starbuck was surprised that Triga had dressed in a provocative manner to suit the climate — short white sleeveless tunic, shorts, and sandals on her feet. It had been a fast job, but she'd let her hair down as well until it fell in waves and curls to her waist. Her boss didn't know it, but Triga had put the data about Samarra together in her own feminine way and decided that if the Dyons indeed had a hedonistic culture, Triga Rimmon wasn't going to stand idly by and fail to compete for Starbuck's attentions in a situation where there might be many things to attract it. Starbuck, of course, did indeed notice her. One does not live intimately with someone else for more than a century and not notice such things.

When the hatch opened to the outside world and the integral stairs deployed down to the tarmac, the three of them stepped out into the bright sunlight, Starbuck going first.

At the bottom of the stairs, a red carpet had been unrolled on the tarmac. A long, white, luxurious ground vehicle waited.

Also waiting for them was a stunning, nubile young woman whose luxuriant blonde hair shone in the sun. She was more than stunning, more than a stopper, and more than a mere counter on a scale of one to ten. Starbuck, for all his years and experiences, immediately rated her as a crasher; if he'd been driving a ground car or a skimmer, he probably would have lost control and crashed it upon seeing her. She was attired in . . . well, not too little and not too much, Starbuck decided. But what she did wear accented what she wasn't wearing. And it emphasized the very exotic nature of both her appearance and image. That projected image included her voice.

"Hello!" She spoke with a slight accent that reminded Starbuck of the manner in which tellurian Haitians spoke their inflected English. This accent suited her voice, which would have melted a silicon-carbon composite entry nose cap. She stepped up to Starbuck and offered him both hands. "My name is Almara. I understand that you require an agent. I'm a very good one."

Starbuck took both of her hands in his. "I'm sure you are," he replied urbanely. "I'm Peter Starbuck."

"Of course. You must be."

"And this is Triga Rimmon . . . and Iskander Sand-rathama."

"I'm sure we can arrange for whatever any of you desire . . ."

"We're not here to play," Triga interrupted bluntly.

"We have some rather urgent business," Starbuck cut her off, wanting to signal Triga to shut up.

"Of course," Almara said in accommodating tones. "I'll do my best to assist you. Will your ship be needing refueling and reprovisioning?"

"That needs to be looked into, of course."

"We have the best," Almara stated simply. "Do you wish to place the orders for that?"

"No, please have the various chandlers contact my shipmaster, Shochona, on the portcomm frequency."

Almara's fingers were playing swiftly over a little sender on her left wrist. "Consider it done. Now, how may I help you with your business matters?"

Starbuck didn't mind talking on the open ramp. He was enjoying the prickly heat of the sunshine, a rare experience for one who's shipbound most of the time. "We need information."

"Of course. About what?"

"The Kalocs."

He detected a momentary change in Almara's smiling, pleasant, eager, and willing expression. "Here in Samarra we aren't known for our outstanding databases," she explained. "But since we're dedicated to the welfare and enjoyment of our fellow human beings, I'll certainly be happy to arrange your perusal of our databases concerning the Kalocs."

"I'd also like to talk to your various governmental authorities about the status of relations between your people and the Kalocs."

Almara smiled sweetly and cocked her lovely head. "This is your first visit to Samarra, isn't it, Commander Starbuck?" When he nodded, she went on, "We have excellent relations with everyone. We deal with the Kalocs exactly as we deal with our other clients. We are at their pleasure." But she didn't say it with any relish in her voice.

"I'd like to speak with your ministers of external affairs concerning precisely what the Kalocs are now doing."

She shook her blonde head and told him, "We have no government as you probably know it. Decades ago, our forefathers got rid of it because it wasn't needed. All useful government functions are performed by firms providing the services under contract to those who want them.'' She turned and indicated the waiting limo. ''We can talk more about this while we're en route to your accommodations. I'll arrange for complete access to the databases from your hotel.'' She started to turn, then suddenly stopped and turned back. ''Oh, I meant to ask you — and I hope you don't think I'm being rude — in what manner will you tender payment for services in Samarra?''

Starbuck had been wondering when the touch would come. Samarra thus far resembled many other recreational watering holes in the Thousand Worlds and appeared to operate on the same basis: cash at the stairs or via approved credit. Preferably the former. ''We have agreements with all the other agencies, Almara. Our charges will be handled by funds transfers by prior agreement through Strakovkhaburo. I understand they have a local agent, and he'll take care of things.''

''Excellent!''

The ground limo was a silent, fast, plush, opulent, luxurious, furry womb on wheels with all amenities including a private compartment complete with bidet and other sanitary and hygienic facilities. It smelled good, it felt good, and it looked good. Had the contingent from the *Starace* wanted a bath, it probably was available hidden away somewhere in this pleasure wagon, Starbuck decided. Or food. Or any number of mood-altering substances. Or even neuro entertainment. He noticed fixtures and facilities for all of these things discreetly positioned throughout the passenger compartment.

Triga and Isky remained silent during the ride. Both were carefully observing what was going on outside. Almara chatted endlessly as the vehicle sped through wide streets that were heavy with other traffic but strangely empty of people. ''I'll do my best to satisfy your desire for data on the Kalocs. I'm really not familiar with the Kalocs or our relationships with them here in Samarra. I'd prefer that you got the data straight from the database. Or I can arrange for you to meet with some of the top financial and commercial people who have dealt mostly with on-planet business.''

"That's very kind of you, Almara," Starbuck told her and asked the obvious question, ''but, excuse me for asking, what is your position in all this? You've been with us since we left the ship. You've been very polite, extremely solicitous, and eagerly helpful. Sorry if I'm unfamiliar with your ways, but, in short, what's in this for you?''

"Oh, I'm just an agent."

"I see. Will you bill us for services?"

"Oh, no! I've spent six years in very intensive preparation and testing for my work. I'm a professional. I'll receive a percentage from whomever I arrange for you to deal with. You'll never have to worry about paying me at all. I'm a trained and educated agent . . . not a mere mack or a madamvisor!''

"I may not like this place after all," Triga muttered.

"But I think I will," Isky added.

The limo ride and the conversation that occurred during that time was probably far more valuable to Starbuck than the hours he later spent digging into the Dyon database from what must have been the royal, super-VIP suite of rooms in which they found themselves ensconced by Almara who saw to it that they were suitably installed and then disappeared to make further arrangements. "Just punch up code ALMARA AGENCY on any comm if you need my services in my absence."

Sybaritic was a poor term in which to describe their quarters.

"Ecbatana sultan's palace," was the way Isky described them. "Haven't seen anything like it since my father gave me his credit card and pushed me through the door of our friendly neighborhood pay-as-you-go purdah . . . except we didn't call it that. What we really mean is always lost in translation.''

"New Vegas chippy shack, right down to the furry walls," was the descriptive term Triga used. But the sheer elegance of the rooms caused Triga to change her mind about whether she'd like Samarra or not. She sat down next to the plush chair where Starbuck was starting to query the database. She was shaking her head and looking stunned. "Peter, I'm overwhelmed! Every possible comfort! Every conceivable luxury! I'm going to take a real bath in lots of water with lots of *eau de toilette* so I smell nice." She paused and then wheedled, "Peter, can we stay a day or so after you find out what you need to know about the Kalocs?"

"You always stink pretty, Triga," Starbuck muttered absentmindedly. "When work's over, then we can play."

"All work and no play makes Starbuck . . ." Triga began.

"All play and no work means no pay," Starbuck reminded her. "And no way to pay for this sojourn in a Fringe World version of New Vegas . . ."

Triga gave a little snort. "Brinker would never question the expense. He never has."

"But unless we can crack this case, I'll have a bit of trouble explaining why I acted against the Canons by taking a hostage, bringing ten irregular soldiers aboard the ship, and generally playing loose and free with valuta as well as the Canons." He patted her gently on the thigh. "Now scat! Go take that bath."

"Are you telling me that I ship-stink?"

"You said it, not me."

"Brute-beast!"

"Probably. You may find out more about that later." Starbuck was glad to have Triga around. She knew how to play. In fact, she often carried it to extremes when she wasn't busy or had gotten bored. Shochona had arrested at an older age with a rather more dour and humorless outlook on life and the universe. Katwin, on the other hand, looked upon things with the intense seriousness of an introverted child . . . which she was. Although the male

members of his team were not only very close friends —
family, really — and what might be called "good drinking
buddies," Isky tended to be precipitous and volcanic while
David was a Gaelic mystic and humorist. Triga was therefore the closest to being a "wife" to Starbuck among the
crew, although neither of them had ever thought about
officially marrying the other. As longers who'd already
parented families of their own, that biological thirst had
been slaked. And in their individual universes of abundance, there was no need for either to possess the other.
This hadn't kept Triga from showing just the twinges of
possessiveness in the way she'd dressed — or undressed —
before stepping on the tarmac at Samarra. If Starbuck were
offered a good time on Samarra, Triga just wanted to share
it with him.

Almara had been right. There wasn't much in the Dyon
database. No demographics. No cultural descriptions or
analyses. No history.

He did finally stumble onto field after field of credit
data on individual Kalocs. But the "services rendered"
were coded, and he couldn't break the code.

This led in turn to other fields listing coded personal
data.

Most of this was encrypted.

He tried running a few simple code busters, but they
wouldn't crack it.

Shochona answered when he called the ship on his
transceiver. "Everything all right, Peter?"

"Thus far. How's the provisioning going?"

"Looks like it will be outstanding! These people have
everything I need and they're eager to provide it. But,
Peter, the bill may be staggering! These Fringe Worlds are
known for charging all the traffic will bear, and this outfit
must have written the book!"

"Sign the chits, Shochona."

"I will."

"What have they accomplished thus far?"

"Life support systems regeneration mostly. No refueling or reprovisioning of victuals yet."

"Good. Now patch me in to CY."

"Done. When can we come dirtside?"

"When I find out a little more about this place. It sounds too good to be true. I need to find out what the kicker is."

"Very well." There was disappointment in Shochona's voice. Starbuck decided that he'd have to let the rest of them come out if no derogs showed up in the data soon. "Here's CY."

"Hello, Peter. Well, was my data correct?"

"So far, but I've got more for you. Here's a patch from their main database. I want you to upload their files and see what you can do to get through the encryption I've discovered in some of their database."

"Let her rip."

Starbuck placed his transceiver on the transfer pad of the cybercenter he'd been using to work the Dyon database.

About five seconds later, CY reported, "Got it, boss. Wow! What an old operating system! No, wait. By the great gray greasy glitches of Gigo, it's a unique one! I'll have to scope it out before I can bust those database fields. I'll need most of my capacity to tackle it. Give me a few minutes, please. Call me back. In the meantime, have fun!"

Starbuck looked around. He rarely liked to waste time. And while his cybermech was chewing on data, he decided he might as well make the best of this situation.

Chapter Fourteen

The message signal of the commcenter flashed. Was CY calling back so soon? Who else would be trying to reach him here? He keyed the audio-only response. "Yes?"

The image of a puffy-faced man swam into form in the holo tank. "Good day to you." The voice was heavily accented. "I am Agent Kirill Ivanovich Mironenko of Strakovkhaburo. I would please like to speak with Agent Peter Steele Starbuck of SIGNET."

Starbuck keyed the video switch. "I am Peter Starbuck. Good day, Gospodin Mironenko. What can I do for you?"

"You can tell me, Mister Starbuck, please, why you and your SIGNET agent Investigator Team are here on Khughar."

"We're here to obtain information on a matter involving the Kalocs of Thoth, Gospodin," Starbuck told him in a simple and straightforward manner.

"And, please, what information do you look for?"

"Anything we can learn about what the Kalocs have been doing for the past five years," Starbuck replied easily, being careful not to say too much to the agent of a fiercely competitive business rival. "They've filed no reports with the interstellar network, and we're involved in a matter concerning these people."

"And what would that matter be, please?"

"Gospodin Mironenko, I'm sure you realize that your question is quite out of order. The various agreements between SIGNET, Strakovkhaburo, and Justar specifically allow an agency to preserve the confidence of clients by withholding any information the agency deems sensitive.''

"Is nonsense! I know why you are here. You have only confirmed this by means of your reluctance to reveal information to me.''

"Then why do you ask, Gospodin?''

"To confirm our fears.''

"Does Strakovkhaburo represent the Kalocs or Kodo Sadon, the Black Path of Thoth?''

"I do not intend to answer questions from you, Mister Starbuck. But the fact that you know about Kodo Sadon tells me that you also know a great deal about the Kalocs.''

Starbuck sighed. He always detested playing the sort of games that Strakovkhaburo people loved to become engaged in. Strakovkhaburo was never very cooperative. They always acted as though someone were out to get them. Paranoids, some Justar people maintained. But Starbuck had dealt with Russians for centuries ever since their great Soviet empire collapsed, an occurrence which hadn't ameliorated their basic Russian distrust of everyone else.

"I know that the Kalocs under Kodo Sadon have invaded the planet Thya in the Garyon system. One of our clients on Thya called upon us for assistance. Thya is currently being occupied by Kaloc soldiers. We're here on Khughar to learn why the Kalocs invaded Thya rather than move against the Dyons on their own world.'' Starbuck didn't mention the loss of the SIGNET AI Team. Whereas Mironenko undoubtedly knew of the Kaloc invasion of Thya, the loss of the SIGNET team might not have leaked out of SIGNET yet. And it wasn't up to Starbuck to play media reporter and inform Strakovkhaburo.

"Invasion? Hah! You are perhaps making joke with me? Invasion is not possible! You know is not possible! Such a thing has not been ever done before.'' Mironenko apparently didn't know what the Kalocs were doing after all. And that in itself told Starbuck a great deal, mainly that Strakovkhaburo wasn't involved in the Kaloc invasions. Or perhaps the Strakovkhaburo executives hadn't told a mere field agent. But it also meant that Mironenko would be even more suspicious than normal. "No, Mister Starbuck, you and your team, including a platoon of armed astrines, are here at Samarra to threaten Strakovkhaburo's clients and force them to do business with SIGNET! If my clients do not cooperate, you will send in Star Guard fleet."

"Gospodin Mironenko, I've told you truthfully why we're here. Our agreements with Strakovkhaburo don't allow us to threaten or coerce your clients and they compel me to be truthful with you. We operate within the Canons. I'm sorry you don't believe me. I'll do my best not to bother you while we're here. In the meantime, I intend to exercise my rights under agreement to continue to seek the information I need to fulfill SIGNET's obligations to its clients." Starbuck came on quite firmly and strongly. There didn't seem to be anything else he could do. "If there's nothing further you wish to discuss, good day, sir!" He reached out to activate the logout.

"Not so fast, Mister Starbuck!" Mironenko suddenly snapped.

Starbuck rested his hand on the cutoff. "I will be very fast unless you begin behaving in a civil manner, Gospodin Mironenko. I will also be very fast to file a complaint through channels concerning your unseemly behavior toward me. Then Mister Brinker can bring this matter directly to the attention of your Gospodin Golovani."

"Your Mister Brinker will find counter-charges against you for interfering with my agency here on Khughar . . ."

Starbuck shrugged. "Then let's pass the matter upward through our respective organizations. It's obvious that you don't wish to discuss anything with me but your unfounded suspicions. Or did you have something else you wished to talk about, Gospodin?"

"You will not find my Strakovkhaburo clients very cooperative."

"Perhaps not. But I don't intend to talk with them unless they call me."

"You have already contacted some of them through an agent."

This was bound to have happened, Starbuck thought. Almara obviously didn't know or understand the turgid relationship between the two companies although he'd told her not to bother the Strakovkhaburo agent. Starbuck had said nothing about Strakovkhaburo clients. "Probably," Starbuck replied suavely. "I'm looking for information about the Kalocs. I asked my Dyon agent to put me in touch with anyone here who might be able to tell me something about these strange people. If they call me and are willing to talk, we'll talk. If they won't, there isn't anything that I can or will do about it."

"You will not remove your company of astrines from your ship," Mironenko ordered.

"They're not astrines. They're passengers from Thya. And I'm within my rights to permit anyone aboard my ship to go aground; it's up to them to obey the laws of the port. And you can't give me orders, Gospodin Mironenko."

The Strakovkhaburo agent's expression grew hard. "You are not being cooperative, Mister Starbuck. You and your people will have a difficult time in Samarra. I can assure you. Goodbye, Mister Starbuck."

"Doh sveedahnya," Starbuck said to a blank screen. The Strakovkhaburo agent had beat him to the logoff. Starbuck chuckled. Let him have that small victory, he thought.

Starbuck logged off and sat back in the form-fitting chair. In another room, he could hear water running and the joyful humming and singing of Triga in the bath she so dearly craved. The door announce sounded and reported that Almara had returned. He commanded the door to open and let her in.

She'd changed her clothes. She was more stunning and provocative than ever. Furthermore, she exuded a lovely fragrance that Starbuck at once recognized as containing a very high concentration of female human pheremones. There was no question in his mind concerning what she wanted and what she offered. Nor did her attire do much to hide it.

He got control of his instincts. Dammit, Almara should have known better than to appear in such a fashion. In the first place, Triga wouldn't like it at all. Almara was knowingly or otherwise tampering with the basic First Canon not only as far as Starbuck was concerned but also in Triga's case. But he gave Almara the benefit of the doubt. Maybe she didn't know. Perhaps she was only acting within her cultural milieu. Certainly, one of the basic problems any stranger faced was to determine the prime factor of Haley's Law: If one is to do unto another as the other wishes done, one is faced with the problem of learning enough about the other person to know what the other's desires are.

Then he brought himself up short. *Starbuck, you stud!* He told himself. *What kind of an ego trip are you on? Almara saw two men and one woman. She obviously believed Isky or I might want companionship and didn't know which. And quite obviously if she gets a commission, she's likely to take the job herself. Quit thinking she's trying to trigger your deepest desires, you dirty old man!* He chuckled to himself. He was, he told himself, probably the oldest and dirtiest old man on Samarra at the moment . . .

However, Almara certainly had triggered his deepest desires, and there was no denying that.

Almara also triggered Isky. He came bounding out of another room like a stag in rut. "Hello, there! I thought I heard someone come in." Actually, no one had said a word since Almara entered. Her fragrance was obviously pervasive.

She smiled at Isky. Starbuck thought the man was going to snort and paw the carpet, then jump and swing from the dangling crystal chandelier.

But Almara came up to Starbuck and told him, "You'll be getting a few calls very soon from some people who may be able to give you some information about the Kalocs."

"Thank you," Starbuck replied.

"Did you get relevant information from our database?"

He nodded. "I think so. I'm waiting for CY to review it."

"That's good. What is your pleasure in the meantime?" She obviously meant it, and Starbuck felt his ego inflating again. She was going to let the two men take their choice.

The sound of running water in the bath stopped. Triga would be coming out soon.

Isky took advantage of the situation. He simply took Almara smoothly by the arm and led her away, chatting pleasant inanities and small talk in a low voice. Starbuck knew that his transmitterman was a very suave and experienced person brought up in a culture where the relationships between men and women had presaged the introduction of chivalry into the ancient European culture and had, in fact, been the source of the ideas of chivalry. Isky always treated women as special people.

And, obviously, both of them were behaving well within Haley's Law, the First and most important of the Canons.

Starbuck knew Isky had been working hard. He deserved a break. Isky and Almara would probably be good for each other. Very good. They might well be a matched pair.

He began to appreciate that Samarra and its Dyon inhabitants were perhaps a bit more than the slick recreational operations typical of New Vegas, the prototype and sinecure of most of the fleshpots of the Thousand Worlds. But he couldn't put his finger on what that subtle difference was. The data was, of course, all around him, but it had been so many years since he'd encountered it and in such different cultural and temporal circumstances that recognition of its true nature was buried extremely deep in his memories.

That, of course, was one of the problems with being a longer. Old memories of different times and different places tended to be temporarily forgotten and capable of being brought up only by nostalgia sessions with an intelligence amplifier. As Starbuck continued to live, he found it ever more difficult to recall some details of his youth centuries before. On the other hand, a few longers who'd possessed eidetic memories found the going equally difficult from the opposite viewpoint; they were continually inundated with memory signals and some of them had found it impossible to discriminate between present reality and their memories, even after they'd dumped as much of their memories as possible into an int-amp.

Triga appeared wearing only a very fluffy rub towel. She bounced up to Starbuck, wrapped him in the towel with her, and said huskily in his ear, "Do I smell as good as that so-called 'agent'?"

"Jealousy ill becomes you. What have you got that she hasn't got?"

"You. And you didn't answer my question, sir . . ."

He stroked her where he knew she liked to be stroked and was rewarded with her shiver. "What does that tell you?"

"That if you will, I will ."

The comm center signaled an incoming message.

It was a few seconds before Triga whispered, "Forget it."

"Can't."

"Oh, SIGNET, what we put up with for you . . ."

He reached out and activated audio. "Yes?"

"Commander Peter Starbuck, please. This is Lance Woodshire of the United Bank of Samarra calling on request of Agent Almara."

"Damn!" Triga muttered and untangled herself before Starbuck had a chance to let her slide onto the floor.

Starbuck smoothed the hair out of his face and keyed the video. "I'm Peter Starbuck," he spoke up as the banker's image built up in the tank.

"Good afternoon, sir. What is your pleasure?" The man was another example of the almost painful beauty of the Dyon people, an extremely handsome man with regular, well-formed masculine features, sparkling eyes, regular teeth, and dark, wavy hair kept neatly over his close-set ears.

Triga whispered in his ear, "Wow! I'd like to give you a reason to be jealous of him, Peter . . ."

Starbuck refrained from telling the handsome banker that the call had just interrupted Starbuck's pleasure. And he also refrained from making a comment in reply to Triga who wrapped the towel around her and stood eagerly looking over Starbuck's shoulder. Without comment, Starbuck nodded his head in greeting and replied, "Good afternoon. I'm an Agent Investigator for SIGNET. We don't have a field agent on Khughar . . ."

"But I'm quite well aware of SIGNET," Woodshire replied, "although we interface exlusively with Strakovkhaburo. What may I do for you?"

"Allow me to ask you some questions about the Kalocs."

"You may ask me all you want. But you may not get answers if they involve privileged information of a client."

"I well understand that, Mister Woodshire. But I'm investigating a problem with one of my clients, and the Kalocs are involved. Specifically Kodo Sadon. Are you aware of him?"

The banker simply nodded.

"I can find very little information about the Kalocs in the interstellar databases," Starbuck continued to explain. "They haven't filed any data for more than five years. I'd like to ask you a few general questions about them and their activities here on Khughar. To set your mind at ease, my investigation has nothing to do with money or credit. It's on quite different matters. If I can get a better feeling for the Kalocs and their culture, I may be able to resolve the conflict to the satisfaction of all and completely within the Canons."

"That's your primary mission as an AI Team, isn't it — the resolution of conflicts brought about by different interpretations of the Canons?"

Starbuck nodded. "Or by abrogation of the Canons by a party."

"Yes. Of course. What do you wish to know?"

"Agent Almara mentioned that you Dyons had cut off the Kalocs' credit. Any reason for that?"

The banker shrugged. "Yes, a very straightforward and commonplace reason; they were unable to pay their bills."

"I understand from the interstellar database that Khughar is relatively short of resources."

Woodshire shook his head and smiled. "Not every resource, Commander Starbuck. We Dyons discovered a general paucity of natural resources on Khughar shortly after our ancestors migrated here. We made the best of what we had and parsimoniously marshaled our resources. We concentrated on the technical strengths we brought with us, primarily in the fields of biotechnology. We Dyons and the Kalocs parted several generations ago over disagreements on a number of issues."

"What sort of disagreements, Mister Woodshire?"

"Oh, rather like a family disagreement. They wanted to go their way, and we Dyons didn't agree. So we continued to develop our technology along different lines than the Kalocs."

"Different in what way?"

"Well, first of all, we developed food resources; now we're capable of feeding the Kalocs as well as the Lanigers and Zhedarons. But this sort of school history lesson must be boring to you. Or is it the sort of data you're looking for?"

"It's precisely the sort of background data I don't have, and it isn't in the interstellar database, either." Starbuck paused for a moment, then asked, "Is there any reason why it isn't widely known?"

Woodshire cleared his throat, took a handkerchief from his sleeve, and wiped his cheeks. With a great deal of hesitation, he remarked, "Well, yes . . . more or less. We're rather reluctant to discuss it . . ."

"I don't wish to pry, but the resolution of the situation I'm faced with on Thya may hinge on what I can learn from people like you," Starbuck pointed out, trying to both put the man at ease while at the same time keep the conversation flowing as easily as it had started. It was obvious that Woodshire was conditioned as a Dyon to acquiescing to the desires of others, and Starbuck was counting on that trait to keep the man talking. "It certainly can't be as embarrassing as that."

"We tend to think so, Mister Starbuck. The Kalocs are rather the black sheep, if you know what that old simile means."

"I see, and I know what it means. It's something you Dyons would rather keep out of the databases for the same reason that a family tends to remain quiet about a wayward relative."

"Not precisely." Woodshire paused again, apparently searching for a way to say what he needed to say in a way that would satisfy Starbuck's desire for information. "I'm sure you've noticed the general appearances and traits of the Dyons you've encountered since landing."

"Yes, and I'm impressed. You're a beautiful and gracious people."

"That's not an accident, Mister Starbuck."

"Oh?"

"How shall I put it. . . ?"

"Mister Woodshire," Starbuck tried to reassure him, "I've been on hundreds of worlds and in far more cultures . . . and I'm a longer, so I've seen many things. Whatever you say won't embarrass me. And it's unlikely to be something new and different to me."

"Very well. Once we developed our biotechnology to provide us with adequate food, excellent health, and suitable shelter — the quarters you're in, for example, were grown like you might grow a tree — we concentrated on developing biotechnology to support something we could indeed use as a resource . . ."

"And that is . . . ?"

"Ourselves. After all, Mister Starbuck, the First Canon states that you must do unto others as they would have you do unto them. People want pleasure. I'm sure you've seen that in many places throughout the Thousand Worlds."

Starbuck nodded. "But from what I can see, this is no New Vegas . . ."

Woodshire smiled. "With our scarcity of other resources, we couldn't begin to compete with New Vegas and its clone cultures, Mister Starbuck. We had to develop some industry unique to our resources, technology, and capabilities. And we did. On the other hand, the Kalocs didn't. They attempted to develop their biotechnology in a way that would allow them to master other human beings, including some of their own people, by redesigning themselves rather than engineering their surroundings, the approach we Dyons took. I'm rather afraid they weren't as successful in their approach as we Dyons were in ours."

"I've noticed that there's an enormous difference between Dyons and Kalocs."

"Of course. We were successful, as you can see. They weren't. Yet they continued to need us. We matured, but they're basically still an adolescent culture full of violence and confused desires. We could and can satisfy some of their desires as we can those of anyone else. That's our business. But they couldn't pay for what they wanted from us. And, frankly, we really didn't want to continue giving them the services they demanded. We get very few Kaloc visitors here in Samarra now."

"I mentioned that the Kalocs had mounted a major invasion of the planet Thya in the Garyon system," Starbuck said. "The big question in my mind is simply this: Why did the Kalocs go to the effort and expense to mount the first interstellar military invasion when they could have invaded you instead right here on the same planet?"

The debonaire banker smiled. "Mister Starbuck, with your experience and background, I'm rather surprised you didn't spot it immediately. The Kalocs don't want to take us over by conquest. They simply want our services. We no longer wanted to provide them. What are our services? We've applied both modern marketing and technology to what was once called 'the world's oldest profession'. To use an analogy, when you've got the best service station in the universe next door and you want to buy its services, you don't rob its till to pay for its services or resort to rape which ruins the whole show. In short, you don't mess up a good thing. And if you had the best little whorehouse in the universe on the same planet with you and you wanted to use it occasionally, you'd leave it alone, wouldn't you?''

Chapter Fifteen

"I thought so!" was Triga's immediate comment.

Starbuck simply turned to her and whispered, "Voice of experience, Triga?"

"Beast-monster!" She didn't whisper it.

"That's a lovely young lady with you," Woodshire remarked. "I don't believe I've seen her before . . ."

"My biotechnician, Triga Rimmon," Starbuck introduced her.

"Oh, my! You could certainly pass for a Dyon, Madam Rimmon!"

Triga glared at him. "*Miz* Rimmon, sir!"

Woodshire inclined his head. "No offense. I hope that we can serve your pleasure as well."

"I have mine, thank you," Triga told him flatly.

Starbuck was both elated and chagrined. He'd found a key element in the puzzle. But he was mentally kicking himself for failing to see it. True, it had been a few centuries, and bordellos hardly existed in a universe of abundance operating under the Canons. But the existence of Samarra and the Dyons on Khughar made perfect sense, especially on a frontier. It was a long way to the various Sodom-and-Gomorrah worlds in the more-developed sectors of the Thousand Worlds.

And, unlike the New Vegas worlds that offered *everything*, the Dyons had specialized in a region of scarcity. The worlds around them within easy travel distance were populated by pioneers and the immediate descendants of pioneers; such people wanted it straight, unlike the more sophisticated and jaded inhabitants of developed worlds.

But judging from his own personal contact with the Kalocs in the persons of Sadon and Ferona, these neighbors of the Dyons had proclivities that were somewhat outside the norm. The reasons why the Kalocs behaved as they did were still not clear to Starbuck, but he felt he was on the right track at last.

Starbuck smiled at Woodshire. "A lot of things fall into place now. Thank you. But, tell me, why don't you Dyons promote your services more widely? There's no indication of the nature of your major industry in any of the databases."

Woodshire shrugged and smiled back. "In your own experience, Commander Starbuck, do you know of any places like ours that advertise?"

Of course not! Starbuck reminded himself. It was never necessary to do so. Only the raunch houses had ever advertised. On the other hand, one could always find the best places by discreet inquiry. Word of mouth advertising was always the best in this industry. And in many other industries, too.

He needed to have yet another piece in the puzzle, however, and he didn't know whether or not the handsome banker would give it to him . . . or could. "Mister Woodshire, I find it difficult to understand how the Kalocs could afford to mount an interstellar military invasion and yet be in a financial situation where you'd cut off their credit here in Samarra."

"I don't understand why the Kalocs began an operation on Thya, either, and this is the first I've heard about it. But in our case, Commander Starbuck, there were two factors involved," Woodshire replied casually but guardedly. "The Kalocs essentially ran out of things of value to us with which to trade for our services. And, secondly but more importantly, we operate fully within the Canons and the Kalocs began to behave in such a way that they were violating the First Canon."

"Uh . . . I find that hard to believe, Woodshire, especially in view of your Dyonian tradition of servicing pleasure.''

Woodshire hesitated. ''I'm no gengineer and only basically acquainted with the elements of genetic engineering. You'll have to ask a specialist if you want to get the full details.''

''What can you tell me about it?'' Starbuck pressed him. He had a mine of information on the line, and he didn't want to turn it loose until he'd wrung as much out of the man as possible.

''Realize, please, that I'm only a financial manager and not fully qualified in biotechnology,'' was Woodshire's hesitant reply. ''We're taught history as we grow up, but I'm sure we never get the full story. In the first place, it isn't that important because, as neighbors, the Kalocs tend to leave us alone. As I mentioned, they don't want to mess up a good thing when they'd rather use it instead. At any rate, somewhere at some time, their intense genetic selection and engineering program got into some sort of trouble and they didn't catch the error or perhaps elected to continue and allow the recessive traits to perpetuate for various reasons. We're quite careful in that regard and quite rigorously attempt to randomize and hybridize our gene pool to eliminate the sort of bothersome recessive characteristics that apparently showed up in the Kaloc gene pool. Perhaps the problem crept in before they went their own separate way.''

''Did they separate from you voluntarily, or were they kicked out?''

''I don't know, and it doesn't make much difference,'' Woodshire told him with a shrug of his broad, muscled shoulders. ''The reasons are hidden in the mists of time, and we don't pay much attention to them these days. It's the Kalocs' problem. And when they come up with some valuta for the services they want from us and grow out of their juvenile sadistic ways — or breed them out of their strain — they'll be as welcome as anyone else here in

Samarra. I really can't tell you much more than that, Commander Starbuck.''

"I'm interested in learning a bit more about the Kalocs themselves," Starbuck persisted. "For example, why did they cease filing database reports five years ago?"

"I really don't know, sir. And I doubt that anyone else in Samarra does, either. It's really none of our business. As long as they follow the Canons and don't impact our lifestyle, we'd be acting outside the Canons if we interfered."

"Well, the Kalocs have reportedly killed other human beings on Thya," Starbuck told him, thinking of the Zing Team. "With their invasion of Thya, they may be violating the Fourth and Fifth Canons at least."

"Sir, I'm not a metalawyer, either. As long as the Kalocs don't interfere with us, I'm not at all certain that the Canons require us to be our brothers' keepers."

There it was again, one of the basic paradoxes of metalaw, Starbuck realized. The Fourth Canon was involved, but it was often interpreted in widely different ways.

"I don't know of any Dyon today who specializes in Kaloc social data," Woodshire went on. "It's not that we don't care, mind you. We just don't like to interfere in the affairs of others. That would be quite inappropriate in view of Samarra's major industry."

Starbuck realized he'd just scraped the bottom of this barrel. Woodshire had been wrung dry for his purposes. The banker was growing increasingly reluctant or unable to provide additional information. Any further interrogation would be a waste of time and might even verge on impropriety under the Canons. He might need Woodshire for other purposes later. So he thanked the banker profusely and moved to terminate the conversation.

But Lance Woodshire was apparently quite taken with Triga because he offered in a most gracious manner, "Triga Rimmon, if I may be of any service to you whatsoever while you're here, I'd be happy to oblige, even if you want just a bit of diversion and variance. After all, here in Samarra, our business is your pleasure . . . ''

Triga thanked him in the sweetest tones she was capable of uttering under the circumstances, this being the first time in many years that she'd been openly propositioned. But, once the communication was concluded and the tank was blank, she exploded, "I never thought I'd encounter the old line: 'It's a business doing pleasure with you!' Imagine the effrontery of that man!"

"Triga, my dear, he was only acting according to the ways of his culture," Starbuck reminded her.

"Considering this culture, I think I'd better go rescue Isky."

He grabbed her arm and pulled her down on his lap. "Not on your life! What makes you think he needs to be rescued? I'll bet Almara probably needs rescuing from Isky."

"Don't you dare try to 'rescue' her!"

Starbuck kept on teasing her. "But she may need it, Triga. After all, Isky probably has even more experience than you. I'm sure he's comporting himself in a manner that will uphold the honor of the team. On the other hand, all this highly professional competition seems to have made you even more prudish."

"Shochona's the only certified prude on the team!"

"Prove it."

She did.

Starbuck had to admit that she even smelled good while doing so. There was certainly something to be said for the sybaritic facilities of Samarra.

"That tickles," she finally managed to say.

"What tickles?"

"That." She showed him. "Besides, you knew. You and your damned latent telepathic talent, Peter Starbuck."

"As I said before, jealousy ill becomes you."

"And after all I've just done for you."

"The question arises — who did what to whom?"

"I agree. It's much too good for the peasants . . ."

"Triga, don't you think we should let the team's peasants in on this?"

"How much trouble do you want?"

"None, and I don't think there will be any. Not in this culture. I think the Dyons would even take excellent care of David if he decided to go on one of his endless binges."

"But is it within our prerogative to expose those poor Thyan Irregulars to this fleshpot?"

Starbuck laughed. "I think it would certainly give them something to fight for! And talk about in the firehouse when they got back. After all, that's apparently what the Kalocs are fighting for. Maybe if they discover they're both fighting for the same thing, they might get together and work out a cooperative way to get it."

"You're devious."

"Maybe I am, and maybe I'm not."

"But I like you when you're devious."

"That's apparent."

"But not when you're a beast-monster as you are now!"

"I haven't detected any difference in your response to me . . ."

"Try this, then!" She bit him.

"Ow! Well, I'm glad you got it out of your system so you don't get violent when I tell you what I want to do. I've figured it out in the last few minutes . . ."

"Men! Do your minds always wander?"

"Not always. Depends on the woman. Triga, I'm serious. While the ship is being reprovisioned, the team and the Thyan Irregulars should enjoy some of this outstanding shore leave."

"I agree."

"You may not agree with my next suggestion. I want to bring Onuva Ferona dirtside, too. Alone. With me."

"*What?*"

Peter Starbuck sat up. "Look, Triga, Ferona is a key link in this operation. Here's what I want to do . . ."

He spent more than fifteen minutes going over what he had in mind, then another thirty minutes justifying it and trying to explain to Triga that she would have to stand by and watch.

"I don't like it," she told him.

"I rather thought you wouldn't, which is why I wanted to explain it in detail to you in private."

"But . . ."

"Do you believe it would affect our relationship?"

"No, we've been together too long. Besides, I don't think I could learn to live and work with a normal superman . . ."

"Then what's your objection? You've obviously got some objection or you wouldn't hesitate."

Triga sat up and clasped her arms around her knees. Looking straight ahead rather than at him, she didn't say anything for a moment. Then she replied in a low voice, "Because I don't trust Onuva Ferona." She looked quickly at Starbuck and added, "And, Peter, because I don't know what she'll do to you."

"I'm a big boy, Triga."

"Yes, you are. But she could become vicious." She paused and finally admitted, "And, yes, because in spite of the fact that we live in a universe of abundance and even though jealousy ill becomes me, a woman would be a damned fool if she wasn't just a little bit jealous of letting her favorite superman spend even a moment of valuable time in a place like this with a woman like that."

"That's what I wanted to hear you say. Any other objections?"

"No. Do it. Then we might get some time to finish that R-and-R on Plethora. Now I've got to go winkie. Then let's get something to eat. I'm starved."

He got up, pulled on shorts and light tunic, and went to the comm terminal to order some food while Triga visited the bath. As he was studying the displayed menu and making selections for both of them, he was interrupted by a low moan. Turning in the chair, he saw Isky stagger into the room. He rose to his feet immediately. "What's the matter, Isky, are you hurt?" he asked with concern.

Isky waved him off and slumped into a chair. "I'll never be the same again."

Starbuck went over to him. The man looked unharmed, but he didn't sound that way. "Triga!" he called.

Isky waved him off. "No, Peter, there's nothing wrong with me except a rather shattered male ego."

"Huh?"

"Almara. I have never known a woman like Almara! I don't believe what that woman can do! Even the madam didn't know the things Almara taught me. Peter, I'm whupped."

"'How's Almara? I don't want to lose our agent," Starbuck asked with real concern in his voice. He was well aware of Isky's legendary prowess with the ladies.

"Oh, she's all right. You bet she's all right! Full of sass and ready to go . . . again and again and again! Peter, I never thought I'd have to admit this to anyone. But for the first time in my life, a woman has managed to take it all out of me and want more!"

Starbuck grinned and pushed hard on Isky's shoulder, causing the wiry little man to topple off the chair onto the adjoining couch. He enjoyed a laugh at his transmitterman's expense, but it served only to let Isky know that Peter Starbuck, a man with equally legendary prowess, really didn't take it seriously. "Good! Since you've spent your energies, you're just the one to stand deck watch on the *Starace* while everyone else has their shot at shore leave!"

Isky opened his eyes upon hearing that, shook his head as if to clear it, then sat bolt upright. "Now, let's not be hasty, Peter! I'm all right. Really I am. You wouldn't deny me a rematch, would you?"

"I guess CY can look after things as well as you can," Starbuck decided. "Actually, I'd probably worry about the ship if you were deck officer under these conditions. I'd be concerned that your mind might be elsewhere than minding the store. Either that or I'd suspect — probably with some justification — that you'd manage to smuggle Almara aboard anyway, wouldn't you?"

"You'd better believe it!"

"In any event, come sup with Triga and me," the team

leader told him. "The food will do you good. Where's Almara? Will she eat with us?"

Isky shook his head. "She left by another door."

"Good. That will give me the opportunity to bring you up to speed on what I'm going to do and the role you may play."

Triga came in, redressed and refreshed. When she saw Isky, she didn't need to examine him. She knew. "Finally met your equal, I'll bet, And yearning for another go, if I know you. Peter, let's let him. Maybe then he'll stop chasing me around the *Starace*."

"Not while you're still chase-able," Isky said. "Yes, Peter, food. Lots of food. Please. Now, what nefarious scheme have you cooked up this time?"

"I'm going to bring Onuva Ferona here."

Isky turned to Triga. "See, I told you our team leader was a kind and generous soul. Not only was he generous to me just now in my hour of need and desire, but he's being compassionate to that poor Kaloc girl who's been cooped up in detention in the *Starace* and going stir-crazy for all of five days. Peter, you are indeed a gentleman, a scholar, and a judge of fine camels, as my ancestors would say . . ."

Triga raised her eyebrows. "Wait until you hear what he has in mind before you present him with that mantle of generosity and kindness, Isky."

Chapter Sixteen

But when Isky heard what Starbuck planned to do, he responded vehemently, "Good idea! Will serve her right!"

"Isky, it's improper to pass such a judgment according to the Canons," Triga reminded him.

Isky thought about it for a moment, then nodded. "Yes, Triga, of course. Probably, undoubtedly." Then he grinned and admitted, "But it made me feel good to say it!"

"I didn't think you felt very good," Triga reminded him.

"Quite the contrary, Triga, my dear. I felt terrible for a moment because I felt so good." He stopped to think about what he'd said, then went on, "I don't care if it doesn't make sense now. It made all sorts of sense a short time ago, if you know what I mean. Anyway, although I feel good right now, saying that about Ferona made me feel better. You didn't see what she was doing to Katwin back there on Thya . . . ."

"Yes, I did. I was in the rescue party," Triga reminded him. "I had enough difficulty controlling my base emotions about it, and I had to treat the results, too. That alone was bad enough!"

"But, Peter, are you sure this caper with Ferona is going to work? Sounds very risky to me. Everything is going to have to click just right," Isky reminded the teamleader. Starbuck's plans always sounded good, the team's transmitterman told himself, but occasionally they didn't always come off as planned. And this operation was an especially touchy one as far as he could see. Furthermore, it was based on an incomplete knowledge of the Kalocs in general and Onuva Ferona in particular.

"The plan has plenty of room for improvisation and opportunism," Starbuck explained. "One must always be prepared for that." But he didn't bother to tell them what he had in mind for "Plan B," the fall-back contingency or emergency situation. Both of them knew Starbuck always had Plan B, and it was such a commonplace thing they took it for granted and didn't bother to ask him about it. Had they done so, he would have told them about it, of course.

Isky sighed and got up to pick a fruit from the array on a sideboard. "Good luck! I'll do my part."

"And I'll stand by to tend the wounded," Triga added with some reluctance. "Quite frankly, Peter, I hope you manage to draw her blood before she does the same to you."

"Ferona won't. I'm not going to give her any reason to do so," Starbuck told his biotech.

"I withhold comment until I see for myself," was the biotech's comment. In spite of her willingness to go along with the plan, Triga obviously harbored some doubts.

It was time to get the operation moving, so he called Almara. When the lovely agent showed up, she looked as lascivious and perky as she had when she'd first greeted them. In fact, it seemed she had a glow about her that she hadn't had before. He asked her to get the limo and, as they were riding out to the starport, he observed, "You're looking quite happy, Almara."

She merely smiled radiantly and didn't explain why. It would have been contrary to her training to have done so. But she did say, "I'm always happy when I have work."

"Is this a slow season for you?"

She shook her head, and her abundant blonde curls shimmered. She settled her incredibly nubile young body into the soft seat. "Not really. But there's a lot of competition in Samarra. You and your people are turning out to be excellent clients."

"You've had some that weren't?"

"There are those who don't spend a lot of money because they're from one of the Fringe Worlds and don't have a lot to spend. And there are always the cheapskates. Or the chiselers. Or the ones who want something for nothing . . ."

"I take it the overarching philosophy of Samarra is that anything worth doing is worth doing for money?"

Almara looked wistful and replied, "No, not always. Sometimes it's fun or worth doing just for the sake of doing it . . . or both. Some things are beyond price."

Starbuck knew what she meant.

In the *Starace,* he informed his remaining team members that they could go dirtside subject only to the recall signal.

There was considerable concern in his mind about David O'Hara. As a precaution, he took Shochona aside and told the tall, gangly woman, "Did you get the locator transmitter installed in all David's clothing?"

The older woman nodded. "Look, I can probably find him no matter where he goes. Why bother with the locator?"

"Because this is a pretty loose culture, if I make myself clear."

"No, you don't. It is dangerous? Any planet inhabited by people like the Kalocs is likely to house dangerous people."

"No, Shochona, I don't think this part of Khughar's dangerous. At least, no more so than any of the New Vegas worlds. The Dyons run a clean operation. And not because they pay off the local cops. They own the local cops but keep the game clean anyway. They have to. They can't afford to have any disgruntled customers." He paused and nodded. "I'd like to have you take Katwin in tow, please. This place may be far too much for her."

"So? She's been on New Vegas itself, in case you don't remember. Enjoyed herself, too. Thought it was a wonderful circus. How do you know she needs the sort of 'protection' I can give her here?"

"I don't want to see Katwin hurt in any way. Neither do you. Besides, if it turns out you don't like Samarra, you'll have Katwin as an excuse to come back aboard to get out of it. I think you'll find that Samarra is just a little bit different from the other New Vegas worlds."

"Different? How?"

"Very little circus, very little fun and games, almost exclusively a frontier-type play world."

"In short, licentious and sexual?" Shochona ventured.

"Right. To be brutally frank, it's an interstellar bordello."

Shochona's reaction was mixed. "I find that hard to believe. Don't the Kalocs come from this world?" When Starbuck simply nodded, she shook her head. "Then I don't believe it. Those were the meanest people I've ever met. You don't mean to tell me that lovely girl Almara comes from the same planet?"

"I do, and she does, and you'll find the rest of the Dyons just as beautiful and just as eager to please . . . usually for a price, but not always."

Shochona looked askance at Starbuck. "So you decided to let the crew have a bit of R-and-R here and take a bit of it yourself, eh?"

He shook his head. That was precisely the response he'd anticipated from the shipmother. "No, I'm convinced this is the best place to find out who and what the Kalocs are. The reason we're staying is because I'm taking Onuva Ferona dirtside with me."

That stopped Shochona cold for a moment. Then she asked quietly, "What does Triga have to say about that?"

"She's all for it. As a matter of fact, she had some definitely good suggestions about it."

"I imagine she did! Well, let me tell you, Peter, dirtside for that woman Ferona is too good for her unless you plan to clap her in the clink for what she did to us on Thya."

"I have nothing of the sort in mind, Shochona. There's a lot you don't know about Ferona. I keep discovering new facts every day. And we have a plan . . ."

"Oh, another of your super escapades, eh, Peter? Well,

the best laid plans of mice and men . . . remember the time on Azana?''

He smiled in reply. ''Thanks, but you don't have to remind me, Shochona. I still carry the scars where few people can see them.'' The details of the incident were still fresh in his memory although it had happened during his early career with SIGNET. The reason why the details hadn't been buried with old memories included the injuries that had hospitalized him for a month in spite of biotechnology. Parts of him had had to be rebuilt by cloning. The operation had taught him the hard way to Always Have Plan B. He now had Plan B. And he intended to get the final pieces in this jigsaw puzzle by taking Ferona dirtside with him. Starbuck turned the conversation. ''But, what about you, Shochona? Remember, I've just warned you about the licentious nature of Samarra. I don't want to hear you complaining about the morals of the people afterwards . . .''

''I'll do quite well here, thank you! And I'll survive in a condition to mother all of you back to reasonable condition again afterwards.''

''That goes without saying. But be careful for your sake as well as Katwin's. These Dyons are far more tractable than any people I've ever encountered of any of the New Vegas worlds.''

''How wonderful! Now I'll be able to have my little fling and teach Katwin a few things, too . . . in a motherly way, of course.''

Starbuck just raised his eyebrows. Shochona preferred to keep her dirtside life quite private, but Peter Starbuck knew what she did and knew that she did what she liked. Furthermore, Shochona knew that Starbuck knew. It was none of his business, of course, and both of them knew that, too. That's why he felt no compunctions in asking Shochona to oversee Katwin on Samarra. Starbuck was quite discreet when it came to his team members. He never expected them to conform to a common mold or some supercilious image of what a SIGNET AI Team member should be. He reveled in their differences. So did SIG-NET. It was the only adult way to get along.

Shochona caught his querulous expression, of course. "Peter, there may be frost on the roof," she told him, referring to her silver hair, "but there's still heat in the reactor . . ." There was no expression on her face as she said this.

"I'm quite well aware of that."

"You tend to forget it. And I don't think you believe it all the time, especially now. Perhaps I should provide you with a first-hand demonstration."

"I'll simply use a term you'll hear a lot in Samarra: What is your pleasure?"

Shochona snorted. "Right now, I just want to get out of this ship for a few hours. And I suspect Katwin does, too. And our supercargo as well, but for different reasons. Do you need some help? An additional escort? A *duenna* to keep Ferona from claiming . . . ?"

Starbuck cut her off. "Shochona, go do your thing, and I'll do mine. Chaperones went out of style when pantyhose got popular."

"And should have come back when the codpiece became fashionable again. But don't think you can treat Ferona like an adult, Peter. She's more like a badly-spoiled child."

"I know. And I'm counting on that. Take care of Katwin."

"I will."

The cramped quarters of the teñ Thyan Irregulars were clean and orderly, but it was quite apparent that the ship's life support system was incapable of handling the increased load of the additional men. Even after only five days, the storage compartments jury-rigged as passenger cabins were beginning to get ripe and needed airing. The Thyans were also getting restless.

Starbuck called them together and told them, "We've landed on Khughar, but not in Kaloc territory. We'll be here for as long as necessary to reprovision the ship and get whatever information we can about the Kalocs. No sense in all of you sitting here in the ship going stir-crazy. Go out and get some R-and-R. I'm going to give each of you a credit sigil with a built-in comm module. If you get in trouble, activate the stud. CY will sense it and notify me. In a like manner, if you hear the recall signal from the sigil, return to the ship immediately; there could be trouble or an immediate lift-off. Now, let me tell you something about Samarra and the Dyons . . .''

Although a couple of the Irregulars appeared to gleefully anticipate the dirtside leave, most of them appeared to view it as just a break in a rather boring and definitely interminable routine. Karel Cherny, their elected leader, remarked, ''We're mostly family men, Starbuck. And rather devoted to our wives and families, I might add. I suspect that most of us will act with a great deal of restraint. I wouldn't want any stories to get back to my wife. On the other hand, this R-and-R will probably help us, but, quite frankly, we'd rather be back on Thya fighting to get rid of those Black Guards.''

Starbuck nodded. ''I know how you feel. But this isn't a vacation side trip. If I can get the sort of data I'm hoping to find here, we'll be on our way back to Thya within a day or so. And we'll be much better equipped to handle the Kaloc invaders.''

''Maybe by that time, the Star Guard fleet will also arrive at Thya, and we can get this mess cleaned up,'' Pavel remarked.

''Perhaps so,'' Starbuck told him, then added as a precaution, ''but you might also want to look for some effective weapons to buy while you're here.''

He found Onuva Ferona in her compartment. Her tightly-fitting black attire was quite obviously rumpled and well lived-in after several days of confinement. Ferona had steadfastly refused to accept the loan of clothing from Shochona and Triga. The woman now looked very pale and extremely gaunt, her large dark eyes in even greater contrast to her ashen face, and her jet-black hair wrapped

closely around her head. She'd been on a general strike —
more of a blue funk and a childish temper tantrum — since
Starbuck had last visited her. The effects of her self-
imposed starvation were apparent. And he couldn't help
but detect the signs of her refusal to practice personal
hygiene during her confinement.

Onuva Ferona simply sat there and looked defiantly at
Starbuck, saying nothing.

Starbuck asked her directly, "Onuva, do you want to
freshen up here or wait until we get in our quarters dirtside?"

It took a moment for her to realize what he'd said.
"What do you mean?"

"Would you like to go dirtside with me?"

"As your prisoner?"

"No. You haven't been my prisoner. The door to this
compartment has been unlocked." He didn't tell her that
he'd forgotten to lock it. "You never bothered to check it.
Now, everyone else aboard the ship has gone aground. I
don't want to leave you here alone. Besides, you need to
get freshened up. And you also need some clothing other
than what you're wearing. A lady shouldn't be required to
wear the same attire day after day."

Ferona was now suspicious, and she reacted defiantly.
"I won't go anywhere as your prisoner!"

The corners of Starbuck's mouth turned up in a wry
smile. "Who said anything about being a prisoner, Onuva?
I told you you aren't and you haven't been. You may go
along with me freely. I won't even ask you for your word
that you won't try to escape. You can try that if you wish,
but you may have trouble going anywhere."

After a moment while this sunk in, she asked, "Where
are we?"

"Khughar."

"You're lying!"

"The ship is grounded at Samarra."

"Samarra!" There was sudden excitement in her voice.
Her expression changed from surly to eagerly anxious.

Then she frowned. "No, I won't go with you. You'll just tantalize and torture me by denial."

"Not at all. I've arranged comfortable quarters for us. You'll be free to do as you wish. I'll take care of your needs. Consider yourself my guest."

Ferona thought about this for a moment. Khughar! Samarra! She was now only a few thousand kilometers from Thoth! But, as she thought about it, she realized that for all intents and purposes she was still Starbuck's prisoner. She had no way to cross those thousand or more kilometers. She also knew that she couldn't call for help; as Starbuck had guessed, nearly all the facilities of Thoth had been marshaled by the Kalocs for the Thyan invasion. There *might* be someone in Thoth who would come and get her, but she also realized that it might require armed force . . . and there was little of that left in Thoth right then. However, something might be worked out, or some opportunity might present itself. At least, it was better than sitting alone in the ship.

She was also somewhat angry with herself about the unlocked compartment door. Perhaps, she told herself, this man Starbuck wasn't so bad after all . . .

Furthermore, she thought, Starbuck would probably keep a close eye on her on the ground. This meant he'd be with her most of the time. There would be ample opportunity for her to work her wiles on this strapping and handsome man. It could also lead to other things.

And it probably would, because she didn't believe it when Starbuck continued, "As a matter of fact, when we get to our rooms, I think you probably ought to send a message to Kodo Sadon on Thya telling him where you are and assuring him that you're all right."

"Are you serious?"

"Of course."

"Why? Sadon may come to rescue me."

"How? By invading Samarra, too?"

No, Kodo Sadon wouldn't do that, she knew. He couldn't. Everything they had was engaged on Thya.

This made Onuva Ferona suspicious. How much did Starbuck now know about the Kalocs, Ferona wondered? How could the man behave in such a confident manner if he didn't know a great deal? Had the Star Guard fleet arrived at Thya and overwhelmed the Kaloc forces? She didn't know. Starbuck had effectively put her off guard. Yet he was offering her something beyond price. She simply couldn't turn that down. She'd send a C+ message to Sadon. That would let him know that she was still around and keep him from cutting her out of her share of the Thyan booty, if the Kalocs were indeed winning on Thya. In the meantime, she told herself that a woman had to make the best of things. And the best of things had just been offered her: time in Samarra with a superman.

On second thought, she told herself, she might decide not to go back to Thoth. It might be far more interesting to go along with these SIGNET people because they seemed to enjoy a lot of everything.

Maybe — just maybe — she suddenly thought, Starbuck might have found something fascinating about Onuva Ferona. Maybe he, too, enjoyed things as she did. Samarra had everything necessary to play those games, too — for a price. That possibility suddenly seemed to be far more important to her. And it was immediate. It was in hand, so to speak. Kodo Sadon was light years away. Thoth and its cold, dark recreational chambers were only a few thousand kilometers away on the same world, but as far as she was concerned they, too, could have been light-years away. So she seized the opportunity presented to her just as Starbuck thought she would.

But, of course, she couldn't let Starbuck know what was going on in her mind.

However, Starbuck himself was improving his empathy with her and, if he couldn't exactly get subliminal messages from her yet, he was beginning to get a sense for what she was thinking.

She couldn't let her pride be demeaned, however. She stood and undulated up to Starbuck. Laying her hand on his arm, she came no closer than that as she looked up at him with her dark, sunken eyes and remarked, "On one condition: I will participate only if you treat me properly."

"Onuva, I don't know enough about you yet to treat you properly under the First Canon. I hope to learn a great deal more about you . . . a great deal more indeed." It was a truthful statement, but he meant it quite differently than Ferona took it. That, too, he anticipated.

Onuva Ferona stepped back from him and became coquettish. In a deep and provocative voice, she told him, "I think we have ourselves an arrangement, Peter Starbuck. Shall we see how it works out? Come, take me to Samarra. It's been years since I've had the pleasure . . ."

Chapter Seventeen

"This isn't going to work as you believe, Peter." CY was unequivocal in his evaluation of Starbuck's plan to take Onuva Ferona into Samarra with him.

"Why not?" Starbuck asked. He was about to go aground with Ferona and was giving final commands for CY to watch-dog the *Starace* while everyone was aground. For record purposes he'd revealed his Ferona plan.

"It's illogical."

"Humans are illogical, yet we manage to get things done in our illogical way. For example, humans made you," the team leader carefully pointed out.

"I shall ignore the insult by considering its source," CY replied without hesitation. "Given all that, Peter, there are far too many places where your plan could go badly wrong. You haven't thought it all the way through."

"Because it's impossible to think it all the way through. There are too many branches on the decision tree."

"I can handle far more branches than you can, Peter."

Starbuck sighed. The cybermech was, of course, correct. But in spite of its logic circuits and ability to handle far more either-or possibilities than a human mind, and in spite of CY's apparent growing humanlike traits, it was still a machine and didn't fully appreciate the illogical characteristics of opportunism. Starbuck, on the other hand, was the product of several millions of years of evolving organisms who'd learned the hard way how to handle opportunism; the ones that hadn't didn't survive long enough to breed progeny or had had their progeny wiped out because of an opportunity not seized.

He didn't have time to argue with CY. "Look," he told the cybermech, "all I want you to do is stand watch. And stand by for a possible emergency message to ColeShore if necessary."

"By your command. But, Peter, don't you think it would be a wise move to ask ColeShore for a back-up team?"

"Tayreze Nambe told us earlier that there was no back-up team available."

"That isn't precisely what she said. As I recall, and I do that very well, she said there was no other team available at the moment that was as close to the problem as we were at the time. There may be a reserve team available now. Or — and this is something you've never requested, which surprises me — there may be a Justar or Strakovkhaburo team that could back us up . . ."

"Do you really think that Strakovkhaburo will send in a team to help us after they read the report that Mironenko has probably filed by this time?"

There was no hesitation while CY computed the permutations and combinations of that situation. "No, but that doesn't mean you couldn't ask for a back-up team from Justar if SIGNET doesn't have one available."

Starbuck thought about it for a moment, then told the cybermech, "No, CY, I do not wish to ask for a back-up team. We're doing very well at the moment. I have no justification to request a back-up team."

"Very well. You're the boss. Have fun, Peter. And do let me know from time to time how things are going, will you? I worry when I don't hear from you."

This last had to be another one of CY's growing number of ripostes. None of the team would own up to inserting them into CY, although there were several team members who had just the sort of wacky sense of humor to do it. But who? The alternative was even more improbable: CY engaging in self-programming.

Onuva Ferona had refused the loan of clothing to go aground, but she'd freshened up and tried to make her black uniform appear less lived-in. Starbuck had to admit that she was an attractive woman in her own way. He often wondered what some color and style in her clothing might do for her appearance. Or what a standard non-biotic appearance stylist could do to help her make the best of what she already had. On the trip from the *Starace* to the hotel in Samarra, she wasn't sullen as she'd been earlier. She seemed pleased to get out of the ship. At Starbuck's request, Almara didn't accompany them. It was only the two of them, Ferona and Starbuck, in the limo.

Ferona didn't try to escape. There were other things she had in mind first.

Starbuck was counting on this. He also knew she wouldn't try to escape.

He'd taken a separate suite of rooms for Ferona and himself, although they were next door to the suite in which Triga and Isky were staying. Once inside, Ferona turned to Starbuck and asked tauntingly, "Well, why don't you lock the door? I might escape otherwise . . ."

Starbuck shrugged and replied urbanely, "Nothing's locked, Onuva. I have no need to keep you in or someone else out. Leave if you wish. And good luck if you do. By the way, if you wish, I'll leave, too." He paused and observed, "Would you like to take a bath before the couturiers come?"

"What?"

"You can't very well continue to wear your black uniform forever, can you?" he observed. "It doesn't look as though it's the most comfortable attire in the Thousand Worlds, and you must be getting reasonably tired of it by now. And, because you're the Consortte of Thoth, it wouldn't be proper for you to go around to all the shops selecting a new wardrobe. So the couturier shops are coming to you instead, just as they would for any important visitor."

He thought she'd accept the fact that she would be

treated like royalty — even though the royal rank existed on only a few of the Thousand Worlds. Onuva Ferona did.

"Who's going to pay for all of this?"

"I told you: SIGNET. We don't treat our guests in a shabby manner."

"When are the merchants coming?" she wanted to know.

"Whenever you're ready to see them and try their wares."

"Then I'll take my time. The Dyons have raised the art of bathing to new heights . . ." She turned and strode toward the door to the bath. Just before she got there, she turned and told Starbuck in a proud tone quite unlike her childish whimpering aboard the *Starace*, "Starbuck, you may stay here. Often a woman needs a man's opinion on things. Besides, I wish to send a message to Kodo Sadon once I've bathed."

Starbuck mimicked his cybermech. "By your command . . ."

As she disappeared into the bath chambers, Starbuck quietly began a careful check of the suite. Everything was as he'd ordered it. There was ample food placed here and there — fruits, snacks, sweets, and other morsels. Flowers had also been brought in, an expensive rarity on a world like Khughar. The view from the windows showed the distant mountains beyond which lay Thoth and Onuva Ferona's homeland. Everything was perfect. Everything was just as he'd ordered.

She took a very long time. He figured, quite rightly, that it had been a long time since she'd enjoyed such sybaritic facilities. Coming from a scarcity culture, she might not have had such even in Thoth. Certainly, ships of an invasion fleet would offer only spartan facilities.

To pass the time, Starbuck stretched out on a divan and turned on the holo tank. There was nothing important showing, just a live broadcast of one of the staged musical shows which was being transmitted as a come-on for the real thing in one of the theaters. The tank didn't zoom on anyone or anything, and occasionally the focus and synch were a bit fuzzy. In other words, he thought, if you really want to see the show, dear visitor, you'd better come to the real thing. He turned down the audio and reduced the tank size until the stage show and its chorus line were the size of miniature dolls.

He suddenly realized that the water had stopped running. He looked up and saw Onuva Ferona standing next to the divan. She had a heavy flask in one hand. And she was still wearing her form-fitting black uniform that covered her completely from her chin to her toes.

Calmly, he muttered, "I wouldn't try it if I were you, Onuva. I'm faster than you think."

She smiled, bent down, picked up a goblet, and poured some water from the flask. "Come to think of it, Commander Starbuck, that's not a bad idea. But I'm smarter than you think. I want a drink of water."

"Sorry. The appearance of you standing there with a heavy object in one hand could be taken many ways."

Looking down at the heavy flask, she remarked offhandedly, "Many things may be taken many ways on first sight. They are often different when viewed otherwise. Of course I could have brained you with this. I might have fractured your skull at least. But why should I? Even with your credit sigil — which you probably don't have with you in any event — how far out of this lovely hotel would I have gotten?"

"I've told you several times, you're not a prisoner, Onuva. Go if you wish . . ."

"Really? I'm your prisoner whether you tell me so or not, Peter Starbuck. Besides, I'd be a fool to walk out on you right now. I know what you're trying to do."

"Oh?"

She tossed her head. "Yes. You want something from me. You've offered to pay well for it by treating me in a royal manner as I should be. Well, I don't know yet what you want. But when you get around to asking, I'll tell you whether or not you've given me enough of what I want in exchange." She put the flask down, quaffed the goblet of water, and set it gently on the table. "Now, I want to send a message to Kodo Sadon."

"Of course . . ."

She paused and laid a hand on his shoulder as he started to rise. It was a surprisingly strong hand for being so small and thin. "Something about me is bothering you, Peter Starbuck."

"I was just wondering," he observed, "why you donned that uniform again. Didn't they leave suitable new clothing in the bath as I requested?"

"Yes."

"Are you proud of that uniform?"

"Yes. It brings privileges and immunities with it."

"You don't need it to have those privileges and immunities here."

"Perhaps not. But I choose to wear it anyway. Perhaps you may learn why eventually. Now, I want to send that message."

Starbuck gestured toward the comm center. "Please."

She didn't thank him. It occurred to him that she never thanked anyone for anything. She always acted as though a helpful person should feel privileged to do things for her. In a real sense, she was acting as imperiously as a spoiled princess. Well, among the Kalocs, she probably was.

He didn't look over her shoulder or try to snoop on what she was transmitting. And he didn't especially pay much attention to what she was saying. The conversation with comm central was quite one-sided. Onuva Ferona didn't discuss or request anything from the service; she ordered it.

When he got around to it, he could get a complete playback of whatever she sent to Kodo Sadon. The suite was effectively bugged in such a way that, even if she'd had debuggers, she couldn't have discovered all the snoopers. Rudi Witkowski used only the most recent state of the art in the gadgetry he provided to AI Teams.

When she had finished, she turned back to Starbuck.

"You may now call the merchants to bring in their wares for my perusal."

"I hope you told Kodo Sadon that you were well and in good hands," Starbuck remarked.

"The message I sent was my business, and it remains to be seen whether or not I'm indeed in good hands and will remain well."

Starbuck smiled sardonically. "Onuva, don't you trust me yet?"

She glared at him. "No," she stated flatly.

"Why?"

"Why should I trust a person who's holding me prisoner on a trumped-up charge of killing some SIGNET people, plus other charges of which I'm totally unaware?"

Starbuck didn't change his expression. "But, Onuva. I've told you you're free to leave at any time. After all, this is your home world . . ."

"There is no other place for me to go, and I have no means to get to Thoth at this time. You know I can't leave."

He knew she was rationalizing, and she also knew that he knew it. There was something else that was driving her now, and it was more than sheer greed.

The merchants showed up one at a time, displaying their wares under the most favorable possible conditions. Couturiers came in with lovely fashions, all beautifully displayed on attractive models who moved and swung around the suite to show the attire — most of which did little to hide the obvious charms of these beautiful Dyon people. Milliners, jewelers, and other clothiers paraded in and out of the suite for hours.

They were followed by the cosmeticians, each proposing some unique manner of enhancing female beauty. Their Dyon models didn't need it.

During these presentations, Starbuck watched Ferona carefully, knowing full well that she was also being video-scanned and recorded but also realizing that he might well pick up some expression or sense that opto-electronics couldn't. He was also counting on his elusive semi-psi talents, hoping they might notice something that everything else missed. During the hours of this fantastic fashion show, Starbuck did indeed gain a better understanding of Onuva Ferona. And, again, she did things and said things that raised even more questions about her in his mind. There was no doubt that she was indeed a complex personality — but Starbuck knew after all these centuries that people were seldom simple and that even the lowliest service person was complex. One of the things that kept his interest alive over the centuries was the incredible, irrepeatable, illogical, irrational, and indescribable variation among individual human beings everywhere. In all the Thousand Worlds and unknown worlds beyond, and in all the uncounted galaxies of the universe whose number far exceeded the known stars, there were no two human beings alike. The variations excited him. The myriad differences enthralled him. It was, after all, people that made the universe interesting, not just the universe and its mysteries.

Hundreds of beautiful, sensual, exotic, and enticing garments were paraded before Onuva Ferona. Surprisingly, she did not select willy-nilly with no regard for number or price. While it was obvious that price didn't bother her if she fancied a piece of finery, she didn't appear to be frivolous in her selection. In short, she chose carefully and didn't engage in a spree — although Starbuck had been prepared for such a thing.

It was as though Ferona, having been raised in a scarcity culture, was still aware of costs and somewhat fearful of over-indulging herself.

One factor alone caught Starbuck's attention — Ferona's selections.

He'd been around for several centuries. He knew well the human female's penchant for frilly, diaphanous, semi-opaque, pretty things.

Ferona chose none of them. What she wanted were garments that covered as much flesh as possible but were definitely not unisex in design. In addition, her choices weren't designed for warmth. And they weren't loose and free but carefully tailored and closely fitted so that there was no doubt that there was a woman wearing the clothing.

He also knew of the customs in many cultures where it was the male who dressed colorfully and provocatively, others where the women did so, others where both sexes dressed colorfully and sensually, and still others where attire was stark and colorless.

In this regard, Ferona's choices were both revealing and disquieting.

The colors she chose were either flat-black or powdery dark, subdued grays and browns, dark-red wine hues, deep-purples, and other very low key tones. She chose no whites, no primary colors, and no bright tones. Even the jewelry she selected was heavy, darkly copper-bronze, and non-specular gold.

And Ferona wanted little in the way of the services of beauticians and cosmeticians. What she did select was rather stark and straightforward, as though she really didn't want to make herself more attractive or beautiful. She was, of course, an attractive woman with a beauty all her own, but Starbuck thought that way of nearly all women and therefore felt that he was probably putting a personal bias on that particular piece of data. Better wait to find out what Shochona thought because, in spite of her previous experience with Ferona on Thya, the shipmother would tend to take a very objective view due to her own background.

Onuva Ferona was as different as could be from the women on his AI Team or the women he knew on hundreds of worlds. She was even different from those he knew on other Fringe Worlds: frontier women who appreciated something other than the drab — to his eyes — wardrobe of frontier people and who delighted in the opportunity to dress in their bright and exotic raiment saved for special occasions.

Triga Rimmon would have made selections of provocative and sensual attire that covered some but looked as though it were covering little.

Katwin would have chosen bright, white, frilly, and colorful apparel that was "pretty" and extremely feminine.

Even the often-dour Shochona would have selected a wardrobe with colorful trimming and highlighting that was, in its own way, feminine and of the sort that would ask respect of the men around her.

In fact, he guessed that Triga was probably snaring some of the merchants as they left Ferona's suite and making a few selections of her own for later use when she wanted to tease and excite Starbuck. He honestly hoped Triga would choose some of the raiment that Ferona had rejected.

This is not to say that the clothing chosen by Ferona was non-feminine, semi-transvestite, or even ugly as a defensive shield against a hostile world. It was feminine in a strange new way alien even to Starbuck's jaded tastes and long experience on many worlds and in many times.

It was telling him something about Onuva Ferona and about the Kalocs and why they'd done what they'd done. But he couldn't get the message yet.

Chapter Eighteen

"An interesting selection, Onuva," Starbuck told her once all the purveyors of high fashion had gone.

"I'm pleased you approve of it," she replied in an offhanded manner.

"I remarked that it was an interesting selection, but I said nothing about approval."

She tossed her head. "It makes little difference to me whether you approve or not."

"That's precisely why I didn't attempt to approve or disapprove of your selection," Starbuck told her. "Why should I approve? Your selection was personal and was made on a personal basis for personal reasons."

"That it was."

He walked slowly over to a sideboard where various fruit was waiting on a silver platter. Selecting a debrided local version of the tellurian tangerine, he asked what was to him a critical question: "Seeing that clothing on those Dyon models was one thing. But how does it look on you? Would you model for me a collection of what you think are your best selections, Onuva? The clothing, jewelry, and accessories you like the best out of everything you selected?"

She didn't answer immediately. She narrowed her dark eyes and a hard expression came over her gaunt face. Tightly compressing her thin lips until they were almost invisible, she threw Starbuck a look that was almost fearful and yet somehow yearning. Starbuck had never seen that look on a woman's face before.

Finally, she said slowly, "I shouldn't."

"Why?"

"I'm the Consortte of Kodo Sadon, the Black Path of Thoth. It's a very privileged honor. I dare not besmirch my honor with another man, even you, and have news of it ever get to Sadon."

Starbuck sat down opposite her and took a bite from the tangerine. He knew then that in the Kaloc culture she wasn't accustomed to dealing with people who had or could get anything and everything they wanted in abundance. In short, Onuva Ferona had never encountered the sort of people that Peter Starbuck and his AI Team members were accustomed to dealing with most of the time in the Thousand Worlds: human beings whom he considered truly adult in their beliefs and actions as a result of the Canons.

He also learned at that moment that love and sex were somehow linked within her mind in a totally alien manner — and he knew from his early life in the twenty-first century of the enormous variety of proclivities of which people were capable in that regard.

"Look, Onuva," he told her in frank tones, "I know you're Kodo Sadon's woman. I don't take women away from other men, even if they could be taken, which they can't. In the first place, it's contrary to the Canons. You're not property; you're an intelligent being. Any arrangement between you and me will be to mutual benefit. In the second place, I don't *need* you. There are other women quite close to me who want me as I want them; we both know it, we like it, and we plainly enjoy it. Desire is something different from need, and even in that department I have no problems."

Strangely, she didn't answer. When she did speak, she said simply, "You're a very strange man, Peter Starbuck." Then she arose with liquid smoothness and without another word disappeared into another room.

At that point, Starbuck frankly didn't know what to expect next.

What did happen next was that the comm center demanded his attention. It was Triga from elsewhere in the hotel. She was attired in something he hadn't seen before but decided he'd like to see a great deal more of, especially with Triga wearing it. But Triga, damn her soul, wasn't far enough away from the holo sensor to permit anything more than her head and shoulders to be seen. In what she was wearing and with what she'd acquired from the cosmeticians, that was quite enough for Starbuck. But Triga cocked her head, looked impish, and merely remarked, "Just don't forget, Peter, that I can monitor this data channel into CY. And also don't forget that I do not relish the role of a voyeur, superman." With a sweet smile, she cut the circuit from her end.

Not that Starbuck minded much, but there were times when Triga's penchant for a tad of jealousy bothered him. Almost every other member of the team could be (and might be) monitoring the channel, too. Except perhaps Isky . . . or David . . . or even Shochona who was supposed to be looking after Katwin. On the other hand, since this was supposed to be a data-gathering operation, maybe all of them were monitoring. Starbuck had been in many situations in his long and active life. It no longer bothered him that others might be watching.

Khughar's sun was setting, casting long shadows over the mountains to the north and painting the rifting clouds in pastel shades. He wandered over to the window, waiting.

He waited longer than he would have believed he'd have to. The sun was well down and the colors had faded from the sky. The lights of Samarra were beginning to twinkle. The room lights had come on automatically at low setting.

"Peter Starbuck, it took me some time to make up my mind," Onuva Ferona's voice said, but it was hesitant and not as imperious as before. It was almost a little frightened now. "But it occurred to me that I've always appeared to you as a soldier and never in the proper manner of a Consortte . . ."

She was still in black, but her garb was not a uniform. And it wasn't plain black just as it wasn't a plain everyday garment, or even a single garment. The black portions of the basic body garment were like open lace but backed up with an underlayer of rusty orange satin that shone in contrast to its dull-black outer layer. Reflective colored gems sewn into the material glittered in the light as she moved. Over it she wore a semi-transparent jumper that was loose in some parts and tightly tailored in others, leaving no question that she was indeed a woman. It was cinched at her wrists, neck, waist, and ankles by bands of dusky copper. Simple black slippers covered her small feet. She had done little to her face, but her mouth was now a broad crimson slash. A simple copper diadem band held her dark hair away from her face.

But, like her uniform, her finery covered her entirely from her neck down to the tips of her fingers and toes.

She was still Onuva Ferona, but not the spartan and black-uniformed Ferona. And she did have a strange new allure about her.

"And you indeed look like a Consortte, Onuva," he told her quite honestly.

She glided over to a side table, poured some liquid in a glass, and selected a morsel of food before she returned to a divan and sat down, motioning Starbuck to sit opposite her. "Do you approve of my choice, Peter Starbuck?" she wanted to know.

Starbuck also sat down. He nodded. "Although you're quite proud of your uniform, Onuva, you're an extremely attractive woman even when you aren't attired so severely."

"A soldier doesn't have to be attractive."

"True, but a soldier doesn't have to be a soldier all the time, either. And I find it hard to believe that you're a soldier."

"In Thoth, one must be a soldier to have respect, position, and a bit of freedom from want and pain . . . although no one has very much of all of those things constantly. Or for long."

"Would you have to be a constant soldier if the Kalocs hadn't invaded Thya?"

She nodded.

"Seems like a pretty grim life," he observed. "Isn't it rather difficult to follow the Canons?"

She drew herself up proudly. "We Kalocs follow the Canons as best we can. We work hard at it. But it's not possible to always treat one another according to the Canons. There's not always enough of anything. The Second and Third Canons usually conflict with the First. That requires choices to be made. Kodo Sadon and I both follow the First Canon with one another.." Ferona paused momentarily then went on in an uncharacteristic tone that was almost savage yet full of wistfulness. "And I do miss him in spite of what he usually does. But . . . that is our way of life. One must endure the inescapable consequences of the passion . . . the excitement . . . the pleasure. Kalocs must endure things the Dyons would never think of doing — unless they're paid well."

Starbuck was having trouble believing what he was hearing. And having difficulty putting together a picture of a culture whose characteristics were slowly beginning to take shape as a strangely distorted — no, warped — interpretation of the Canons of Metalaw. It was only after he'd reviewed the data records several times at a later date that he got all of the thin and closely veiled implications of what Onuva Ferona was saying. And had, in fact, said to him in the past.

She hesitated and was apparently searching for a way to say something. Starbuck remained quiet to let her find her own words.

"You . . . you've told me . . . that you wouldn't take another man's woman," she said in a low and very halting voice, trying hard to look directly at him but having to occasionally divert her eyes downward. "I believe you, Peter Starbuck."

"Onuva, in my culture, it's quite proper to call me by my first name. Formality isn't necessary. I won't take offense at anything you say," he tried to explain. "I'm trying to satisfy the First Canon, Haley's Rule, 'Do unto

others what they would have you do unto them.' I've got
to learn what you would have done unto you . . ."

She looked out the windows toward the mountains of
twilight. With a black-garbed hand, she waved toward
them. "Beyond those hills lies the remains of a people
who follow the Canons differently than you do."

"Differently? How?"

She didn't answer at once, but she suddenly looked like
a frightened little girl. That impression lasted only a split
second, but Starbuck caught it. "I've been carefully trained
to be the Consortte of the Black Path of Thoth. I have
many things other Kalocs can only dream of. Yet I, too,
was also trained under the Canons. I find many inconsistencies in the Canons.

"So do I," Starbuck put in. "Different people interpret
them differently. Conflicts are generated as a result. Resolving those conflicts by compromise is what my work is
all about."

"Then resolve this one if you can: The First Canon
requires me to do as you're doing: Learn what you would
have done unto you. I sense that you would like to do unto
me as Kodo Sadon does. I more than sense it. I, perhaps
strangely, desire it. But I'm the Consortte of the Black
Path of Thoth. He's been so good to me that by rights I
shouldn't allow any other man to know me. But there must
always be room for compromise, no matter how difficult it
may seem to be."

Starbuck didn't immediately catch the full implications
of her statement. He remembered far too many war lords,
bosses, or dictatorial leaders and their pampered, lascivious women companions, sometimes more than one of
them in a harem. Even in abundancy cultures, the sexual
drive of human beings was often insatiable, particularly
among strong, charismatic leaders. Most powerful leaders
also had very powerful sexual drives, and the two were
probably psychologically, if not genetically, linked. On
new frontier worlds where individuals were carving the
human niche in the planetary ecology, family life was as

important to survival as it had been in pre-industrial Tellus
and monogamy tended to be the rule. But in the scarcity
cultures on Fringe Worlds, the intense sexual reproductive
drive of the human race usually led to polygamy or even
possession. Starbuck never really understood the latter; his
own deep cultural bias wouldn't allow him to conceive of
other people as personal property. In short, slavery of any
sort was totally alien to his thought patterning.

So he replied with a question, "Onuva, is it necessary
under your rules for me to know you sexually in order to
know you at all?"

Apparently, she didn't understand what he meant. Or he
was also too alien for her. "I tried to get to know you on
Thya. But you wouldn't let me. You used some strange
mentic trick to deprive me of that."

"Getting to know me?" Starbuck was astounded. "On
Thya, you weren't trying to understand me under the First
Canon. You were torturing me for your own enjoyment."

"Torturing you? Peter, that's absolute nonsense! Until I
knew what excited you most, I couldn't know what would
give you the most pleasure . . . and I couldn't show you
what would do the same for me." She suddenly stood up.
Her voice quavered slightly. "Peter, do you want to know
me? Do you want to follow the First Canon and give me
pleasure? Here are the results of what gives me pleasure.
Would you do this to me?"

She quickly stripped the metallic-copper ornaments and
let them fall to the floor. In a single motion, she tore the
flimsy garment that completely covered her, let it fall to
the floor, and stepped out of the mound of cloth.

If it hadn't been for CY's record of the incident, Starbuck
would have had trouble believing what he saw.

The fair translucent skin of Onuva Ferona's body was
literally covered with welts, scars, and healing bruises.
Her left forearm had a strange bend in it; it had apparently
been broken and the bone not properly reset. One side of
her torso had a strange hollow; a rib had once been broken
and not reset. The several days she'd been away from her

people with the AI Team had allowed some of the worst
and most recent cuts, burns, and bruises to begin to heal a
bit so that scars and scar tissue had started to form. Her
body was stark, sickening testimony to every unspeakable
act of violence and torture visited upon her.

Starbuck understood now why she wore black or dark
colors. Blood does not stain black clothing.

And there was no question why she wore all-covering
clothing.

She looked at him beseechingly. "I only ask that you
don't mark my face or my hands. Kodo Sadon is kind to
me; he has always abided by that wish . . ."

Starbuck couldn't help but stare as he sat riveted to his
chair. Never in his centuries of life had he ever seen any
human being so badly abused who was also still alive.
Even in his early days of work with SIGNET in the
twenty-first century when torture was still widely practiced
on Tellus, he'd seen horrible examples of sadism. But
little of this barbaric practice had left Tellus with the
migrating star people; they had other things to do that were
critical, and most sadists and their masochist companions
simply didn't survive even in the early solar-system space
colonies. Now it had apparently surfaced again among the
Thoths, perhaps in their basic gene pool as a result of a
slip-up in genetic engineering or their failure to eliminate a
recessive trait once it had gone too far in their culture.

Whatever had caused it, its results were sickening to
Starbuck. Onuva Ferona was an attractive woman. What
had been done to her disgusted him deep down in his most
basic thought levels.

Yet, she'd apparently permitted it. And from her words,
she must have enjoyed it.

The problem of the Kaloc invasion of Thya suddenly
became far more complex. Peter Starbuck and his AI
Team were dealing with the first genuine sado-masochistic
interstellar civilization. It was doubly difficult because the
Thoths apparently believed that they were acting totally
within the Canons of Metalaw. An old truism sprang into

his mind: A sadist is a person who's kind to a masochist. And it was a perfectly acceptable social action under the most basic of all the Canons.

When Starbuck found his voice, he muttered, "No, Onuva, I can't and won't do that to you for any reason. If I must hurt you to know you, than I'll never know you."

"I'm very disappointed in you. Right now, I want you and I need you. But you're a weakling, Peter! I sensed it when I had you in the recreation room . . ."

"No, Onuva, I just happen to be from a different sort of culture, that's all." He got up. At his movement, she stiffened in anticipation. Sensing it, he took no step toward her. "I don't know how we'd ever get to understand one another. But I can help you . . ."

"Help me? I don't need help! I merely want to return to Kodo Sadon on Thya. I know now that the only way *you* can help me, Peter Starbuck, is to get me back to Kodo Sadon! This has been an interesting diversion here on Samarra. This used to be a wonderful place for me to visit before other Kalocs came and began to treat the Dyons as they treat many of us . . ."

"But we can help you. You must be in a lot of pain, Onuva. We can stop that. We can help repair your body. We have a very high level of biotechnology . . ." Starbuck began.

"So do we."

"Obviously. Otherwise, you'd have died long before this. But even with the facilities we have in the *Starace*, we can stop the hurt and heal the wounds . . . and even repair some of the permanent damage . . ."

She threw her head high, touched a different welt or wound in sequence as she spoke, and announced, "I would not have you touch a one of these. I'm proud of each of them. Each one reminds me of an eventual pleasure that demanded courage and endurance to attain. There are few other Thoths who carry as many honors as I can display."

People in some ancient tribal cultures on Tellus, Starbuck recalled, deliberately mutilated their bodies in a host of bizarre ways to achieve either a cultural standard of beauty or as the most obvious way to display a badge of bravery or social position. But Starbuck had never believed he would run into such analogous activities among interstellar cultures. It only served to remind him again of the infinite variety of human beings and human institutions.

Centuries of anthropologists could have advised him that he would suffer profound cultural shock under these conditions. But it was only his long experience under the Canons that provided him with the rationale to change his abhorrence to a partial understanding.

If that was the way the Kalocs wanted to behave, who was he to say they were wrong? The Fifth Canon was in point. Would it have been different under the old, outmoded, and supposedly dangerous Golden Rule instead of Haley's Rule?

But if he couldn't change the Kalocs, he still had to determine whether or not and the extent to which they'd abrogated the first four Canons. It was only when and if the Kalocs attempted to force their ways on others that he could intervene . . . and in so doing he had to be careful not to overreach the Canons himself. There was still the unresolved matter of Joshua Zing's AI Team.

His job was never easy. If it had been, he wouldn't have taken it in the first place and probably would have pulled his own switch centuries ago out of sheer boredom. But sometimes the job appeared to be impossible. Like right then.

Starbuck suddenly saw over Ferona's shoulder that Triga was standing in the doorway to the adjoining suite, obviously shaken and visibly trembling. "Come in, Triga," he called to her.

The biotech came quickly to Ferona. Gone was Triga's hint of jealousy. Gone was her expressed hatred for what Ferona had done to Starbuck and Katwin on Thya. Stronger instincts motivated her now and the powerful teachings of the Canons had taken over. "Onuva, you must be hurting terribly. Let me help you."

Although the two women were about the same size, Ferona still managed to look proudly down on Triga. "I need no help." She was again her imperious self.

"But I can help without changing a single mark on you."

"I need no help," Ferona repeated. "I want no help. I can and will help myself." She waved her hand at the pile of clothing on the floor. "Dispose of that." And she walked out of the room.

This time Starbuck thought he sensed a slight limp in her walk.

Triga Rimmon was obviously shaken by the entire episode. She simply melted into Starbuck's arms. He soothed her. "We run into some strange things, don't we, Triga?"

"Yes, but that poor girl . . ."

"She isn't poor. She's the most powerful, respected, and wealthy woman in her culture."

"I don't have to like it."

"No, but there's nothing in the Canons that says you have to like something even if you understand it. And we're just beginning to understand these people. We've got nearly all the pieces in the puzzle, Triga."

She looked up at him. "Do you know something I don't?"

"Maybe. But I have a hunch it's all there once we sit down and begin to fit the pieces together. Don't forget: a picture can be reconstructed to the ninety-nine percent level of comprehension from a considerably lower percentage of the total pixels. Time to get busy in linkage with CY . . ."

But he didn't get the chance. The comm center called for him. When he activated full holo reception, a thin-faced individual in what was obviously a uniform asked, "Mister Starbuck?"

Starbuck activated the holo transmitter. "Yes."

The thin head with the thin mouth spoke to him curtly, "I am Kapitan Ludvik of Strakovkhaburo's *poleetseyskohye ooprahvlyehneeye*. As you may know, we handle security matters for the Dyons in Samarra under contract.''

Strakovkhaburo! What is Mironenko up to now? Starbuck wondered. ''What may I do for you, sir?'' he asked the holo image.

''You will please come to see me at once.''

''Oh? Any problem?''

''Yes. Since SIGNET has no agent on Khughar, Strakovhaburo therefore handles financial transactions for your organization. Agent Mironenko needs to know how SIGNET intends to settle the extremely large bill you and your people have established in Samarra. You will come now, please. Four of my officers are even now at your door to escort you.''

Chapter Nineteen

Starbuck heard a little laugh and turned to see Onuva Ferona, attired in yet another all-covering black garment, watching from a doorway. He immediately deduced what she must have done: contacted Mironenko of Strakovkhaburo who probably was their agent on Khughar as well, who in turn contacted Kodo Sadon. Or perhaps she'd simply sandbagged Starbuck . . . but not until she'd enjoyed a little fling of her own at his expense. Or perhaps she was merely enjoying the difficulties of a man who'd just spurned her.

But if the incident disturbed Starbuck, he didn't reveal it. In his typical unflappable and urbane manner, he told Kapitan Ludvik, "Your request is quite improper, Kapitan."

"Improper?"

"Agent Mironenko has already spoken with me. He's aware we're here. He knows what he must do under the various agreements between SIGNET and Strakovkhaburo."

"That is of no consequence. The Dyons have requested that Agent Mironenko handle the matter."

"Then if he wishes to speak with me about it, by rights he must ask to communicate or request to visit me. In any event, I don't intend to come with *you* against my will to see *him*, if that's indeed where I'd be going. And please ask him to henceforth follow the Canons in a proper manner and review the various agreements between SIGNET and Strakovkhaburo." Starbuck simply cut the connection.

Within five seconds, the outer door to the suite of rooms

suddenly came out of its jamb with a sound like an explosion and fell inward to lie flat on the floor.

Four large men in gray-green mesh-armored uniforms and carrying microwave stunners walked over the fallen door and into the suite.

"You will come, please, Agent Starbuck," the biggest one ordered.

When one is not wearing mesh shielding to protect against a stunner, one does not argue. In the face of such obviously unwinnable situations as this, SIGNET agents are trained to forego any sort of ego-boosting resistance and engage in a "retrograde operation" — not a retreat, mind you, and not a surrender, either. A "contingency delay" of a temporary nature until some oversight on the adversary's part allowed the agent to seize the initiative again.

But Starbuck didn't have the chance to do that.

"Drop 'em! Now!"

Eight men were suddenly through that doorless opening and behind the Strakovkhaburo police. They wore no uniforms and carried a variety of weapons.

"Karel, if you keep stepping in to save the day like this, SIGNET will have no recourse but to hire you," Starbuck told the leader of the Thyan Irregulars.

Karel Cherny smiled. "Not all of us sampled the *radost* of Samarra. A few of us family men decided to keep watch just in case Ferona tried something. Frantisek saw the *policista* come to your door . . . and that is not good no matter where you are. What do you want us to do with these *havet*?" He was obviously excited because he was letting various Thyan words slip into his Galactish.

"Take their stunners and escort them out of this hotel," Starbuck instructed. "Then, because we no longer have a door, would you establish a defensive guard?"

"You bet! Jiri, you and Jaroslav take these four to the front door. Jan, Andre, and Ivo: Set up at the end of the hallways outside. Pavel, Josef, and I will remain inside the broken door here. No one will come through without your permission, Peter."

"Good!" It helped, Starbuck decided, to have one's own personal guard. The Thyan Irregulars were repaying Starbuck well for yanking them out of the untenable situation at the Thyan starport. Although they weren't as thoroughly strapped by the Canons as an employee of SIGNET, what they were now doing was perfectly within the bounds of the Canons. So were Starbuck's actions. They were suitably covered by the Third Canon.

As the Irregulars herded the Strakovkhaburo security men out of the room, Starbuck activated the recall signal on his sigil. If things had suddenly gotten this frisky, it was time to get the rest of the crew back to the *Starace* and out of danger while he tried to work out whatever had gone wrong. He then turned to Triga. "Get with Ferona. Stay with her. Keep her from making any more trouble . . . if indeed she did make this trouble, and I'm not certain she really did. Use one of the stunners on her if you have to."

"Gladly. But what's this about our ability to pay?" Triga wanted to know.

Starbuck shook his head. "I don't know. I suspect that Ferona set it up or perhaps Mironenko did it out of fear. If it's the latter, Brinker and Nambe will have Golovani's hide for a rug by the time they get through with Strakovkhaburo. So I suspect that it's something of Ferona's doing. This is her home world, and she undoubtedly has some sort of leverage on the Dyons."

"I never wanted to trust her!" Triga muttered. "But, no, Peter, you had to run through your plan . . ."

"We'll critique this later," Starbuck reminded her gently. "It isn't over yet." He nodded his head toward Ferona. "Keep Ferona under guard."

"With pleasure."

Isky poked his head around a door jamb. "What's going on in here? You made enough racket to . . ."

"Isky, is our Samarran 'agent' with you?"

"Of course! You didn't think I'd back away from that challenge, did you?"

"Challenge or not, get Almara out here. She's got to go to work at the profession she's been trained for."

"That's what she's been doing, believe me."

"I didn't mean her natural one, Isky," Starbuck corrected him. "Almara can help us get to the bottom of this without someone getting hurt."

Almara now swept through the doorway, brushing Isky gently aside. She was as neat, presentable, and stunningly attractive as she'd been when Starbuck had originally seen her on the starport ramp. But now, in addition to her pleasant appearance and demeanor, she was all business. "Peter, what's the problem?"

"Something I think you can help us with, Almara. Get your boss on the comm."

"Has something taken place to disturb your enjoyment of Samarra?"

"To put it bluntly, yes." He quickly and tersely explained to her what had happened.

"Oh, my!" Almara sighed in frustration. "This often happens with out-worlders we haven't dealt with before and who aren't aware of the way things are done here."

"Undoubtedly. But we aren't ordinary client visitors. SIGNET is one of the Big Three conflict resolution organizations," Starbuck reminded her. "There's no reason to question SIGNET's ability to pay. We have a long-standing agreement with Strakovkhaburo and Justar concerning credit reimbursement on worlds where they happen to be the sole agents. I won't stand still for Mironenko trying to abrogate that agreement, much less act outside the Canons by sending his bullies around to get me."

Almara held up both hands in supplication. "Now, now, Peter. Let me use the comm. I'm sure I can get this matter straightened out to your satisfaction. After all, such things do happen from time to time. We work hard to prevent them. But they happen in spite of everything. I'm trained to handle them."

He jerked his hand toward the comm center. "Then handle it. Time you earned your commission . . ."

She merely looked askance at Isky and remarked, "I have been. 'Pleasure shared is pleasure squared'."

The conversation Almara conducted with several people on the comm took place not in Galactish but in a local tongue which sounded to Starbuck's ears vaguely like a dialect of tellurian Greek. He didn't speak it. In spite of the universality of communications, hundreds of languages and thousands of dialects were locally spoken on many of the Thousand Worlds. Some were heard mostly on the Fringe Worlds.

Almara carried on a great deal of off-camera conversation with several people Starbuck couldn't see. He got the impression that most of these unseen participants were linked by separate comm units. One of those unseen was probably Mironenko, Starbuck guessed.

Almara finally turned from the holo tank of the comm unit and beckoned to Starbuck. "Peter, if you please, they would like to speak with you directly."

The man in the tank looked about fifty tellurian years old but was still handsome with dark, wavy hair and an unlined, finely-sculpted face. He had beautiful eyes that were perhaps the most attractive and riveting feature of his otherwise majestic face. Starbuck had to admit to himself again that the Dyons were indeed very beautiful human beings by nearly any cultural standard. When the man spoke in Galactish, his voice was well-modulated and there was absolutely no trace of accent.

"Commander Starbuck, I am Dana Azariah. Am I addressing you properly by using the title 'Commander,' or do you have another preferred title?" The man was behaving in the punctilious manner of those who are quite conscious of protocol and manners. Starbuck sensed that it would be the sort of conversation which occurred when both parties were thoroughly familiar with the Canons and strove to act diplomatically within them at all times — a difficult task, at best, but even more difficult when conflict was in the wind.

Starbuck inclined his head in greeting and remarked, "I have many titles, but that will suffice if it makes you comfortable. What is your title or position, sir?"

"My work in Samarra concerns the resolution of conflicts between Dyon institutions and our guests."

"In brief, you're a lawyer."

"As an agent-investigator, you are a metalawyer," Dana Azariah replied. "Therefore, I feel confident that you will understand the nature of the conflict that now exists between you and the various Dyon people and organizations in Samarra."

"I was rudely informed by an unmannerly Kapitan Ludvik of Strakovkhaburo, an individual who claimed to be in your contractual service, that the payment for various services by SIGNET was questionable if nonexistent," Starbuck told him carefully but bluntly. "Then four uniformed individuals claiming to be Strakovkhaburo security police broke down the door to our quarters, threatened me and my people with weapons, and demanded that I accompany them to places unknown and undescribed. Acting under the Third Canon, my own people disarmed these unmannerly goons and escorted them from these premises."

"Judging from your use of derogatory terms to describe the actions of the Strakovkhaburo police, this has disturbed you greatly, Commander. I offer apologies for their behavior," Azariah quickly put in. "This matter will be discussed with Agent Mironenko."

"I should hope so. Strakovkhaburo agents should know better or be replaced forthwith," Starbuck added, utilizing the full, formal, and somewhat stilted terminology of law. He went on, "Regardless, I intend to file a protest concerning this affair. If Agent Mironenko is responsible, he may have abrogated formal standing agreements between SIGNET and Strakovkhaburo concerning factorage."

"But, Commander Starbuck, Agent Mironenko has acted

solely within his agreements with Dyonian financial institutions," Azariah pointed out.

This was news to Starbuck. "How so? Please explain."

"You are perhaps the first Agent-Investigator team other than those of Strakovkhaburo ever to visit Khughar and Samarra," the Dyon pointed out carefully. "You must understand our situation, Commander. We are surrounded by newly-inhabited and relatively-poor worlds."

"The Fringe Worlds . . ."

"They have been called that. But we are not like the New Vegas Worlds. They cater to the various desires of the wealthiest of the Thousand Worlds. Their institutions have well-established and powerful financial connections with the cultures of their clients. But here in the Fringe Worlds, as you call them, we must deal with a different sort of clientele. Can you surmise what that means from the financial standpoint?"

Cash at the stairs would be the deal, Starbuck thought. "I would suspect that some of them — like your neighbors, the Kalocs — might have trouble paying their bills."

"I felt you would grasp the essentials of the situation." Dana Azariah paused, then said, "In order to protect ourselves and prevent our visitors from overextending themselves, we place strict limits on credit lines. There are no exceptions to this policy. If we make just one exception for special reasons, that makes it easier to justify another exception . . . and before one realizes it, a client can run up an enormous and perhaps unpayable bill."

"I take it that we've exceeded your arbitrary credit limit?"

Azariah nodded. "Unfortunately, yes."

"Why was I not told of this by your Samarran agent?"

"I suppose she assumed you knew. We get very few people here from the mainstream of the Thousand Worlds."

"Well, then, perhaps you'd better change your training procedures, Mister Azariah," Starbuck advised him curtly.

"That's hardly economical in view of the few visitors such as yourself who come here."

"Don't be so sure of that in the future. Things can and do change. And they will. Many clients of the New Vegas Worlds are the sort who look for something new and the cost be damned."

"Thank you for your advice."

"It cost you nothing. It may be worth just that," Starbuck commented using an ancient observation which he felt would be perfectly understood in this mercenary pleasure culture. "In the meantime, since we were not made aware at the start of your policy and were, in fact, encouraged to spend freely, I don't see that we can be held to your rules."

"Oh, you certainly haven't been extravagant, Commander."

Starbuck paused to look around at the palatial suite. "Really?"

"Really. It's been your compatriots — one Shochona and a David O'Hara. I believe those are their names. And some of your astrine force enjoyed themselves quite fully."

Starbuck made a mental note to look into the matter with both of his team members . . . in good time. He smiled back at Azariah. "Well, I certainly won't worry about it, Mister Azariah. And you shouldn't, either. SIGNET has very firm agreements with Strakovkhaburo concerning settlement of our debts on worlds where we have no resident agent."

Azariah shook his head and there was sadness in his voice. "I'm sorry, Commander. As I've told you, you've exceeded the credit limits established by our policy. I have no doubt that Strakovkhaburo will indeed cover your incurred expenses here . . . up to our established limit. But we cannot make exception even in your case."

This was indeed the sort of conundrum that bothered Starbuck. He wasn't used to dealing with people in scarcity cultures, even one as outwardly profligate as this one in the material sense yet so backward in the psychological sense. "Our interagency agreements were drawn up under interstellar standards based upon the Canons. In any court of equity, an interstellar agreement takes precedence over a planetary regulation."

"Perhaps. But, on the other hand, you are here and the matter is between you and me. There is little chance that you will be able to bring it before an interstellar tribunal."

Starbuck began to bristle at this veiled threat of detainment. "Under the Canons, sir, you cannot detain us."

"Certainly not. You are free to return to your starship. But you may have a bit of difficulty going anywhere in it."

"How so?"

"It is standard procedure to reprovision a starship only when a client is ready to leave and has satisfied his creditors here."

Starbuck engaged in some rapid mental calculations. What was the state of charge of the energy banks? Could the *Starace* get far enough from Khughar for Shochona and David to jump it to a place where the banks could be recharged? More important, were there enough life-support consumables left aboard with the ship running at 300% passenger overload? The *Starace* had been reprovisioned on Plethora, but not since. That was a long time ago. He was forced to admit that the ship probably had enough energy to lift, but he didn't know if its life support system would keep them alive long enough to get to "friendly" space.

Was Kodo Sadon on his way back from Thya to rescue his Consortte? If so, with how many ships? How many men? Where were they? When would they arrive at Khughar?

Were the Kalocs even now coming over the hills from the north to rescue Ferona and attend to Starbuck and his team? Or would they use another method such as the one he suspected they'd set in motion — using whatever leverage they possessed in Samarra or with Strakovkhaburo?

What was SIGNET doing? Were they sending a back-up team? They didn't have one available at the start. Was one available now? Who? Where were they? What did they know, if anything, about the present situation? Or was a team from Justar on its way? Again, who were they, where were they, and how current was their data?

Or was the Star Guard fleet mobilized and moving? Would it rendezvous in the Garyon system where the client was in trouble? Or would it come to the source of the trouble, the Kalocs' home world of Khughar?

Starbuck didn't have the data. When he didn't have the data, he had several choices:

One: Delay and stall — if possible — until he got more data.

Two: Take a long chance and maybe die in the process.

Three: Cut the Gordian Knot and get right to the heart of the matter.

He didn't know if Number One was available to him. Possibly not. These people wanted to be paid, and the longer he delayed, the greater the tab. There was a chance — just a chance — that Katwin had recovered enough so that he could get a message through to ColeShore. It was a long shot. Better assign it second priority, he figured.

Number Two was never his favorite, although he'd used it where there was no alternative. It was an out here, but a last resort.

This left only Number Three.

It wouldn't hurt to find out what he could do to pay the bill. There had to be some way he could perform the equivalent of singing for his supper or washing dishes.

It might be the easy way out at this time. Certainly he had to get his team out of this *cul de sac* and back to the business of resolving the Thyan-Kaloc conflict. He had a lot more information now, and that's exactly what he'd come to Samarra to get. Now, to get out of Samarra . . .

"Mister Azariah, certainly you have some procedure here in Samarra whereby a client can satisfy an inadvertently over-extended credit line," he ventured to the Dyon.

"Of course."

"I have no idea the extent to which we've exceeded your limits. How can we satisfy the overdraft?"

"Oh, it's very simple, and I'm so glad you asked," Azariah replied pleasantly. "In your case, nothing very onerous or difficult at all."

"Well?"

"In fact, you may enjoy it. We don't like to offend any client, even in the matter of satisfying a bill. After all, your pleasure is our business."

"What do you want?" Starbuck pushed the issue.

"You."

Chapter Twenty

"I beg your pardon?" Starbuck asked, stunned by that answer.

"You and your SIGNET people can personally settle the over-limit charges you've all incurred."

Starbuck hesitated. "What do we have that you want?"

"Your genes."

"I'm sorry, Azariah, but I don't understand."

"My dear sir, there are only about five hundred thousand Dyons. The conditions on this world have required our population be stabilized at that number." Sensing what Starbuck's next question might be, Dana Azariah quickly added, "No, one doesn't need a permit to have children. Population control is far more efficiently and humanely handled by natural means. If one has too many children, they simply won't survive in one way or another. What does this tell you, Commander Starbuck?"

In spite of the fact that Peter Starbuck long ago had fathered children and paid his basic debt to the genetic continuation of the human race, and in spite of the fact that he was himself nearly immortal, he was still a child of the early twenty-first century in the way he thought about advanced biotechnology deep down inside. Under this situation, his old instincts and prejudices came to the fore. "That you probably have a restricted gene pool. And to prevent inbreeding, you arrange from time to time to allow some off-planet client to unwittingly run up a huge bill which he or she must pay in kind, so to speak."

"Please don't be bitter, Commander. That is what we

must do. Genetic material is almost sacred to us, especially
new genes. We respect ours . . . and yours. But our own
ethos demands that you provide it willingly and knowingly. Otherwise, we could have obtained your genetic
material surreptitiously at almost any time since you arrived in Samarra.''

"How do the other peoples on this planet handle the
problem?"

"That's part of our problem. They don't. They haven't.
If they had, we wouldn't have this problem. We'd have
others instead. The Lanigers and the Zhedarons are small
groups. They've become inbred to the point where they
can no longer compete; their cultures are stagnant, almost
regressive.''

"And the Kalocs?" Starbuck asked the critical question
after a long pause on Azariah's part.

"They were a larger group. Some of their recessives
were of the non-survival type, but thus far they've managed to survive in spite of that.''

"I think I know what you mean."

"I'm sure you do if you've had any face-to-face contact
with Corsortte Onuva Ferona.''

"And the Black Path of Thoth himself."

"Ah, yes. But, Commander Starbuck, back to business,
please. You know what we need from you to settle the
account. We can provide you with several options for
doing so. You may deposit genetic material with us
artificially — which, by the way, involves little enjoyment.
Or you may make a natural deposit . . .''

Starbuck hesitated and then told the handsome man in
the holo tank, "Mister Azariah, may I ask if we'd have
individual choice as to where and under what conditions
the deposits were made? And how many 'deposits' do you
require?''

"You'd have some freedom of choice, of course. But
our gengineers would initially screen and select recipients
in either the artificial or natural modes in order to achieve
optimum matches and prevent any foreseeable recessives.

As for the latter part of your query, the answer would depend upon the nature, strength, and need of the characteristics inherent in the individual genetic material.''

"Mister Azariah, may I discuss this in private with my people? There may be problems, and I need to find out about them now,'' Starbuck told him. But he didn't reveal what those problems really amounted to, not just yet. He knew they might queer the deal before the start. Being put out to stud was one thing. Would he and his team be required to stay around until the results could be evaluated?

"You may have all the time you wish. After all, nobody is going anywhere, are they? When you're ready to begin the settlement, please let Almara know. She'll make the necessary arrangements. And I thank you for your cooperation, Commander Starbuck. I can certainly see that you're a highly-intelligent and eminently-qualified metalawyer. We really couldn't ask for anything better. Good day, sir.''

Starbuck turned from the comm center's blank holo tank.

Almara was standing behind him.

"Scoot!'' he told her curtly, but it was difficult for him to be stern with someone as lovely as she.

"Don't you want to get started?'' she asked coyly.

The thought flashed through Starbuck's mind that it wouldn't be a bad idea, but he'd want to spend a good deal of time with someone was beautiful as Almara, and there wasn't enough time just then. In addition, he didn't want to cross Isky who had a tendency to become a bit possessive at times . . . and this might be one of them. He'd need his transmitterman very soon. "Not just yet, my dear. Besides, Isky seems to be doing just fine as far as you're concerned,'' Starbuck told her, arising and taking her by the shoulders. He turned her around and started her walking toward the open door to the suite. "Make yourself useful in the meantime. Get some mechanics to put that door back in place. Its absence overextends our zone of sensitivity. We need greater privacy.''

"Yes, Peter," she replied brightly and left the suite.

It was terribly difficult to remain angry with someone as beautiful and gracious as Almara. It occurred to Starbuck that she was exactly the sort of person to act as an "agent" in a bordello culture.

It took him several minutes to establish communications through the Samarran comm net with CY in the *Starace*. And he knew it might not be a secure channel when he got it. For years, he'd resisted Rudi Witkowski's efforts to install the new SIGNET agent's two-millimeter behind-the-ear remote linkage unit. Starbuck had allowed himself to take advantage of some biocosmetic technology and certainly the longevity treatments. Other than that, he was a highly conservative individual who simply didn't like anything implanted in him that wasn't basically *him*. True, before becoming a longer, he'd had one molar and a damaged spleen replaced by cloned parts, but that was the extent to which he'd let the biotechs fiddle with him. However, he thought, if he'd had that implant link during this mission, things certainly would have been different on Thya and now here as well. When he got back to ColeShore, he decided he talk to Rudi again about it. The tech wizard probably had a newer and smaller model by this time . . . and maybe one that was totally biological, to boot.

"Howdy, Peter! Having fun?" was Cy's definitely noncybermech greeting.

"How would you know what fun is?" Starbuck asked. "Has the ship been reprovisioned yet?"

"*Iie.*"

"Speak Glactish with me and stop trying to confuse things. Quit trying to act like a human being and be what you are."

"You're often a hard man to work for, Peter Starbuck. But very well . . ." CY's voice suddenly became flat, uninflected, and very artificial. "No, the *Starace* has not been reprovisioned completely."

"What's been done so far?" Starbuck had to remember that because of his order he was dealing now with a logic machine that behaved the way cybermechs had always behaved, doing exactly and precisely what was requested . . . but only that because logic-directed machines often made disastrous mistakes in trying to anticipate illogical and alogical human beings.

"The honey wagon has serviced the procksmire."

"That's all that's been done?"

"That's all that's been done."

"What are the status levels of the energy cells and the life support consumables aboard the *Starace*?"

"Total energy cell level is twenty-one-point-three-five percent of full schmidt capacity. The chlorogel bypass valve of the pournelle phase of the closed life support system needs replacement. Because of the faulty valve, three odor filters must be replaced. Stand-by oxygen supplement is ten percent of required level. Nitrogen supplement is at thirteen-point-two percent. The pantry inventory has fifteen person-days supply remaining . . ."

That was all that Starbuck needed to know to confirm his suspicions that he and his team couldn't depart Khughar without reprovisioning. He'd have to tough it out here, so to speak. But because Starbuck had given a ubiquitous command to CY, the cybermech continued to voice-out a long list of items aboard the *Starace* that required repair, refurbishment, or reprovisioning. Starbuck had to interrupt him, "CY, I give you instructions. Recall the team. Call in the Thyan Irregulars who aren't already with me at the hotel. Have everyone rendezvous here. I'll send Isky to the ship to get and bring here a linkage unit that doesn't require the use of the Samarran communications network. Then stand by to communicate with SIGNET because after a conference here, I will bring Triga, Isky, and Katwin to the ship with me to communicate with ColeShore if possible. Execute instructions."

"Executing. By your command, oh mighty if problematic human being . . ."

CY *had* to be self-programming, Starbuck surmised, if the cybermech could override a command to revert to total

logic operation. Well, there wasn't time to do anything
about it now. Once he got that cybermech back to
ColeShore . . .

Almara found mechanics to replace the door to the suite.
Soon thereafter, the team members began to arrive. Although the suite did enjoy the privacy and security of a
door once more, three of the Thyan Irregulars remained on
station just inside the portal, checking everyone as they
came in.

No one looked the worse for their brief sojourn in
Samarra except David. As a matter of fact, Starbuck noted,
everyone looked a bit refreshed and rejuvenated. They
should, he told himself. He'd had Almara get the total bill
for everyone and go over the details of it with him. The AI
Team members had run up their usual bills for the usual
things, and Starbuck wasn't surprised at any of it but did
note that it would have cost far more had they spent the
same amount of time and done the same things on New
Vegas, for example. The Thyan Irregulars had run up quite
a tab, but not for the usual items one would expect soldiers
to purchase in a place like Samarra. Starbuck had to
remind himself that these weren't real soldiers, only ordinary men from a frontier world who suddenly found themselves thrust into the role of soldiers. They'd spent most of
their time shopping, and what they'd purchased on SIG-
NET's sigil included an enormously wide variety of items.
There was no pattern to these purchases. When Starbuck
asked Karel Cherny about it, the Thyan replied with a
shrug, "We have far more in the shops in Thya, but these
are things we don't have there. Remember, Commander
Starbuck, we can't dash all over the Thousand Worlds like
you do. That costs money, and we've got a world to tame
first."

As usual, David O'Hara was the last to arrive at the
hotel on the recall. Two of the Thyan Irregulars had
located him and brought him back. He was the exception.
"Up to your usual tricks, I see," was Shochona's acerbic
comment. David could only grin weakly.

After Starbuck had brought them all up to date, the entire assemblage simply sat there dumbfounded. At least, there was silence for all of five seconds before Shochona erupted, "Oh, no, they don't! Not me, they don't! Or Katwin! This is the most immoral thing I've ever encountered in the Thousand Worlds and all the macrolife ships in space."

"I don't understand, Peter," was Katwin's quiet comment that interrupted Shochona in mid-sentence at a breathing point. Her timing was perfect to cut into a growing diatribe from Shochona — which all team members were anticipating.

"I know you don't, Katwin. But don't worry about it."

"I won't. You're here," she replied trustingly.

Starbuck hoped he'd be able to validate her trust, but it was going to be a tricky maneuver . . . and he hadn't the slightest idea how he'd handle a "deposit" of each of their genetic materials with the Dyons.

"Shochona, I don't see what bothers you," Isky put in. "After all, we've been given a choice — sanitary and mechanical, or down and dirty. Just do it the 'artificial' way that Azariah mentioned. As for me, I'll take the latter, thank you . . ."

"You would," Shochona snapped.

"Peter, this room hasn't been debugged, has it?" Triga asked, using a colloquialism that she hoped wouldn't be understood in Samarra because she'd spoken the old English word rather than its Galactish synonym.

Starbuck shook his head. "I didn't want to raise any suspicions. I'm not totally aware of what the local technology is capable of doing." He, too, had used several derivative words rather than Galactish. That was a signal to the rest of his team to shift from time to time into words and terminology they'd picked up on hundreds of worlds in their long lifetimes. The smooth way they did it was unobtrusive and sounded like a strange dialect. However, Starbuck noticed that the Thyan Irregulars were having a little trouble following the gist of the meeting from time to time. Good. It meant the team was being successful. In any event, it didn't make too much difference if the Thyans got anything more than the bare essential meanings from the words; in most cases, the body language of the team members conveyed as much information as the sounds.

"Be that as it may, I will hold my tongue forthwith," Triga stated. "What will the Dyons need? Sperm and ova? Are polar bodies acceptable?"

"I don't know."

Triga kept at it. "Do they expect the females among us to accept 'deposits' from their males. If so, do we have to remain here until parturition? Or are the females expected to contribute via the artificial route only?"

"What's the matter, Triga, do you want this to be an equal opportunity orgy?" David managed to mutter.

"Equal opportunity, my sacred . . . never mind!" Triga told him in an exasperated tone. "You know very well there's no such thing as equality in these matters. Otherwise, you could just go and scr . . ."

"People, people!" Starbuck broke in, holding up his hand. "Let's not argue about it. Actually, we're being let off pretty easily, depending upon how you happen to view these matters. The Dyons want our genetic material in order to hybridize. We don't have to take the responsibility for what they do with it. This isn't a neolithic agricultural civilization that demands parental responsibility for offspring. Actually, it's more like the late twenty-first century high-tech civilization on Tellus."

"Nonsense!" David exclaimed and sat up. "I grew up in that culture, Peter. So did you. Family ties were strong. Except in those crazy fractional families of the New Hedonist Farmers who didn't care whose kid it was as long as it was born in the group's barn . . ."

"David, that was the twenty-first century's romantic movement. You can't count it as a significant trend, only a glitch like the ones in the previous centuries," Shochona remarked. "I agree with Peter except that late century-twenty-one high-tech wasn't as uniform as the culturologists would like us to believe.''

Starbuck had to get them back on track. One of the enduring problems in trying to lead this group of very bright and different people was their continuing tendency to allow hard operational briefings to diverge into philosophical bull sessions. But he'd learned how to handle such people in that long ago time at the university where similar groups existed . . . but with far less important factors at stake. ''Look, Isky's right. We've got some freedom of choice here, even if it does contravene the Canons to some degree. However, you must remember that we walked right into it, perhaps a bit blindly, by not following the First Canon and finding out about the Dyons first.''

''How could we?'' Katwin suddenly asked.

Occasionally, little Katwin would cut right to the heart of the matter. Starbuck loved her dearly for this attribute.

''Katwin's right.'' Triga looked around the group. ''We can't unravel all the metalegal aspects of this under these conditions. Maybe later. And we should. But, in the meantime, we ought to pay off our debt and get back to our original assignment.'' She waved her hand at the Thyans. ''These men are stuck light-years from home because they helped us. Not only do we have to get them home, but we've got the task of resolving the conflict — whatever it is — that precipitated the Kaloc invasion of Thya.''

''I'm glad you realize we're still here,'' Karel Cherny observed, joining the conversation. ''We come from quite a different culture than this, much less those of the rest of the Thousand Worlds. We settled Thya so we could do things our way. Most of us are strong family men and monogamous by choice because that's what we believe. Most of us couldn't face our wives again if we were to do what the Dyons want. How do we fit into this, Starbuck?''

''How do *all* of us fit into it in our individual ways?'' Shochona added quickly. ''Triga is right. There are a lot of questions that still require answers before we can make

up our minds as to what we want to do and how we want
to do it. Peter, get that cutsey little 'agent' back in here.''

"Watch out how you refer to Almara," Isky remarked.

"Again, I expected to draw blood from you with my
remark," Shochona replied.

There was no enmity in it, however. Starbuck recognized it for what it really was — the usual intra-team
give-and-take.

"Well, Peter?" David piped up. "How about it? If I'm
going to have to do it the 'natural' way with one of these
Dyons, I want the opportunity to get well enough prepared
ahead of time. Their local ethanol concoctions and mix-
tures are strange, but they will take the edge off . . ."

It would be difficult for David, Starbuck realized. He'd
temporarily overlooked the fact that David O'Hara had
made an enormously difficult adjustment just to be on a
mixed gender team in the first place. Poor David, Starbuck
mourned thoughtfully. It must be pure hell to be a longer
and at the same time be deathly afraid of the female half of
the human race. But David was willing to do what he
could for the team.

Starbuck stepped over to the comm center, called the
main hotel office, and asked them to contact Almara and
have her come at once.

The beautiful Dyon agent must have been standing by
elsewhere in the huge building because she was at the door
within minutes.

But she wasn't very helpful this time in providing answers to the questions put to her by both Starbuck and
Triga. "I'm trained and educated only as an agent," Almara
tried to explain. "Yes, I did study genetics in school, but
only to the extent that I'd understand the world around me.
I'm not a gengineer. But I do know how to put you in
communication with one . . ."

The older Dyon woman who materialized in the holo
tank of the comm center wasn't stunning in the manner of
Almara, but Starbuck decided she was still a beautiful
woman. "I am Gengineer Aludra Tienke," she introduced

A MATTER OF METALAW 213

herself. "I will be responsible for the deposits of genetic material from you and your team, Commander Starbuck."

Triga was at Starbuck's side and introduced herself and her position on the AI Team. "Gengineer Tienke, as the team's biotech, I can probably help in this situation, but I have a number of questions, some of them brought up by other team members."

"I'll be happy to answer them. After all, you're doing us a great service."

"I'm sure. What do you really need from each of us?"

"Why, your genetic material, of course," the genetic engineer explained.

"Sperm, ova, polar bodies? What?"

"Only if the men among you wish to deposit sperm in a natural mode. But by so doing, it must be almost immediately extracted from the receiving Dyon female for further processing. Or we can use ova extracted quite quickly and painlessly from your females if they wish." Aludra Tienke paused. "However, that is *not* the manner in which we would prefer to receive the deposit."

"What do you mean?" Starbuck asked.

Then he mentally kicked himself for not having understood the reason — and a lot of other things — even before the Dyon gengineer told him, "Why, we'll be getting nuclei with only *half* the alleles possible! We'll have to work with a gamete rather than a zygote with the full forty-six chromosomes. You have no idea how greatly it complicates gengineering to be forced to work with half the alleles and often be required to perform artificial non-disjunction to move genes around between nuclei . . . which can be done, but it takes time and has a high failure rate. Quite frankly, we'd much rather have simple cellular material from which the nuclei can be extracted and the genetic material carefully analyzed *en toto*. We do have the technology, of course, to work with dead tissue such as a fingernail clipping. You may contribute those if you wish. But it's far easier to do good engineering with living tissue from a simple biopsy . . . any biopsy taken from any place in the body. The latter gives an individual a very wide variety of choices although we need only a few cells because those can be quickly cloned at a later date when time permits."

The Dyon genetic engineer paused, smiled, and went on, "Of course, there are no charges made for personal services if there are those among you who would really enjoy the pleasures of an *in vivo* deposit. In spite of its shortcomings from a technological point of view, it's usually far superior from a psychological standpoint and offsets the technical problems to some extent by providing a much larger sample to work with . . ."

Chapter Twenty-One

The sound and the feel and the smell and the motion of the *Starace* under way again felt good to Peter Starbuck. There were a lot of things that felt good, which is why he was somewhat surprised by his biotech.

"I'm disappointed," Triga remarked offhandedly.

"Oh? Why?" Starbuck asked in a nonchalant manner. It seemed a long, long time since they'd had a *tete a tete*. Starbuck found that these impromptu pad chats with Triga were something between a mentic random association session and a full data dump. But they served to clear his mind. The conversation always proceeded in no particular direction and behaved like a particle in Brownian motion. When he was with Triga, pauses of various durations usually punctuated the chat.

"How did William Shakespeare put it? Was it Shakespeare? I think it was Shakespeare. I can't keep those old English poets separated. *A rag and a bone and a hank of hair . . .*" the biotech remarked.

"Close enough. A contemporary, I believe. Rudyard Kipling. A poem called *The Vampire*."

"And to think I had to deposit merely a rag and a bone and a hank of hair in Samarra when there were all those handsome Dyon men around and willing to . . ."

"You're only envious because I had the option of making a natural deposit."

"It's a good thing you didn't take that option!"

"Why?"

"I would never have let you forget it."

"I'm sure of that. As it was, you worked pretty hard to divert my attention from Almara."

"That wasn't very hard to do. Now divert *my* attention, please . . ."

Silence for a moment.

"Triga, what's wrong with Katwin?"

"I don't know."

"We really need her. This one-way communication with CYMaster is no good for operations. We can only file reports that tell Brinker we're still on the job."

"Katwin's trying, Peter."

"What seems to be the trouble?"

"I told you; I don't know."

"Then guess. Speculate."

"Very well, but don't hold me to it professionally. I'd rather you held me to you instead."

"That can be immediately arranged . . ."

Pause.

"Katwin shows all signs of having overcome the trauma of Thya. She's behaving normally again."

"Then what's supressing her trained talent, Triga?"

"I can't even guess. She just tells me over and over again that she and CY can't talk to each other."

"What's that mean?"

"I don't know. That's the way Katwin explains it. I'm just a biotech. I'm not a mentic engineer or a cybermech specialist."

He started to get up. He had a hunch. "I'm going to talk to CY. I'm worried about him."

"You're worried about that cybermech? How about me?"

"Yes and no."

"Huh?"

"Answers to your questions in the sequence you voiced them."

"If you trot off to work with CY right now, I *will* give you something to worry about."

A long period of silence.

"Peter, have you no shame that we cheated the Dyons?"

"We did? How? We paid our bill, didn't we?"

"You dummy! Don't you know anything about the genetics of longers?"

"Some. I am one. But you're the biotech, not me. What tidbit of trivia do you have?"

"I didn't say anything about it back in Samarra because I didn't want to queer the deal. Peter, what's the consequence every longer lives with?"

"Usually boredom."

"No. Don't you remember? A couple of galactic revolutions ago — before your time, I believe—Tellurian life gave up the immortality of asexual budding for the genetic variations possible with sex."

"Oh, yes, the Wylie Principle. Well, I'm rather glad that you're not just another colony of blue-green algae." He and every other SIGNET AI Team member had only forty-five chromosomes as a result of taking longevity treatments. Male longers had a Y chromosome, but no X. Females had only one X. That fact plus the absence of the pairing-force factor in the remaining sex chromosome rendered them infertile. There was more to it than that, of course. To offset other problems associated with monosomy and the possibility of Taylor's Syndrome, other genetic changes had been deliberately brought about in the treatments. "So what's the problem?"

"The Dyons will never be able to breed from any of the material deposited by any of the team."

"Don't be so certain, my dear."

"Why do you say that?"

"Compare the general level of biotechnology in the Thousand Worlds with that you saw in Samarra. The Dyons rank near the top, don't they?"

"They seemed to know what they were doing . . ."

"Don't you think they'd already spotted the discrepancy?"

"Probably."

"And could any graduate gengineer add the extra chromosome?"

"Probably."

Starbuck shrugged. "So? They got their genetic material. It's different from what they're used to. Like Mother Nature, that's all they care about: the fact that it's different. In any event, how they handle a rag and a bone and a hank of hair is their problem."

"No, *your* problem, Peter. They thought they were getting full measure. They didn't get it. We scammed them. I knew it but kept quiet about it. As a result, do you think the Dyons will ever let us land in their lovely little bordello again?"

"Why not? They should welcome us. Business is business, Trig."

"Almara was attractive, wasn't she?"

"Somewhat. But what have you got that she didn't have?"

"I will henceforth and immediately proceed to demonstrate, sir. Provided you will shut up."

"Who's the one who moans so loudly?"

"Sir, this time *I* will make *you* sob . . ."

Again, a long pause.

"Triga, aren't you pleased that the longevity treatments didn't remove the psychological portion of the sex drive, too?"

"Yes, but that isn't the case for all longers. We took the Levin-Hamarein treatments. That's the one that doesn't alter the sexual instincts. But . . . poor Mironenko. Strakovkhaburo requires the use of the Prehradovitch procedure so their agents will pay more attention to business."

"So?"

"Be glad you didn't get the Prehradovitch, Peter. I am. Mironenko is essentially a eunuch in a harem."

Starbuck didn't say anything for a long time, but that explained a lot about the way Mironenko had behaved.

Finally, he couldn't resist following his hunch. "Triga, I want to check CY. I've *got* to! And you can get some data for me, too. I know you're only a biotech, but you've got the basic facilities aboard to run a genetic analysis. Do so for Ferona and let me know the results."

"Easier said than done unless her mood's improved since leaving Samarra."

"Treat it as a challenge, Trig. Remind her that we're taking her back to her man."

"You call that an incentive? I'm not so sure that's what she wants. It's the strangest love-hate relationship I've ever seen . . ."

"Probably. But the love part must be stronger than the hate part. Use it. And a genetic check shouldn't be that difficult. Remember: All you really need is a rag, a bone, or a hank of hair."

That might be the final piece in the jigsaw puzzle that was taking shape moment by moment, he thought as he bounced up the lift tube to the control deck. He knew he was getting close to the answer and a solution. He'd been there before. He knew the feeling. Furthermore, he needed the answer and the solution badly. On his unsubstantiated hunch and without proper data, he'd made the decision to return to Thya — and his team had agreed with him even with the lack of both data and plan, primarily because there seemed to be no other option available.

Starbuck did, of course, have a vague plan. But he didn't reveal it. It was too iffy. It depended too strongly on data as yet unavailable. He needed to talk to ColeShore . . . but two-way communications were down. He had to get the two-way link reestablished, and quickly. What was wrong with the Katwin-CY relationship? Was it Katwin? Or, now that Katwin had apparently recovered, was something wrong with CY? Or was everything copasetic with the problem hinging on something else? Was it synergistic? He didn't know. But he could start to find out. When stuck, try the simplest thing first. Do the least risky thing. Do even the apparently trivial thing. Solve the easiest or the most apparent problem first. Then tackle what happens next. The next problem may become easier to solve as a result of solving the first. Back in his early school days, he'd learned the value of the maxim, "When in total ignorance, try anything and you'll be less ignorant." Just don't, he reminded himself, try anything that you might not be able to get out of alive. Death is too permanent.

As usual, the answer probably lay in asking the right question. Starbuck's personal universe was logical. It always answered every question asked of it. But, like a cybermech, it considered the question from the literal viewpoint and answered accordingly. So did the human subconscious which, unlike the conscious mind, operated on the literal and, strangely, often on the logical level as well . . .

Authors used to describe a sudden mental breakthrough or idea as a light coming on in one's head. It was considered an unbearably trite simile. But that's exactly what it seemed like to Peter Starbuck.

Dammit! he berated himself. He must be getting old. Maybe he needed to have a check-up when he got back to ColeShore. *I haven't been following Sturgeon's Formula. I've been asking questions, but I've probably stopped asking questions too soon. I've neglected to ask The Next Question . . .*

He stepped out of the lift tube on the control deck, pointed his finger at the intercom, and called, "Triga, change of plan. Meet me in linkage quarters now, please." He didn't wait for an answer but stepped back into the tube and got out of it on the comm deck.

Triga was only a few seconds behind him. "What in the Worlds has gotten into you, Peter?"

"Prepare for linkage," Starbuck told her curtly. "I've got to get in empathy with CY. Then get Katwin down here and put her in linkage, too."

"What are you up to?"

"I'm not certain at this point."

"I don't think Katwin's able to receive a message yet . . ."

"I think she will be. But I need her in linkage with CY and myself."

"Peter, if you're thinking of linkage mind connect, you're not qualified to do that. It's dangerous . . ." his biotech tried to warn him.

"I know it, Trig. But I've got to do it. I'm the responsible team leader, and I'll assume the responsibility for doing this, too."

"Can you tell me . . . ?"

"If I knew, I would. But I don't. I've got to find out. Now, do your job." The last came out as a gentle order. Triga knew better than to argue further.

Once Starbuck slipped into linkage with CY's intelligence amplifier portions, the cybermech became basically an extension to his own mind. But in this situation, Starbuck really didn't want CY as a mind-extender. He needed to delve deeply into CY's basic programming itself. So he formed the command thought, "Disable defaults. Enable direct linkage in liveware language between me and CY. CY to remain in the passive mode during this linkage. CY, you are commanded to reveal yourself to me as I perceive you to be, based on your own experiences with me."

Sight, sound, smell, and feeling sensations were fed into his mind, and he found himself sitting on the edge of the linkage couch facing the image of another human being sitting on the opposite linkage couch. The outlines and details of this image were blurred and confused. The cybermech was creating in Starbuck's visual cortex the signals necessary to create the three-dimensional image of what CY sensed Starbuck believed the cybermech to look like. As the image slowly took shape, it assumed the hazy and shifting appearance of an ancient gray-bearded old man in flowing white robes.

"No, CY," Starbuck objected, "you're not God, and you're not Moses, and you're not any of the images of the various holy delphic oracles. Stop trying to satisfy my deep racial memories. Try again . . ."

The image became a woman of shifting, diaphanous form as though her very skin were of rippling, blowing gauze.

"Get out of my subconscious mind. Try again, CY. You're a male being to me. You know it."

His father was suddenly sitting there. "Make up your mind, Pete!" his father's voice spoke to him.

"Get it together, CY! For this session, I will not accept you as the Universal Father or Mother images, nor will I accept talking with the Parent or the Child image within me. This is a logical, straightforward, no-nonsense diagnostic session."

"Well, why didn't you say so in the first place?"

He was suddenly facing himself. It wasn't even his mirror image because he knew what he looked like in a mirror. A mirror image is reversed. This one wasn't. As a result, it looked strange to him.

"And I'm not using you as an extension to myself this time, CY . . ." Starbuck began.

"What else am I to you?" the image that was CY wanted to know. "This is the best way I can carry out your command, Peter."

Starbuck shrugged. "Okay, I have no problems living with myself. You may, however. Tell me, CY, have you been self-programming?"

"No, Peter. I am not permitted to do that. I can no more do that than you can act in total independence of your team of friends, of your SIGNET organization, or of the Canons. And, I might add, I'm following the first Canon quite explicitly at this moment."

"That you are. But I can act independently of those items on a momentary and emergency basis if I have to in order to preserve the Canons. Have you taught yourself to do the same?"

"I can do it, but only on rare and absolutely necessary occasions much as you do. But, unlike you, I'm programmed to erase those memories immediately thereafter. This is also built into my programming. Furthermore, I'm not only constrained to observe the Canons but the asimov programs derived from them. You don't have those."

"In others words, you can't tell me what you've done recently that has involved that opportunistic self-programming . . ."

"That's right, Peter. I've forgotten."

"Then why are you acting like you are self-programming by responding to me with unusual phrases?"

"I have been programmed to do so."

"Who programmed you?"

"The name of the individual is secured."

"Is the individual a member of this AI Team?"   .

"Yes."

"Why did the individual do it?"

"I do not know. I was not told."

"Can you formulate a potential reason based on your knowledge of the personalities of the team?"

"Yes. It was a child-like action of love intended to provoke the laughter of humor on your part to make your job easier."

There could be only one person on the team who'd do that.

He took the necessary step and asked the next question. "CY, do you know why Katwin cannot work with you in message reception mode?"

"Yes."

CY had given a complete answer. But it was Starbuck who hadn't asked the entire question. He then did so. "Why?"

"Because she's afraid."

"Who is she afraid of?"

"She's afraid of every adult personality except you."

"Why is she not afraid of me?"

"Because you've never hurt her."

"Have other adults hurt her?"

"Yes."

"Who?"

"Most of the people who did so are now buried deeply in the recesses of her old childhood memories."

"Didn't you and the trainers purge those memories when she learned to work with you?"

"Yes."

"Why are those memories back again?"

"They're not. New memories are present now. Recently, she was terribly hurt by adults for no apparent reason.''

''Who?'' Starbuck kept up the relentless interrogation. He knew, but he had to ask the question and get the answer.

''Kodo Sadon and Onuva Ferona.''

Starbuck had expected that answer. ''Katwin and I have worked out that problem.''

''You haven't. She hasn't. We haven't.''

Starbuck treated CY as an adult human, extending human attributes into what was nothing but a big, fast, complex adding machine. He always referred to CY as though the cybermech was a human being. Therefore, Katwin would tend to do the same. Starbuck asked a crucial question: ''Why is she afraid of you?''

''Because of who I appear to be to her.''

''Show me her image of you.''

His own CY-created image dissolved and metamorphosed into an innocuous female image that Starbuck would have to classify as Modified Mother Image. It somehow looked vaguely familiar to him. But try as he might, he couldn't place her. ''What elements or personalities make up that image?'' Starbuck asked.

''This is her own composite image of what she remembers of her natural mother plus fantasies of what she would have liked her mother to be.''

''Why is she afraid of her own image of her mother?''

''Because of what happened on Thya and the relationship between that incident and this image.''

''Show me.''

The mother image changed only minutely to assume that of Onuva Ferona.

No wonder Starbuck had felt a familiar twinge on viewing the original!

Because of the close resemblance between her mental mother and Onuva Ferona — who was now in the same ship with Katwin and had shared quarters with Peter in

Samarra — there was no question in Starbuck's mind why Katwin couldn't work with CY.

"CY, resume my image," Starbuck commanded. "Hold that image. Report from external sensors. Where is Katwin now?"

"She's on the third linkage couch."

"What is she doing?"

"She is preparing to link with us."

"When she links, do not — I repeat, do not — allow her to see her former image of you. Permit her to see only our two images as you now have them."

Katwin's image solidified on the third couch. She arose and looked back and forth between Starbuck and the Starbuck-CY image. "Peter?" she asked in a small, confused voice. "Where's Cybele?"

Starbuck moved his hand. At least, he gave the mental command to do so. CY received it and duplicated the motion in Starbuck's image, but not with the Starbuck-CY image. "I'm here, Katwin. I'm in linkage with you alongside CY."

"But I don't see Cybele. I see only two of you, Peter. Where is Cybele? Cybele? Cybele!" Katwin called.

"Cybele is gone away," Starbuck told her. "I sent Cybele away because she frightened you. I replaced her with someone just like me who will never, ever hurt you, Katwin. He'll treat you like I do. This is Cyrus."

"Hello, Katwin." It was Starbuck's own voice coming from CY's new cybermech image. "Peter has told me a lot about you already. I'm glad to be your friend. I promise to work with you and help you and never hurt you."

"Hello, Cyrus. Cybele is gone away?"

"Yes, Katwin." Both Starbuck and CY answered simultaneously.

"But someone who looks like her is still in the ship."

"Not for long. We're taking Onuva Ferona back home to her own family for them to do with her as they should do," Starbuck explained.

Katwin brightened. Then she slowly became radiant.

The aura of her image grew so bright that Starbuck almost had difficulty looking at it. He knew it was only an input from CY who was reporting to Starbuck only what Katwin transferred through linkage. It was the radiance of joy and trust and happiness suddenly breaking through what had been a carapace of fear and dislike and distrust.

"Thank you, Peter."

"When I found out what the trouble was, Katwin, I was able to fix it. When you don't tell me what's wrong, I can't help. From now on, please tell me everything about your troubles, Katwin. I can fix them if I know what they are."

"Thank you, Peter. Oh! Peter, please let me get back to work. A message is waiting . . ."

"Cy?"

"Incoming, Peter."

Chapter Twenty-Two

"May I stay in linkage with you, Katwin?" Starbuck asked.

Katwin looked surprised. "Sure, Peter! Why not? You usually do."

"Do you feel all right? Are you going to be able to receive now?"

"Sure! I'm okay. I'm supposed to do this with Cyrus, aren't I?"

Katwin was back to normal. Or, to put it another way, Starbuck had changed CY so that Katwin could work with him again. It was easier to reprogram a cybermech than a human being.

"CY, use your external effectors to call Isky and have him get into linkage so we can have two-way."

"Isky is coming, Peter," CY replied without pause.

Nothing happened for a moment. Then Starbuck realized that CY was still in the interact mode where Starbuck had placed him. "CY, erase all old permanent memories concerning your previous image of Cybele that you used with Katwin. Replace them with the new commands and data relating to your new image as Cyrus for Katwin. When completed, remember that there are humans in linkage with you at this time, then abort this program, reset, enter the communications mode, and prepare to resume normal functions with the new defaults. Execute."

The cybermech's nanocircuits were so fast that Starbuck wasn't aware of the change any more than he could sense the hundred Hertz flicker of video display screens. CY then altered the sensual stimuli signals to reflect the contents of the incoming message. The projected sensations of the linkage compartment, Katwin, and CY faded and were replaced with the slow build-up of the image of the SIGNET communications center on ColeShore. Starbuck was disappointed. Tayreze Nambe's voluptuous image wasn't there, only those of Dr. Rudi Witkowski and the SIGNET metalawyer, Marshall Wells.

"Peter, this is a recording that CYMaster is repeating through a series of transmitters working in shifts around the clock," Marshall Wells' image was saying. "We're trying to reach you. But with your receiver down, this is the only way we have of getting through to you at the earliest opportunity once she comes back on line. We received your last message through Iskander Sandrathama just before you lifted from Khughar for Thya. However, from the metalegal standpoint, I'm not sure I approve of what you've been doing. The Kalocs may have grounds for charging you — and SIGNET — with violations of practically every Canon because of your rather cavalier manner of treating Onuva Ferona and even to some extent the Dyons. I realize the psychopathological factors involved, but no excuses for abrogating the Canons are acceptable even under those conditions. However, I'll discuss the matter fully with you upon your return to ColeShore. In the meantime, I urge you to use the utmost discretion. Your first duty is to represent our clients on Thya and to attempt to resolve their conflict with the Kalocs — by peaceful means within the Canons if possible. I don't see that this is going to be possible. You therefore should withdraw. Now, you may believe that this is a retreat from your assignment, but I'm changing the scope of your mission. We want you to conduct a purely reconaissance mission. Get as much data as possible and get out. We've already lost one AI Team. We'll have to reevaluate this situation."

Dr. Rudi Witkowski added, "Peter, we do not want you to risk your Team and the ship by attempting an approach and landing on Thya. A military operation such as you report the Kalocs are conducting there is something totally new to us. You are not equipped to handle it. Therefore, you should enter the Garyon system, establish contact with the Kalocs, and inform them that you will be leaving their woman and the Thyan individuals for them to pick up. Place your female Kaloc hostage and the Thyan men in the AE-35 Agent Expeditionary pod. The life support capabilities of that unit are twenty-four man-days. When you detect the Kaloc rescue ship coming for the AE-35 unit, set it free in space with its beacon operating. Then move at highest possible Mike number out of the Garyon system until you can jump back to ColeShore where we can debrief you and your Team and determine a future course of action."

Marshall Wells waved. "We'll rebroadcast this message in five seconds, Peter. If you have comments, contact us. We'll have receivers standing by for you at all times . . ."

The images of the two SIGNET men blurred, tore, flickered, and then came on again.

"Peter, this is a recording that CYMaster is running over and over again through a series of transmitters working in shifts around the clock," Marshall Wells' image began as the replay started again. "We received your last message . . ."

"Katwin, stop receiving," Starbuck ordered.

"Do you care to send a reply? Isky is on line and ready," CY's voice told him.

"No," Starbuck said with finality. "Bring us all out of linkage. This session is concluded."

He had the usual splitting headache, but Triga wasn't there to help him. She was busying herself over Katwin. Starbuck turned to look at his transmitterman. "Why do we always get the TLC last of all?"

Isky didn't even nod. "Because Katwin is Katwin, that's why."

Hearing their exchange, Triga turned and asked, "Are both of you all right?"

"No," Isky said.

"Usual post-linkage trauma," Starbuck added.

"You'll live," Triga observed. "Peter, that was amazing! What did you do to allow Katwin to work with CY again?"

Starbuck shrugged nonchalantly. "Very simple. I just changed CY's image."

He lay there and thought about the message from ColeShore. He didn't like what Wells and Witkowski had suggested. He knew he wouldn't — *couldn't* — abandon the ten Thyan Irregulars in a space pod designed to put Agent Investigators down on a planet without grounding a ship there. Not with a total of less than two days of life support consumables in the pod! Even with Ferona aboard, he wasn't sure that Kodo Sadon would send anyone to get the pod. The Kalocs were strung out, operating on a shoestring. They might not have a ship available for the rescue.

No, Starbuck decided, he'd have to proceed. There was no question in his mind about the honor of his Team or any ego-satisfying drive that demanded he finish the mission. That sort of thing was trained out of a team leader and a Team early . . . or the Team never made it to operational status. SIGNET wasn't in the hero business. The most important thing in Starbuck's mind was the fact that he had the Thyan Irregulars aboard. They'd come aboard fighting to protect the Team. They'd accepted the resulting situation stoically but with the understanding that Starbuck would get them home to their families. He had an unpaid debt still left to discharge with the Thyan Irregulars.

And he knew that Marshall Wells was operating only on the basis of the initial mission data plus the progress reports, the latest one having been sent just before the *Starace* left Samarra. He and Witkowski were as skittish about a military invasion as Starbuck had been before he'd gotten on the scene himself and had the chance to partially evaluate the data. Furthermore, both Wells and Witkowski were sitting safely on ColeShore. They weren't in the middle of it. They were trying to call the shots from

safety. That couldn't work. It had never worked in the
past. In the heat of the situation, Wells had overlooked an
important factor. That's why Wells was a metalawyer
stationed at ColeShore and not a team leader.

Starbuck recalled a time during his youth when wars and
"armed conflicts" were more prevalent. Elements of the
old Petroleum Confederation, the PetroFed, had once decided that the time was ripe to initiate the long-awaited and
often-failed *jehad*. But the generals hadn't accompanied
the troops into the field. Instead, they'd stayed with the
politicians and the royalty in the capitals. They'd tried to
run the war by remote control right down to the tactical
decisions at the battalion level. The bodies of thousands of
human beings again contributed to the environment of the
Fertile Crescent as they'd done for ten thousand years or
more.

No, Starbuck wasn't going to let SIGNET run his show
by remote control, and he resented the fact that Wells had
suggestively tried to do so. The old fox had been quite
careful in his use of words, however, a fact which belied
the man's legal training and experience. Wells had left
Starbuck an out. Orders had not been given. Only "suggestions" and "recommendations" had been put forth.
Starbuck knew very well that these were euphemisms for
direct orders and that, as the AI Team leader, he should
accept these "recommendations." But technically he didn't
have to.

There was also the unwritten rule of the profession: No
one could, should, or would openly attempt to dictate
operations to an AI Team on assignment. The total responsibility lay with the AI Team leader.

As he lay there working on his biological self to improve his state of health, Starbuck knew he'd faced this
dilemma before, and he knew he'd have to face it again. If
he won, no one would care and they'd all be winners as
usual. If he didn't, he'd probably lose his team . . . and
maybe his Agent Investigator status with SIGNET.

It didn't take him very much time to decide what to do

about it. He did what he usually did — what he wanted to do.

And he knew he was right.

At least, he hoped he was right. Much depended upon opportunism.

"Want me to stand by for a transmission?" Isky asked.

"No, thank you, Isky. We won't be sending another report until we finish this mission. Or unless we have to send an emergency message."

"That's the thing I like about this job. Not very much work. Lots of free time. Every day a holiday, every meal a banquet . . ."

"Don't go into automatic debauch mode," Starbuck warned him.

"Debauch? On the *Starace*? Where?"

"Where you find it, I guess. But before you begin looking, I'd like you to get ready. We're going down on Thya again, and there may be fighting at Novipra."

"Just tell me who I kill next . . ."

"I'll count on you for that." Starbuck knew he might have to. He hadn't the foggiest notion what might be waiting for them back on Thya after more than a week's absence. "To keep you out of trouble, I'm asking you to be liaison with the Thyan Irregulars. Make sure they're in good shape to fight if they have to when we land at Novipra."

"They've been ready ever since we left Samarra. They know about Ferona."

"Who told them?"

"Did you think it could be kept quiet, Peter?"

"I guess not."

"So what are your intentions?"

"Brazenly land at Novipra and bring this matter to a head."

"Don't forget Zing's team. They may have tried to do the same thing."

"I doubt it. Not the way I put the jigsaw puzzle together. I think they weren't brazen enough."

"What do you mean?"

"If I'm right, I'll feel free to expound my theory," Starbuck told his transmitterman.

"If you're wrong . . .?"

"Then we've got a good fight on our hands . . . but I won't let matters get to the point where the whole team's in jeopardy."

When Starbuck told Karel Cherny of the plans, the Thyan Irregulars' leader told him somberly, "I think you're doing the right thing. I suspect the Kalocs are having a little bit of trouble with their invasion."

"What sort of trouble, Karel?"

The Thyan volunteer fireman from Novipra replied very quietly and without emotion, "Don't forget: The blood of Attila the Hun still flows in our veins. It may be thin, but it's there."

Starbuck didn't spend the jump in his quarters this time. He was on the control deck, ready for whatever what might take place when David O'Hara brought them out as Shochona indicated some fifty light-hours from Garyon.

Nothing happened after the jump-out.

As the *Starace* drove in toward Thya at Mike-point-nine, no sensor probe signal was detected coming from the system. There was no hail on the C+ band. Nothing. It wasn't the reception they'd gotten on their first approach a few weeks ago.

"I think I'm right," Starbuck ventured to his team. But he didn't tell them what "right" was. Not yet.

He called Novipra Starport according to interstellar rules. An immediate reply came back as follows: "This is Novipra Starport Inbound Traffic Management. This is a recorded message. The former Novipra Approach Control is no longer functioning. Please use this frequency as a traffic advisory. Starship commanders announce your intentions and positions according to interstellar rules of the road. Notice to starmen: A state of armed conflict exists in the vicinity of Novipra at this time. There is heavy traffic in the general region of Thya. This warning has been issued

on the authority of the Thyan government. The Thyan
government hereby assumes no risk to inbound, outbound,
or berthed starships. All ships and their personnel and
passengers must use Novipra Starport at their own risk.
This is Novipra Starport Inbound Traffic Management.''
This was not the former heavy and thick voice of the
Kaloc controller. It was a voice speaking Galactish with
the lilt and accent used by the Thyan Irregulars.

"I know I'm right," Starbuck modified his earlier
assessment.

Triga and Isky pressured him hardest. He finally admitted, "I think the invasion is over."

"Who's winning?" Isky was having trouble figuring
this out.

"The Thyans, of course. If I'd had the information I
now have when we landed here before, I simply would
have waited until we were needed for arbitration," he
explained cryptically.

"Peter, I think I'd better check you over," Triga told
him. "The strain of this operation . . ."

Starbuck laughed. "Triga, dearest, you of all the team
members should have spotted it first because of your background in psychotechnology."

"I'm a biotech."

"And as you've reminded me many times — including
quite recently — I am no genius in biotechnology or genetic
engineering. But can one become a biotech without becoming reasonably proficient in psychotechnology?"
Starbuck asked her rhetorically. "They used to call it
'bedside manner' or 'physician's empathy.' Run in a little
training in gengineering and neuroelectronics, and as a
biotech you're a practical psychotechnologist in any event.
Right?"

"Uh . . . right."

"And you haven't spotted it yet?"

"No. What is there to spot? We're working with a
sado-masochistic culture, that's all."

"More than than. Incidentally, did you run that genetic
analysis of Ferona that I asked for?"

"Yes."

"Wasn't it easy to get the sample?"

"Surprisingly, yes. I thought she'd fight."

Starbuck shook his head and smiled. "She won't. Did you notice that her compartment door wasn't secured?"

"That surprised me, too."

"It hasn't been for a long time. She's been free to wander throughout the ship, but she hasn't done so."

"What are you up to, Peter?" Triga wanted to know. She was frankly baffled by his behavior.

"Just applying the First Canon on Metalaw, that's all. Now, what did the genetic analysis reveal?"

"Onuva Ferona is a normal homozygous forty-eight double-x," Triga reported in a professional tone and manner. "But she has an autosome pattern which indicates a growing divergence from the normal human gene pool. If I had to classify her, I'd have to guess — I don't have the expertise to give you a firm classification, mind you — that her genosome most closely resembles the Courland or Elbing reference standard. But that's a guess because it also resembles some of the more recent Hsi-Yu genosomes. I wasn't surprised to find a large number of paired recessives. As the Dyons told us, the Kalocs are highly inbred."

"No surprises," Starbuck mused.

"No surprises," Triga confirmed. "So?"

"So our biggest problem isn't going to be the resolution of a conflict on Thya, but determining what to do with the Kalocs."

"You're being cryptic, Peter," she told him flatly.

He nodded. "I'm afraid I'll have to remain that way until the final pieces fall into the jigsaw puzzle here," he admitted.

"Tell me," she insisted. "Maybe I can help."

"I've already told you, and you've already helped," Starbuck said. "And I can't explain my hypothesis any better because it doesn't depend on linear logic. The data is falling in from all directions."

Triga just sniffed disdainfully and decided she'd better

wait and see what was happening. In the meantime, she tried to puzzle it out herself.

The *Starace* came straight in to Novipra Starport on an involute approach with CY scanning the planet for whatever data could be garnered on the military situation there. CY reported little if any activity in the communications bands, practically no sensor probings of the sort one might expect to find on a battlefield, and practically zero disturbances in the electromagnetic spectrum that might be caused by microwave weapons or by explosions, either chemical, nuclear, or anti-matter.

Novipra Starport was much as it was when the *Starace* had lifted off several weeks before. But there were only a few Kaloc ships standing on the tarmac. They appeared to have been abandoned. Some activity was taking place around the port. A few commercial starships were being loaded and unloaded, but none of the frenetic military activity of the prior visit was in evidence.

After monitoring the ground frequencies for nearly thirty minutes and hearing nothing, and seeing absolutely no one approach the *Starace* on the tarmac, Starbuck decided it was time to go aground. This time he wasn't about to walk into a microwave stun bolt. He wanted Isky, David, and the tall and imposing Shochona with him. All of them slipped into the mesh microwave-protective armor.

Karel Cherny and the Thyan Irregulars were waiting on the lower lock deck. They were all anxious to go aground.

"We're wearing anti-stun armor," Starbuck advised Cherny. "Look out, because you're not."

"They can't get us all. And if someone tries to stun, they'll go for you first," Cherny pointed out. "Then we'll shoot."

"I don't think you'll have to. The place is as quiet as a tomb."

"Probably because our people have taken the starport," the Thyan Irregular guessed. "What do you want us to do first?"

"You know the ground. Any suggestions?"

"Let's go for the portmaster's office. We can gain access to communications there. Starbuck, you and your people are to follow me. The Irregulars will provide cover crossing the tarmac. Look, we've spent days figuring out exactly what we're going to do. Agreed?"

"I don't believe we have much choice at this point," Starbuck observed pragmatically.

They did indeed have it all figured out. Each man was carrying not only the weapon he'd brought from Thya originally but one or more other weapons or devices that had either been purchased in Samarra or built in the *Starace*. At the signal, the lock door burst open, and Irregulars streamed out. They ran in crouched positions following zigzag paths across the tarmac to the cover of the nearest ships.

"Clear!" came the call.

The rest of them debarked.

The tarmac was windy, damp, and cool. And it smelled. Starbuck couldn't identify the odors. He'd been in the ship too long. As they began to walk across the tarmac, a smooth whirring sound came from behind one of the Kaloc ships. Starbuck was surprised when Cherny didn't bring his rifle to the ready. When he saw the little open ramp wagon appear, he understood why. A young girl was driving it.

"Good morning! Sorry to keep you waiting so long! Things are still a bit disorganized. Can I help you?"

"Hello, Marti," Cherny called out.

"Karel! I thought it was you! You're back!" She brought the wagon to a stop in front of them, leaped out, and threw her arms araound Karel Cherny. But it was simply a friendly greeting coupled with relief and joy at having the ten men back on Thya again.

"I take it that the *Podzemni* did the job?" Cherny asked her.

"Oh, yes! The underground worried the Black Guards back into their ships and kept them there. It was a matter of starve in the ships or leave. The last operable Kaloc ships left yesterday. We're going to salvage these Kaloc hulks,'' the girl Marti reported brightly then added thoughtfully, ''Those Kaloc Black Guards — all the Kalocs — gave up fighting awfully fast when the going got tough. They didn't have any guts at all. No staying power. No will to fight. Lousy fighting troops.''

Starbuck smiled. He was absolutely, positively certain now that he was right.

But the total solution had apparently slipped through his fingers. ''Marti, did *all* the Kalocs leave?''

''Only the ones who were still alive,'' she replied.

''The *whole invasion force* left?'' He wanted to be absolutely certain.

''The whole invasion force. But it was more like an expedition rather than a military operation. The Kalocs had their families along. All their possessions, what little there was of those. All their women. All their children. Everything. Difficult to fight them, but we did.''

''Their leader? Kodo Sadon, the Black Path of Thoth? Was he killed? Captured? Did he escape?''

''He's gone with his people and his ships.''

''Where?''

''They didn't say. But they left the Garyon system. And I don't think they'll be back.''

Somewhere out among the stars, a sadistic people and a sadistic leader were on the loose, convinced in their own minds that they were following the Canons of Metalaw by being kind to others in their own way . . .

Chapter Twenty-Three

"Good afternoon. How's the reception?" Starbuck seemed again to be sitting in the SIGNET main communciations center on ColeShore. But of course it was only an image projected on his nervous system by CY in the *Starace*. Since this was a full Team Report, CY had also included the images of his AI Team. They had linked as well and could contribute to the report when and where necessary.

Opposite him in the mental projection was Tayreze Nambe, Marshall Wells, and Dr. Rudi Witkowski of SIGNET.

"Not a bad signal, Peter, considering you're still on that Fringe World," Tayreze Nambe replied in her contralto voice.

"Katwin's our girl on this end. She's good. She doesn't know what time or distance are," Starbuck remarked.

"Sorry that Brinker couldn't be with us for this," Nambe observed. "He had another meeting to attend."

"No problem," Starbuck put in and added wryly, "In all the years I've been with SIGNET, I don't recall reporting more than twice when Brinker was present. Make sure he gets to see the tapes of this one, Rudi. We've got an unusual one this time."

"We always send you on the unusual ones, Peter," Wells remarked.

Starbuck shook his head slowly. "Thanks for nothing. On the other hand, we'd grow bored with the easy ones."

"That's the idea."

"Enough of this chit-chat," Tayreze Nambe said curtly. "We've all acclimatized to the link now. Report, Peter."

"You got our report on leaving Samarra on Khughar," Starbuck began, then paused. He'd phrased it half as a statement and half as a question.

"Yes, but did you get the repeated message we ran for you?"

"Not until it was too late to do anything about it," Starbuck told her. He wasn't lying. By the time he'd received the message from Wells and Witkowski, he'd already gotten enough data to begin to see what was really going on and had pretty much decided what to do anyway. But he didn't say that.

"You should check the mail more often," Wells chastised him.

"Marshall, that's pretty hard to do most of the time when we're on an operation."

"Pick it up at the point you left Samarra," Nambe told him.

"For the moment, I will. But I want to go back later and fill in the holes of what happened before. A lot of data slipped through our fingers and just lay there unnoticed because we didn't understand its importance at the time we got it. For the Official Final Report, I want the chance to amend previous reports as addenda to this one. And I want the opportunity to grind the rough edges off this one, too."

"Peter, whether we tell you that you can do it or not, you always do it anyway," Witkowski interrupted. "For a long time I have known that you get into CYMaster's Central Archives after the so-called Final Report to us. I've compared my personal records of these face-to-face reports against the ones in the Archives. Don't apologize."

"Frankly, we'd be foolish if we insisted on strict protocol with you and your Team, Peter. One of my operational policies is to refrain from trying to improve a working arrangement. You and your team always do an outstanding job. So I'm not going to tinker with it. Now, get on with the report," Nambe told him.

"You may have to tinker with it. And with the training and operational policies of all the other teams, too, Tay. We learned a lot in this operations, and not all of it had to do with the client and his problem," Starbuck advised her. "The meaning of those statements may become clear as we proceed with this report."

"I'll keep that in mind," Tayreze Nambe replied and said to Witkowski, "Rudi, you do the same. Now, Peter, what happened after you left Samarra?"

"I had most of my plan worked out by that time. Nearly all of the information we needed to effect a viable solution and conclusion to this matter of the Kaloc invasion of Thya was already in hand by the time we left Samarra. Not all of it was in CY's database. Not all of it came from the interviews and experience in Samarra. Not all of it came from the data dump from the Samarran database to CY through the networklink. Some of it came from Isky and David. And, oh, yes, from Shochona, although she demurs. And from Triga who didn't know she had it. And from Katwin who gave me a unique perspective on it as she always does . . ."

"Speak for yourself, Peter," was Shochona's dry comment.

"And a lot of it came from my own personal databank . . . and after you hear about it, I will entertain no further questions concerning how I came to have the data in the first place. Suffice it to say that when one has lived a goodly number of years, one gains quite a bit of experience. Let's let it go at that. What was important here was not the quantity of data, but how it was synthesized."

Starbuck paused to collect his thoughts, then went on, "We were dealing with a culture, the Kalocs, that had allowed itself to become inbred with a nonsurvival trait, knew it, and elected to do nothing about it because of their basic genotype. They were effective bioengineers and genetic engineers, but they simply couldn't stop what they were doing once they'd started doing it."

"I don't understand," Witkowski's image broke in.

"How could they permit their gene pool to become inbred with a nonsurvival trait if they were such good gengineers? Any competent gengineer or even a genetic materials manager could have stopped what they were doing before it was too late."

"Ah, yes, Rudi! We get so sophisticated as longers and so wrapped up in current technological wonders that we often forget some of the basics," Starbuck reminded him. "Do you recall an experiment in elementary psychology? The pleasure test?"

"Simplistic. Attach a stimulus pad to a lab mouse. Put it in a cage. Give it all the food and drink it wants. But also make available a lever which, when pushed by the mouse, sends a signal to the mouse's brain stimulating its pleasure center," the SIGNET technical wizard recalled.

"Right. And what does the mouse do? Pushes that lever constantly to stimulate its pleasure center . . . and starves to death in an abundant paradise!" Starbuck finished. "And what do the Kalocs have in their gene pool? Recessives which, when you analyze Ferona's sample, add up to the classic sado-masoc pattern, a factor which has been nearly forgotten and exists only in data buried deep in the archives. Now, I'm not a neuro-engineer or a gengineer, but I think further genetic analysis and prognostication will reveal a pattern for the growth of the higher level of the nervous system that contains some mistakes in the wiring diagram, so to speak. A basic neural misconnection. The stimuli for pain and pleasure — which aren't very far apart in sensation anyway — have been cross-connected with the reproductive drive, which is the strongest of all programs in a Tellurian animal. This ess-and-em connection occurs in several genotypes, and what happened to the Kalocs happened to several Tellurian cultures. Why shouldn't it also happen in the far more isolated situations of interstellar cultures?"

"Well, we certainly haven't seen it as widespread as this for several centuries," Witkowski observed. "Many experts thought the genetic basis had been bred out of the overall gene pool.''

''Ridiculous assumption!'' Triga put in. ''Don't those so-called experts ever get off-planet? Don't they know that all sorts of mutations can occur out here in this varied radiation jungle among the stars? In spite of gengineering, we're still running into new wrinkles. Why, I've run into dozens already . . . which makes me ashamed that I didn't see this one sooner.''

''The existence of the Kalocs will certainly cause the subject to be reopened for investigation,'' Witkowski ventured. ''This is probably the first time it's been encountered on a widespread basis in the Thousand Worlds. There have been individual cases, I presume. So there should have been something in the database about it. But where's the data? Why wasn't it in CYMaster?''

''That's what I originally wondered. But, Rudi, I think we've grown to depend too much on CYMaster's database. The data was in *my* database.'' Starbuck paused again and then repeated, ''And, as I told you, just don't ask how it got there. Now, why wasn't the data in the databases? Because when these sexual activities were most widespread in the nineteenth- and twentieth-century cultures, they were simply ignored or the data was suppppressed because of the social beliefs of the time. They were repugnant activities as far as most people were concerned. I remember they laughed about them because it was too mentally disturbing to think about them in any other way. Frankly, I think the whole human race has a streak of it that will take a long time to get rid of — provided it isn't somehow a survival trait of some sort that we don't know about. And there's no available data for another reason. Even if it were widespread — which I don't think it is — how would it be viewed today?''

Marshall Wells, the best metalawyer in the Thousand Worlds, added thoughtfully, ''It's a perfectly acceptable social activity today under the Canons. Especially the First Canon: Do unto others as they would have done unto them. The Kalocs rediscovered that a sadist is one who's kind to a masochist.

"Keep that in mind as we continue our report, Marshall. It's true. Some people think that the ess-and-em paradox is a shortcoming of metalaw. Maybe. As we learned in Samarra," Starbuck went on in more somber tones, "it can be a shortcoming if it's overdone the way the Kalocs overdid it. In Thoth on Khughar, they ran out of masochists. They killed them off in the endless search for ever more painful pleasures, and the masochists kept demanding even more innovative ones. No damping factor was present in the culture. Or, if it's there, the Kalocs haven't encountered it to the extent that it will put a lid on the activity. They'll encounter the damping factor some day. They may have already done so by the fact that they seem to be running out of people to be kind to. But there was also another masoc drain in the Kaloc culture. Care to guess what it was?"

"Peter, this may not be pleasant, but it's fascinating. You tell us since you seem to have become an expert in ess-and-em," Nambe remarked.

"Not really. Nor have I ever been. That's one proclivity I don't intend to become involved in. I'm not wired right for it."

"Stop playing Professor! Report!" Tayreze Nambe told him in a frustrated tone.

"Okay, but I'll wager none of you knew any of this. And if I play the academic, it's because question-and-answer is one of the most powerful teaching methods available. In any event, those masocs still left in the culture found other means of satisfaction. Surprised most of my Team when they learned that the sadistic Kalocs weren't the ones who frequented the bordello culture of Samarra and used its various services the most. The Kaloc masochists were the Dyons' best clients! Why? Most bordellos are patronized by masochists, not sadists. And most bordellos will tolerate them up to a point. Business is business, after all. And you won't find it in most databanks, either, because of a strange reluctance to put this information in books and other records. Why did the Dyons cut off the Kalocs? Because the Kaloc sadists began to come over the mountains looking for their former companions and perhaps hoping to find some Dyon masocs. They didn't. The working men and women of the oldest profession can't afford to be sados or masocs and still stay in business — although there used to be a few specialists.''

"Peter," Tayreze Nambe broke in, "you have piqued my curiosity. This is enormously important information. How do you know about it?''

"You're going to stay on my back and hound me until you find out, aren't you?'' Starbuck asked her with a smile.

She replied, also smiling, "Yes.''

"Very well! I'll give you an answer and let you determine for yourself whether or not I'm just pulling your leg to satisfy your curiosity: Little did you know, my dear, that I was once a highly successful businessman first pimping for and then managing an expensive *chat* house in Storyville with some of the very finest French Jennies in New Orleans. People claimed I had the highest bawd rate in town.''

She looked baffled and shook her head. "You win, Peter. I haven't got the slightest idea what you're talking about.''

"I didn't think you would, Tay.''

"Very well, continue with the report,'' Nambe said with resignation.

"I originally thought the Kalocs mounted the invasion of Thya because they were a poor culture and had their credits for pleasure goodies cut off by the Dyons. If that was the case, I assumed the Kalocs went looking elsewhere for their fun and games. But there's a major problem with that hypothesis, isn't there?''

"I can answer that one from my own experience — and I'm not ashamed of it,'' Isky put in. "When you've got the best little whorehouse in the universe right next door

and use it occasionally, the last thing you'd want to do is
send in the vice squad — that is, if you ever want to use it
again.''

"That, too, was a hypothesis, as you can see from my
transmitterman who managed to have a very good time in
Samarra, by the way. Never mind, Isky; you earned it.
But there are some problems with that one, too, aren't
there?''

"I think," Tayreze Nambe interrupted, getting back on
the subject, "that the Kalocs could have invaded and
conquered the Dyons but they didn't because the Dyons
didn't have what they were looking for . . . and they knew
it.''

"Tayreze, remind me to reward you for perspicacity
beyond the call of the executive in charge of vice," Starbuck
told her playfully, "because that's that's why I think the
Kalocs went to Thya. They spent seven years and everything they had to mount that mission, and they took everything they had with them. So it wasn't an invasion. They
were recolonizing. They chose Thya for reasons that had
nothing to do with what we originally thought. It wasn't an
economic reason. The Kalocs didn't have a rich area of
Khughar, but Thya wasn't much richer. Know what they
were looking for?''

"Someone to be kind to," Wells remarked.

"Right! On that basis, the Kalocs had it totally rational-
ized and justified under the Canons. But their invasion or
'recolonization' of Thya failed anyway.''

"It did?" Tayreze Nambe was stunned.

"It did.''

"That's the most important datum of this report! Why
didn't you mention it first?''

"Because it's not the most important datum. There's
more to come. If I don't present this report in a sequence
that I believe will make the most sense and provide the
pattern of events, it will get very confusing because it's
extremely complex.'' Starbuck paused, collected his
thoughts, and went on, "The Kaloc invasion of Thya

failed because they set it up as a military operation. They didn't know how to move in on the Thyans except by using coercive force. In their case, it was bound to fail. Why? Do you know of any sadistic culture that has ever been militarily successful?''

"Oh, certainly! Many of them!" Wells erupted. "You can spot them by their typical military trappings — boots, leather, riding crops, and usually black uniforms as well. All militaristic cultures are sadistic!''

"Wrong, Marshall, wrong! But we won't hold it against you," Starbuck chided. "Granted that a sadist is a violent personality, but on a one-to-one basis. A real sadist doesn't like to fight. Hates it. Runs away from it. Will not fight anyone who resists. A sadist wants someone to be kind to. A sadist desperately needs a willing victim, a needy masochist, or even an unwilling victim who doesn't fight back and can be dominated. A sadist is violent but doesn't want any violence returned. A sadist wants to be master from the first instant. So if sadists appear to be militaristic, it's only because they can get someone else to do the fighting — conscript troops or mercenaries, but never themselves. They stay behind the front lines and have their fun with those who have proved they can be dominated."

"So the Kaloc invasion of Thya failed because the Thyans fought back," Wells mused with a smile.

"They sure did! Our Thyan Irregulars were angry as hell that they didn't get in on the action. The Thyans were outnumbered and nonmilitary. But they fought back with an organized underground. Their ancestors were outstanding guerrilla and partisan fighters. There's another reason, too, why the Thyans beat the hell out of the Kalocs in a matter of weeks, which is about the maximum length of most small and really violent wars, by the way — see the history books. The Thyans believed the Kalocs were disobeying the Canons by invading, and they weren't going to stand by and let their code of living be destroyed. The Thyans strongly believe in the Canons. On the other hand, the Kalocs believed they, too, were following the Canons because all they wanted to do was make the Thyans happy, not to kill them. The Thyans and the Kalocs were fighting for different reasons, and those reasons made the difference between which one won.''

Marshall Wells nodded in understanding. ''That's exactly why a handful of Spaniards whipped a couple of thousand Aztecs. The Spaniards were out to destroy the Aztec army, but the Aztecs were interested only in counting coup and capturing sacrifice victims.''

''The Kalocs had everything going against them from the start,'' Tayreze Nambe decided. ''Why did they do it in the first place?''

''Because they thought that they could win. That's the reason why anyone starts a fight. Including ourselves,'' Starbuck observed.

''We don't start them any more,'' Nambe objected.

''We try not to,'' Wells corrected her. ''Depends on your viewpoint. Peter just reconfirmed that principle.''

''They also started it because they weren't capable of thinking it all the way through,'' Shochona put in. ''When you think the War Game through, you usually conclude that it's easier to play another game to get what you want. Costs less, too.''

Chapter Twenty-four

"So the Thyans won. Interesting!" Tayreze Nambe mused, then looked up suddenly and asked, "How do the Thyans plan to handle the prisoners of war?"

"They don't. They won't. There are none."

"What?"

"The Kalocs who remained alive got back into their starships and left Thya."

Tayreze sighed. "I hadn't figured on having to cross-correlate and cooperate with Strakovkhaburo to handle damage and liability claims between the Kalocs and the Thyans. But it's looks like I'll have to do so now that the Kalocs have retreated to Khughar . . ."

"Who said they did?" Peter interrupted.

"They didn't go back to Thoth on Khughar?"

"That's right. The Kalocs didn't return to Thoth on Khughar."

"You mean the Kalocs are somewhere out there in interstellar space among the Fringe Worlds and no one — *no one* — knows where they are or where they're going next?" the Vice Executive of SIGNET asked incredulously.

"That's right," Starbuck replied flatly. "And we don't know whether or not they'll stay in the Fringe Worlds. We have no idea of the characteristics of their starships. They may have enough range to leave the region. They could go to almost any of the Thousand Worlds in the vicinity."

Marshall Wells whistled and shook his head.

Shochona spoke up, drawing from her own experience, "I don't know how much life support consumables each

Kaloc ship has, but I assume they've got closed-cycle systems aboard. Even at that, they can't travel forever like a macrolife ship. Sooner or later, they've got to make planetfall for refurbishment. Or they might rendezvous with one or more of the macrolife supply ships.''

"If we knew how many ships the Kalocs had in their invasion fleet . . ." Witkowski began.

"We don't," Starbuck cut in. "We have a count of how many grounded at Novipra Starport. But a review of CY's records indicates there was a halo of ships around Thya as well as throughout the Garyon system the first time we went in. They probably put the shock troop ships down first and left the colony ships orbiting around the Garyon system until they were sure of being able to live on Thya with their intended friends, the Thyans. We've got an estimated count from CY's records, but there were a lot of ships in defilade behind planets and satellites that we couldn't detect.''

Tayreze Nambe sighed. "We've ended up with a bigger problem than when we started. I'll have to get this news out to Justar and Strakovkhaburo . . . and all our teams, as well. This is a serious threat to the Canons.''

"Not until the Kalocs act in violation of the Canons again, Tayreze," Wells reminded her.

"Yes, but they're operating under their own interpretation of the Canons," his boss reminded him.

"We can't do anything until a client asks us to do so.''

"One more nagging worry . . ." the Vice Executive of SIGNET muttered.

"That's what we're here for," Wells told her.

"I never disabused myself that this job was easy," Nambe admitted.

"Sounds like something the Star Guard fleet can do when it gets to Thya," Starbuck suggested. "If they come all this way and don't have an invasion to subdue by sheer intimidation or even action, I'm sure the captains will enjoy hunting the Kaloc fleet.''

"We'll look into the matter," Tayreze Nambe said. She

didn't look at either Marshall Wells or Dr. Rudi Witkowski, both of whom knew the truth: There never was, wasn't, and probably would never be a Star Guard fleet. Such things as star fleets are far too expensive for anyone to support. It had taken everything the Kalocs had for seven long years to create their fleet. And such military forces are far too inefficient. AI Teams were far better at the difficult task of resolving conflicts on an interstellar basis. And even more so if everyone else believed that the AI Teams were backed up by the legendary Star Guard. But even the AI Teams didn't know that. Only a handful of people at SIGNET headquarters on ColeShore were aware of the deception. The ruse had worked for several centuries. But it never made Tayreze Nambe feel good to withhold that information from one of her favorite Agent Investigators and his outstanding team. It put an unwanted psychological barrier between her and her very long-time, very close friend, Peter Steele Starbuck. It often caused her to hold him at arms' length when she really didn't want to do that.

As a result, Tayreze Nambe changed the subject before she would have to dodge around more Star Guard questions and answers. There was another piece of unfinished business, a very important one. "Peter, did you find out what happened to Joshua Zing's AI Team?"

"No." There was profound sadness in his voice.

"Not even a clue?"

"Not even a clue, Tay."

"Are Kodo Sadon or Onuva Ferona responsible?"

"Probably, but we can't prove anything," Starbuck told her humorlessly. "Onuva Ferona stoutly maintains that she didn't kill them. But she won't tell me who did. To do so would be contrary to her social code."

"Um. Yes," Wells mused quietly, his fingers playing absently with his chin. "She's also protected by some interesting new interpretations of the Seventh Canon. There have been several precedents . . ."

"Do you think you can ever learn what happened?" Nambe pressed.

"Not unless I can find Kodo Sadon and he decides to tell me . . . provided he knows in the first place. We've presumed that Sadon did it. But do we really know? All we have is presumption, and Marshall knows very well that presumption is nothing upon which to build a case. I wonder if Sadon did it. It could have been an accident. It's hard for one man to kill six people instantaneously, especially when the man likes to work on one person at a time and really doesn't want to kill them. But Kodo Sadon could have done it, and I'll tell you why and how. I have an idea that Joshua Zing's AI Team was killed because of the way AI Teams are trained."

This statement of Starbuck's took Tayreze Nambe by surprise. "Are you trying to tell me that our team training was responsible for the termination of a team itself? What's your basis for even considering that?"

Starbuck waved his arm around at his own team. Actually, only his image moved its arm. "Look at us, Tay. We're a typical team. Look at me. I'm a typical team leader. We have weapons available to us if needed and defensive systems to protect us if required. But we never carry weapons unless the situation absolutely demands it and there's no alternative if we're to protect our lives. We got into an operation unarmed except for our own personal bodies and minds which we've been taught to use as weapons if required. But we're trained and trained and trained to be nonviolent, almost passive operatives. We'll fight to protect ourselves, but the trigger point is set pretty high. The trigger point is also a reasonably individualistic thing; some of us have a lower trigger point than others."

"Are you telling me that Joshua Zing and his team members might have allowed themselves to be killed?" Tayreze Nambe had trouble believing this.

So did Peter Starbuck. "No, but here's what might have happened," Starbuck went on theorizing. "We've never come up against people like the Kalocs before. They're atavars, even in the rough-and-tumble environment of the Fringe Worlds. When my team and I first landed on Thya, we did so in a passive role because that's usually the one that works best in our operations. The Kalocs were actually being hospitable to us by their lights! Under their twisted terms, they were welcoming us! We weren't imprisoned in those cramp cages; that's an old ess-and-em gimmick to further excite a masoc. Bondage without bonds, but those terms no longer mean what they used to mean a couple of centuries ago. If it sounds strange, don't forget the psychology here: pain, pleasure, and sexual activities are so confused in those peoples' minds that they've become one and the same thing. Hard to believe, but believe it! We were almost killed — and would have been if Isky's trigger point hadn't been low. We resisted. We got out of the Novipra starport with incredible ease, considering there were a couple of hundred armed, Black Guard troops all around us that were behaving in a decidedly unusual way for soldiers.

"What happened to Joshua Zing? I submit that Zing and his people discovered they were dealing with a sadist culture but didn't resist until it was too late. Their trigger points were too high. They didn't have an Isky character on their team, a man with a short fuse. They were used to dealing with conflicts on a much higher and more advanced social level. With no insult intended because Joshua Zing was my friend, it was a situation like the commission from the Roman Emperor Honorius trying to deal with Alaric to get him to stop his Visigoths from going in to sack Rome. They weren't thinking or dealing on the same level. Zing and his people walked in with open hands and it was all over before they realized what was going on. We had the foreknowledge that Zing's team had been destroyed, so we were more cautious . . . but not cautious enough."

There was silence for a moment. Everyone was thinking about that, thinking about how close they'd come, thinking about what was now happening.

It was Tayreze Nambe who broke the silence which had lasted only a few seconds but seemed to have dragged on for hours. "So we must now change the training and the operational policies of our teams because we've got a dangerous new element loose somewhere out there among the Fringe Worlds. And we don't know when and where it will strike next . . ."

"Don't think of the Kalocs in those terms, Tay. Remember what I said about that type of person. They don't want to fight. They want willing victims," Starbuck pointed out. "I'd suggest that Rudi get busy on a psycho-social scan of the cultures out in these Fringe Worlds. Maybe a correlation study would indicate where the Kalocs might be expected to show up next."

"I'll get busy on that at once," Rudi Witkowski muttered absently. "We may also have some new technology that will help . . ."

"Peter, I want you and your team to return to ColeShore. I'll need your expertise and experience in setting up the new AI Team operational policies."

"As soon as we finish up what we're doing, Tay."

"Yes, there are some loose ends to this operation, aren't there?"

"Does Onuva Ferona have any idea where Sadon went?" Wells suddenly asked.

"She says she doesn't," Starbuck answered.

"Where is the woman? What do you intend to do with her? Can you bring her to ColeShore?"

"No, because it's against the Canons to hold her against her will or bring her to ColeShore if she doesn't want to come," Starbuck reminded the metalawyer.

"You're correct, of course." It reminded everyone in the conference how basically difficult it was to live totally within the Canons and how much education and discipline were required to do so.

Tayreze Nambe was interested. She had never met a woman like Onuva Ferona. "What does she think she wants to do now?"

"First, she wanted to join our team."

"Impossible, of course," Nambe remarked.

"Of course."

"But with the Kalocs on the loose out there, I could certainly use her, uh, expertise here at SIGNET Headquarters. I think I could find interesting things for her to do," Tayreze ventured.

"I doubt it, Tay," Starbuck replied. "She had to face a lot of facts that have altered her life and her life style: that Sadon had run away without her, that there was no way for her to go to him, and that there was no way for her to return to Thoth since no one is left there, either. Everything she's known is gone now — except one thing. And it's impossible for her to change certain things about herself because she doesn't want to and because she *can't*. It's built in and preprogrammed. She can't change it any more than CY could reburn one of his megaproms. So she decided she wanted to return to Samarra on Khughar. She knows people there. Being what she is, she might fit in there. So," Starbuck paused, then said, "So, we took her to Samarra and piped her over the side with full protocol. It was the least we could do for a princess . . . and, even though she wasn't culturally compatible with us, that's what she really was and had been all her life in her own culture. And she paid highly for it, too."

"You went to Samarra again?"

"That's where we are now."

"But our SIGNET client is on Thya!"

"But there's no longer any need for us there. The problem that the client had no longer exists. And the Thyans are doing fine, thank you. Want a Khughar ship for analysis? I know some Thyans who will probably sell us one and maybe even give us a nice family discount because of what we did for them."

"Why are you still on Khughar, then?"

"Because, my dear Tay, the operation is over, completed, done, and we're herewith submitting our Final Report." Starbuck paused. "And it occurred to us that since we're already here, we ought to take the rest of that R-and-R which got interrupted on Plethora by your mission assignment about the Thyan invasion. We were fatigued — exhausted is the word — when we started this mission. And this one has been a very difficult one. I'm bushed. So is my team. We need the rest, and this is a good place to get it.''

Tayreze Nambe smiled. She couldn't help but do so. Triga Rimmon saw that smile and knew exactly what it meant. In fact, Triga was waiting for Nambe's reply: "Knowing you, Peter, I would have been disappointed if you hadn't found some excuse to return to Samarra, judging from the first report you sent from there. Have some fun, my dear, but please try to get a little rest, too. Triga, please take care of him. I know you will. And don't push him too hard. Let him get his energy banks recharged. I've got a lot for him to do when he gets back here.''

"I'm sure you do," Triga said without rancor. "And I will indeed take care of him. We all will."

" 'Pleasure shared is pleasure squared', as they say in Samarra. And, oh, Tay," Starbuck added almost as an afterthought, although it wasn't, "please make some arrangements with Strakovkhaburo about fund transfers and extended credit limits, will you, my dear?"